Troubles

BEEKMAN HILLS

KC ENDERS

Troubles

BEEKMAN HILLS

Dedication
To my 'fiends'. There is no way this I could have done this without the support of each of you.
Thank you!

1

Lis

Orphan.
Origin: Late Middle English (noun)-Late Latin _orphanus_
destitute, without parents.

I'm an orphan.

It's an unofficial designation, but it fits. I'm broke as hell putting myself through college, and that's close enough to destitute.

The "without parents" part is tricky. They're both alive. They even live in the same small New York town as me; we just don't interact. At all—no phone calls, no dinners together.

Nothing.

Cutting them out of my life was not an easy choice until it

was. Cut ties, or let them drag me down. If I didn't have Gracyn as my roommate, I don't know what I'd do.

I scoop another handful of ice into the blender and hold the lid in place. Flipping the switch, I watch as the whiskey blends with the lemonade. When the ice is a slushed perfectly sassy pink, I pour the whiskey sours into tall glasses, adding straws and a couple whiskey-soaked cherries. My nana taught me to make these before I hit double digits. Told me it was her "secret" recipe. I don't know that it's any great secret, but it's perfect every damn time.

The sound of the blender is replaced by the whir of Gracyn's hairdryer as I take the handful of steps down the hall to our bathroom. I squeeze between where she's leaning against the vanity and the tub, knocking into her as I pass and hand her a whiskey sour hoping for a distraction.

I shove my arms up into the front of my new tee shirt and pull it away from my body, needing to stretch it out over my boobs a little. Gracyn bought us matching shirts for St. Patrick's Day and, of course, she bought a size smaller than I would have.

"What are you doing?" She slams her glass down and smacks at my hands. "That shirt fits you perfectly. Leave it alone."

"Gracyn," I whine, "we're just going to McBride's. Why do you feel the need to pour me into this tiny thing?" I'm not proud of the whining, but I feel way too exposed.

I prop my hands on my hips and face the mirror full-on. The thin green material stretches tight over *the girls* and the neckline scoops way lower than I'm comfortable with. Gracyn stares back at me, slurping from her glass.

It's fascinating, watching her brain freeze hit, twisting and contorting her features. I try to push down the laughter that bubbles up, but it's not working.

"Lis, you need to stop hiding your curves—use them, show them off. And for the love of God, promise me you'll try and have fun tonight?"

I settle myself on the side of the tub in our tiny bathroom while she finishes her smoky cat-eye. "It's time for you to get back out there. Just a little bit. Maybe flirt a little—kiss someone tonight." Gracyn waves her hands up and down the script on her shirt, like she's presenting prizes on a game show. "Kiss me, I'm Irish-ish" is scrawled across our chests, highlighted with bright red kissy lips. The shirts are cute, but it would be so much better if the lips weren't perfectly centered over my left boob.

"There's not going to be anyone new there. I'm pretty sure I've kissed everyone I needed to in this town." It's mostly true. Beekman Hills is nothing but a sleepy little college town about an hour outside New York City. Gracyn and I grew up here and sadly never left.

McBride's Public House is only a few blocks from our apartment and the walk down Main Street is cold. Our breaths trail behind us in white plumes. I pull my fleece tighter around me and pick up the pace. Most of the businesses along Main Street are closed for the night, but the scent of cinnamon and coffee still linger outside the coffee shop as we hurry past.

The line to get into the pub winds around the white clapboard building that's been here longer than I've been alive. College students and townies dressed in whatever green and plaid they could find—short skirts, ridiculous hats—and frat boys in kilts. All these people are in line, anxious to get their hands on cheap green beer and listen to a really bad Irish band.

Gracyn and I scoot around the back of the building and push through the door into the kitchen. Francie McBride's bright gaze peers up at us over an impossibly tall stack of plastic cups. He juts his cheek out around the tower precariously balanced in his hands for a quick kiss. "'Lo, love. Just gettin' in, are you?" His accent is extra thick tonight.

Gracyn and I have not had to wait in a line here for years. Francie busted me when I was nineteen trying to drink with a fake ID. He sat talking to me for hours instead of calling the cops, taking me under his wing and eventually bought me my first legal drink. He's been kind of a dad to me ever since. My own father couldn't be bothered finding his way out of the bottom of a bottle.

Gracyn pulls her jacket off over her head showing off her creation. "I bought us matching shirts for tonight and she didn't want to wear it. It took some time to convince her."

"No, it took whiskey to convince me." I pull my bottom lip between my teeth and shift uncomfortably.

Francie steps back to look at us as I drop my jacket on a stack of boxes, eyes crinkling above the scruffy beard he's had forever.

"Let me help you take those out to Finn," I say to try and move the conversation off my chest.

"I've got these. Go and have a pint. Off with you, then." Francie pushes past me, chuckling at our shirts, shaking his head. "Come on, then. I've a new lad at the bar tonight, make sure he treats you right, yeah?"

It's tight, but following close behind we get through the chaos pretty quickly. At the scarred, deep oak bar Francie bumps Finn and throws a nod in our direction. Finn turns, his wide smile about splits his face as he makes his way over to us, pouring drinks and collecting money as he goes. He hops up leaning over the bar and lays a kiss on me.

He thinks he's the Irish Casanova, but the boy is too sweet to pull it off.

"Finn, I need a pitcher and two cups," I shout to him slapping ten dollars down on the bar.

"And two shots of whiskey," Gracyn yells throwing down another ten.

Finn slides us our plastic cups before filling the pitcher. "Give us a kiss, Gracyn, and I'll get it for you." He's already reaching for the bottle and a couple of shot glasses.

Gracyn leans over the bar and Finn's eyes go wide with surprise, spilling whiskey as he pours. He thinks he has a chance, but she's a flirt, plain and simple, so the kiss Finn thinks he's getting? Nothing more than a peck on the cheek.

We down our shots and turn, taking in the crush of wall-to-wall bodies. There's a tiny bit of open space by the pool tables, so I grab the pitcher and start making my way through —turning sideways, trying hard not to brush up against strangers. I breathe a sigh of relief when we're through and fill our cups.

The band in the corner launches into their next set, filling the old bar with strains of violin and lilting voices bouncing around the room.

"Have you heard from them?" Gracyn leans in close, not so much for the noise level, but more to keep this conversation just between us.

I take a drink of the crappy beer and shake my head.

"Nothing? From any of them?"

I shake my head and sigh. "Nope. Not a word." I should be

surprised, sad, something, but this is how my family is.

Gracyn walked in on my boyfriend—ex-boyfriend—bending my sister over the hood of my mom's car on Christmas Eve.

Nope, not going there—not tonight.

"I thought I'd hear from Rob when Francie kicked him and Maryse out last month, but, nothing," I say.

"Unreal. What a dickhead. *Hey*—" She lurches at me spilling beer down my front. It doesn't feel cold in the cup, but when it's running down my cleavage, it's frigid.

The icy sneering glare of Rob's best friend, Tyler, is worse. "Watch where you're going, bitch. You wouldn't want to get thrown out of McBride's." Tyler wasn't all that nice to me when I was dating Rob, but since we broke up, he's been an absolute dick.

Somehow, this is my fault. I feel eyes on me from all around. I hate being the center of attention, and with bodies pressing in from all sides, my skin feels hot and too tight. I blink at the ceiling trying desperately to stem the tears starting to form. There's no way I can make it through the tightly packed crowd before they spill and, God help me, the last thing I want is for it to get back to Rob that I'm still crying over him—because that's exactly the story this asshole will tell.

"Oi!" A low growl comes from Francie's new guy as he slices through the crowd like they're not even there. "None of that—apologize to her. Now." His voice, strong and thickly accented, carries over the band and bar noise, leaving no doubt that he's serious. He stands with his back to me, shielding me from the rest of the room.

Gracyn reaches for the bar towel in his hand and he nods to her.

"Not my fault she spilled her drink—looks good on her though." Tyler looks around the broad wall between us, leering at the way my shirt clings to my very obviously cold boobs.

The music has stopped, all attention is on me now and I just want to disappear.

Francie checks me with a quick look and a nod placing a warm hand on my shoulder. "Aidan, take her round back and fetch her a dry shirt from one o' the boxes back there. I'll take care of this one." With a firm hand, Francie collects Tyler's cup and chucks it in the trash. "Out, and ye'll not come back. Go drink wit' that bastard friend o' yours. Off with you, then."

The new guy, Aidan, takes the towel from Gracyn and pauses, his hand between us. He moves to try and blot at my shirt but stops, handing me the towel instead. "Erm, here."

I clutch the white towel to my chest, trying and failing miserably to hide my discomfort.

Grabbing my hand, he pulls me in close behind him leading me to the backroom. He rifles through some boxes pulling out a clean shirt that is huge—huge. "This should do, then."

"Thanks. You didn't have to do that, you know."

"Your shirt's soaked." He rests his hands on his hips, making a point to meet my gaze.

"I meant coming to my rescue. I'm used to his shit. I'd have been fine." I shake out the dry shirt pulling it over my head and wrap my arms around myself inside—hiding a little.

"Jesus, what are you doing?" Aidan turns on his heel, his broad back blocking the doorway. "Hang on, I'll just—" Muttering, he pulls the door shut behind him.

I change quickly, relieved to be dry and out of the cold,

7

clingy shirt.

The door doesn't budge when I push at it. I knock, but the noise in the bar means the sound gets lost. Sighing, I turn to lean back against it, and pull out my phone hoping Gracyn will feel her phone vibrate, or come looking for me soon. Before I slide halfway to the floor, the door flies open and I tumble out, not at all gracefully.

Shit.

"That's twice, I've rescued you now." Aidan's lips quirk up on one side, like he's trying to suppress a smile as he helps me up off the floor. "Sorry, I was leaning on it—making sure no one walked in on you." His warm hand envelopes mine, squeezing before I slide it away.

"So, what does that mean, I have the luck of the Irish?" I can't believe that really just came out of my mouth. I close my eyes and take a deep breath, trying to push my complete awkwardness away with the exhale.

"You're Irish then?" His brow cocks up, disappearing under his black hair falling forward across his forehead. Dark blue eyes dance across my face as he pulls a curl from the collar of my new, way too big shirt.

"Absolutely." I'm not the least bit Irish. Not at all. "Everyone's Irish on St. Patrick's Day."

"Well, then. Let's get you a fresh beer and back to your friend." His touch is hot, low on my back, guiding me away from the quiet and back out to the crowd.

Gracyn hands me a beer and looks up at Aidan. "Thank you."

"Think nothing of it." His eyes crinkle at the corners as he smiles down at me before sliding back behind the bar. His teeth gleaming white against the dark scruff along his jaw. It's perfect, warm and sweet, right down to the slightly crooked tooth, front and center. I miss the warmth of his hand as he falls right into the rhythm again, pouring drinks and smiling broadly at each person.

As we move across the room, my skin prickles again. Turning around, my gaze goes straight to Aidan—only to find him watching me. I smile and turn away feeling my stomach flip and flutter.

Gracyn finds some people we work with, people I know and feel comfortable with, but I feel eyes on me the whole time. That itchy, scratchy feeling that tells me I'm paranoid about Rob and his stupid friends. I know Francie threw those guys out, but I can't help scanning the room, and each time I do, my eyes fall on him instead.

Aidan.

He and Finn are in constant motion. Working the bar like they're dancing, playing to the crowd like nothing I've seen before. Aidan is older than me, for sure, but it shows more in his bearing, the way he moves—the way he commands attention, than anything else. Looking around the room, I see most of the girls are staring at him, or undressing him in their minds, I'm sure.

His green plaid button-down stretches across his broad shoulders as he reaches for the next pitcher to fill. The buttons strain across his muscled chest a little when he takes a deep breath, pulling on the tap. And just a touch of his flat stomach shows as he reaches up to push his black hair back from his face as the green beer fills the plastic pitcher. He surveys the room, brows pinched together like he's searching for something.

I watch as he takes in every corner of the room—scanning the faces—until his gaze settles on mine and his features relax into a smile.

2

Aidan

In the past two weeks of working this pub, I thought I'd seen it busy. Not in the least. Right now, the place is packed wall-to-wall with university students and probably half the population of this small town—and the queue to get in still snakes around the building. If you'd asked me six months ago I would have thought I'd be spending the day in a pub with my brother, but plans changed and I needed to get out of Dublin.

Francie welcomed me with open arms and a cold pint when I showed up at his door. I'd known him most of my life. When he offered me a place to stay and a few shifts in his pub, I jumped at the chance to lose myself for a bit. I moved in with a couple of his bartenders and while it was nothing special—a loft space in their two-bedroom apartment—it was the distraction I needed; a good place to get my head together.

Tonight, though, McBride's is anything but quiet. No time

to think—just pitcher after pitcher of green-tinted beer, and bad decisions being made all about me. Francie warned me that St. Patrick's Day is a bastardization of what it is in Dublin. Last week he painted the double lines on the road out front bright green. He's been paying a huge fine to the city for years for the stunt, but smiles while the police write him his summons and calls the whole thing good advertising.

He's a good man, Francie is, making sure one of his bartenders has the night off to celebrate—works his arse off to make up for the missing man, keeping supplies up and things under control with the patrons.

The stacks of cups coming from the storeroom grabs my attention well before I see Francie. At least people make space letting him through. Maybe it's the realization that if they don't, then the shite beer he's tinted green stops flowing.

I reach for a wad of bills and the next pitcher, chuckling at Finn laid out across the bar top giving a peck to a girl. I've seen her in here once before, the night I arrived and laid my heart out for Francie.

She laughs at Finn and his *moves*, comfortable with him —but maybe not entirely comfortable in her skin with the way she's tugging at her shirt. When her friend leans in—her lips puckered at Finn, I see him pause like a deer in the headlights. He fancies himself a ladies' man, but generally can't hide the bit of surprise when his plans actually work.

Time passes in a blur of people and pitchers, flirting and laughing—until it doesn't. I don't see the lead up to it, but some knobhead just shoved some blond thing, spilling her beer down the front of her friend. The poor girl is soaked.

I am over the bar and plowing through people before things can escalate—or because I can't stand that shite and have to make him apologize for being an arse. It's not until I turn to check on the poor girl drenched in beer that I see it's *her*. And I'm about to mop the towel across her soaked chest. Thank Christ, I stop myself just before I have my hands on her gorgeous tits, overflowing from her tiny shirt.

She's fighting tears, looking absolutely miserable. My heart clenches and I want to protect her—give her some cover. So, I pull her in tight behind me as we make our way through to the back of the bar.

"What d'ye do, give her the biggest shirt ye could find?" Finn quips as I pass behind him getting back to work after helping *her*.

"It was the first one I grabbed. Thought it'd do fine." That's not at all true. Something about her being exposed after all of that bothered me. She didn't look particularly comfortable in the tight shirt she was in before it was plastered to her round, perfect tits. *Jesus*—I covered her up so no one would be thinking of her that way.

Reaching for the next pitcher, I get back into the rhythm of the bar. "What happened anyway? I didn't see."

Things have settled a bit and we're able to stand side by side and chat for a moment. Finn's cheeks go full red as I tell him what I saw and he starts cursing switching to Gaelic for the full effect. "—and Francie threw him out, yeah? Lissy's okay?" His jaw ticks and eyes dart around the room.

"He did—he's gone, mate." I follow his line of sight and see her smiling at her friend finally relaxing a bit. "What's her story? She's gorgeous."

"Don't. Just leave that alone. She's special." He makes a good effort of puffing up his chest and trying to make sure I know he's serious.

"Right." No way I'm intimidated by this pup, but we're obviously done talking for now. Scanning the room, I can't help but to find her in the crowd—her pull magnetic.

She's beautiful—gorgeous, really. Auburn hair cascades in a mass of curls down her back. I think of the silky strand that passed through my fingers in the storeroom—and her deep green eyes.

I fill several more pitchers answering the same question I've heard all night long. *You're new here, right? So, are you really Irish?* The accent and a little bit of flirting can accomplish just about anything I need it to, and the girls here are drawn to it like flies to honey. My tip jar is full up again, and there's still hours yet to go.

The night feels like it'll never end. Pushing my hair back again and holding it there, I glance slowly around the room, hoping to see it starting to clear out. I'm completely disappointed to see it's just as packed as it has been since we opened today. My gaze bounces around the room until I find her.

Finn mentioned her name, but that was hours and hundreds of pitchers ago. I wonder about her story, trying to work it out in my mind as I think about the timid, self-conscious way she holds herself. The way Francie and Finn seem to wrap her up and look out for her. The photographer in me wants to capture her image. Tease out the sadness she holds in her eyes. This girl is absolutely gorgeous. Stunning. But she's seen some troubles.

She darts her gaze away from me, back to the conversation flowing around her. I can't help my smile and shake my head, chuckling under my breath. As much as I was working her out in my mind, I just busted her checking me out. And that's okay. I like that she was looking at me. The idea that maybe she's trying to figure out my story as well. *I don't want to think of that tonight.*

It's coming on four in the morning when Francie finally starts ushering the last of the people out the door. I head to the back and put the keg of Guinness back on tap and pour one for myself and Finn. There's no way I'm closing out this night without having at least one. Francie's shrill whistle hits me from where he's shuffling people out the front door. He nods at the tap with a little bit of longing in his eye, so I pull a pint for him as well.

Coming around the bar, with three pints in one hand and snagging a bag of rubbish with the other, I do a quick scan and see the last handful of people heading for the door. What I don't see is the blur of luscious curves coming out of the storage room. I have no time to move—barely time to brace myself—I drop the trash, and wrap my arm around the stumbling girl to keep her from falling.

Again.

"Ohmygod, shit. Ohmygod."

The minute I realize who I've got my arm wrapped around, I pull her a little closer, hold on a little tighter. "You're alright, then?" Her arms are trapped between us, one hand pressed flat to my chest. Everywhere we're pressed together, from hip to shoulder, tingles like there's some kind of current running between us.

Slowly, she tilts her head back and looks up at me, her eyes wide and sparkling. "I'm so sorry."

"That's three." I smile down at her, not quite ready to let her go. Her brows pinch together as she purses her lips, confusion washing over her perfect features. "I've saved you three times tonight."

"You have." She straightens, pulling away from me.

"Thank you...really. I...I—um, thank you, for everything." Her voice is soft and shy. I keep my arm wrapped round her a bit longer than I need to, because I *want* to. But when I finally let her go, I feel the loss of her body pressed up against me far more than I should. She steps back with an awkward smile quirking at her lips.

"G'night, then."

"Good night." She turns away, going straight to Finn and Francie, hugging them and gracing each with a kiss on the cheek. Her attention briefly lands on me as she and her friend trip out the door a little unsteady on their feet. Arms linked and heads tilted together like they're sharing a secret.

"Francie." I prop the door open with my shoulder, letting the early morning air sweep through the pub. I watch the two girls walk away, the streetlights spotlighting their path as they go. "They're alright walking home this late, yeah?"

He stands on the walkway out in front of his pub; his pint in one hand and the other stroking his beard as he narrows his eyes on the girls. Several blocks away now, she turns and waves before disappearing into the small apartment building. "She knows I've got her back." Francie fixes me with a pointed stare, brows pinched in earnest.

That message is delivered loud and clear.

3

_____

Lis

Gracyn and I are completely holding each other up as we pick our way down the sidewalk to our apartment. We share a second-floor apartment in an old building just off the town square. "Holy shit, Gracyn. What even happened tonight?"

"Did you kiss him? Were you licking him in the storeroom?" She tries to hip bump me but misses, and I have to grab her so she doesn't fall. "You were so kissing him, right?"

"Nope." I sigh, but I really wanted to.

"Liiiissss," she draws my name way out dramatically, "but, did you see? Did you see how he rescued you? It was like a fairy tale." Gracyn's leaning all her weight into me, her head tilted—almost resting on my shoulder.

I did see it, and I can still feel the heat from his touch lingering on my back. Where our bodies were aligned from my hip all the way up to my chest. If I closed my eyes, I swear I can feel the hard planes of his chest against the palms of my hands. But if I do close them, I'm pretty sure the two of us will bust ass and I know Francie is watching from the doorway to make sure we get home safe.

"Which time?" I swing my still-wet shirt back and forth, trying to keep my mind from wandering back to Aidan. The feel of him. "He saved me more than once tonight, G." Rob never went out of his way to do anything for me. *He just broke my heart.*

Gracyn climbs the steps to unlock our door as I turn to wave at Francie. But Francie's not standing outside alone. Aidan is with him—leaning against the door drinking his pint. He raises his glass and nods to me before we each turn, disappearing into the warmth inside.

GRACYN PLOPS down on the couch with a bottle of water and a bagel, scrolling through her phone, her body swirling as though the world spins around her. I toss my wet shirt into the laundry basket and start peeling my beer-soaked bra off. "I'm gonna shower off before bed, you okay?" Gracyn doesn't even look up from her phone as she waves me off.

While the water heats up, I stare into the mirror, assessing myself. I take a deep breath and remind myself to stop focusing only on my faults. I try to see myself through someone else's eyes, but I end up falling into old habits, finding my eyes too wide, my boobs too big and my thighs too thick. I twist my hair up into a messy bun, not wanting to bother with drying it tonight.

I step under the spray and let the warm water fall over my shoulders, washing the stale beer away.

I knew something would happen eventually.

It's been some kind of a game to see who could humiliate

me more since we broke up. Can you even call it a breakup? Was I supposed to let Rob just have his fun with Maryse until they were done? Or wait until he picked the time most beneficial to him and his fucking political aspirations to publicly break up with me? I think not. Catching them in the act on Christmas Eve was all the humiliation I needed.

But this is the new me. One my family didn't expect, the me they didn't think I was capable of being. I walked as far away as I could in this little town, from the toxicity that is my family—the people who are supposed to love me unconditionally. Gracyn has a theory that Maryse is jealous of me but that thought is ridiculous. I can't help but laugh at that as I step out of the shower and make the usual comparisons. Height, hips, and hair—I've been told since forever that she is the standard and I fall short in every way. I'm still working on being okay with me just the way I am.

By the time I brush my teeth and fall into bed, the sun is ridiculously close to rising. I burrow down into my crisp sheets and close my eyes, thankful that I don't have to work until late in the afternoon. On the edge of asleep, I feel my bed dip and hear Gracyn mumble, "Not gonna talk about it?"

"Talk about what, G?"

"Any of it—all of it. Rob and Maryse. You think they asked Tyler to do that, to embarrass you at McBride's?"

"When did he change, Gracyn? When did he become this pompous asshole?" I know I missed all the signs. I was too busy working to pay my rent, buy my books—too wrapped up in keeping my own GPA up for my scholarship.

Rob's finishing up law school with a position already waiting for him in his father's law firm, Barrett & Barrett. It sounds far fancier than it is—that second Barrett in the title, that's Rob. When we started dating there wasn't any of this pretentiousness. He was just a normal guy who wanted more. Wanted to make his dad proud by following in his footsteps, make a difference in the world.

"Mmm...about the time he started dating your sister? All of those people are evil, Lis. You're better off without them." It seems simple enough when she says it, but knowing how little my mom and sister—let alone my dad—consider me hurts in a way that I can't just shrug off. "Even the most perfect little families have skeletons. At least yours are all out in the open."

The mattress bounces as Gracyn flops over to face me, her waggling eyebrows contrasting with her drunk, droopy eyelids. "Let's move on. Francie's new guy—you gonna tap that? It's time to move on."

"Jesus, Gracyn. Really?"

She falls onto the pillow and her breath evens out. She starts to snore, leaving me staring at the ceiling thinking back over the past couple months. How crushed I was. How my mother implied it was my fault that Rob cheated on me.

You're too independent, Lisbeth. If you had made yourself more available to Robert, been more interested in his goals like your sister is, he wouldn't have looked to spend time elsewhere.

After that, I really had nothing to say to her. Anna Rittenhouse has an unbelievable talent for rationalizing everything to suit her purpose. And her purpose once again, was to boost up her favorite daughter, Maryse.

Gracyn is the one who put me back together. She spent Christmas with me like we usually did, but instead of hanging out in our apartment after family dinner, laughing at Maryse and my mom, Gracyn consoled me. She sat with me on the floor handing me tissues until I ran out of tears. She filled my wine glass until we ran out of that too.

She went down to McBride's and made sure Francie knew what had happened. She also talked Finn out of finding Rob and *taking care of him* for me. They were my true family. These people who wrap me up in love and support that I've never felt from the ones who were related to me by blood.

I WAKE up with Gracyn's hair across my face and a desperate need for coffee and greasy food. "Unng—are you drooling on my pillow?" I whine, shoving myself out of bed to head for the kitchen.

"Coffee…" The morning drama with her is real. She's capable of little more than grumbling until she's had her caffeine.

"Go take a shower. You smell like the stale beer and we have to work—" I look at the clock on the microwave and groan. It's almost one o'clock. "—soon. We have to work soon." I start the coffee and drink down a full water bottle as fast as I can. I'm not hungover—I slept through that whole thing—but I'm thirsty, and tired, and a little sad.

Gracyn shuffles into the kitchen, her hair wet and her eyes still half shut. "Are we going to the diner for food or straight to the bistro so Tony can cook for us?"

"Diner."

"Or should we go to McBride's and get food there? You can flirt some more with…" She looks at me over the top of her mug, searching her fuzzy memories for his name.

"Aidan. His name is Aidan. And no, I'm not going there, I've gotta get through the rest of this year, graduate and get a job that pays better." I turn away, looking for my car keys.

"Lissy, you've got to start dating again sometime. He's perfect—TDH, muscles for days, and probably only here for a minute."

"TDH?"

Gracyn shrugs like it should be obvious. "Tall, dark, and handsome, sweetie. He can be your rebound, no pressure." She's serious. How can she be serious about this?

"For the love of God, Gracyn. No. I'm fine."

4

Aidan

It's been almost a week that I've been looking for her with every chime of the bell. Hoping to see her come back through the door of McBride's. I've worked every shift I could in that time, not wanting to chance missing her. Francie went all protective when I asked about her, and Finn's been useless for anything beyond her name and that I need to keep my distance. Jimmy, the other bartender who shares the flat, talks about her while we clean the bar and pour drinks.

He's told me she's at university, almost done with her program. That she works at Bistro Antonio across town— waiting tables and pouring cocktails. I went in there for lunch a couple days ago, hoping to see her, wanting to chat her up, but she wasn't working. I hung out as long as I could without bleeding over into the dinner rush, but she must have been to class and I had my shift at McBride's. I caught sight of her friend, the one Finn fancies, as I left, but no sign of Lisbeth.

Tuesday, I spend most of the day in New York City. I was

able to arrange a meeting for a photo shoot. It's not the journalistic side that I'm used to, but I miss being behind my camera, and shooting a few weddings for the right people will get me back to doing what I love.

The train ride in to New York City is a little over an hour, giving me plenty of time to think about what's next for me. The rhythmic sway of the train lulls me deep into the introspection I've been trying to avoid lately. Tending bar has been a great mindless distraction, but with all the time I've taken off since Michael died, I probably need to focus a bit back on my career. After university, I fell into photojournalism and made excellent use of my cameras and passport. *Until I got the call home.*

If this meetup goes well, I'll be able to fill more of my hours doing what I'm really good at—and pad my wallet as well.

A flash of auburn hair on the platform brings my thoughts back to the pub. It's not her. I wouldn't be that lucky, but I want to see her again. Spend an evening chatting her up. There's something magnetic about her that draws me in. She's stunning, yeah, but there's something else—something more to it.

MCBRIDE'S CAR park is quite empty when I stop in on the way home from the train station for a pint and some dinner, and to plan for the photography job I just booked. I'm sure there's nothing to eat at our flat since it was Finn's turn to get food in.

Francie's chatting with a man at the bar and Finn, of course, is busy with yet another girl.

I head to the kitchen and drop my dinner in the fryer. It's just easier to do it myself than trying to get Finn's fucking attention. And after setting my chicken tenders and chips on the bar, I start my pint and take stock of the bar. Finn is truly useless when he's flirting, so I clean the glasses he's let pile up, stock the fruit trays and wipe down the bar before topping up my pint, adding a shamrock flourish in the foam just for the hell of it.

As I reach out to place the glass next to my dinner, I'm met with the most beautiful green eyes—an almost olive green with gold and brown twisting through them. And they belong to *her*.

Dear God, help a poor bastard like myself.

"Hiya. What can I get for you?"

She smiles brightly, plump pink lips spread wide, and gives my plate a little nod. "That looks perfect. Did you know I was on my way?"

I smile back and wink, grabbing a glass for her. "I was hoping...only hoping." She chuckles and points to the Guinness when I raise the glass and nod toward the taps. "Are you wanting some dinner as well, then?" I ask, leaving her pint to settle.

"Seriously, I'll have exactly that." Her eyes crinkle as she looks at my basket of food. "This guy's obviously got fantastic taste."

Chuckling, I place her pint in front of her and head to the kitchen dropping more food in the fryer. With a hard squeeze to his shoulder, I let Finn know to listen for the timer, grab the vinegar, and head 'round to settle in next to her at the bar.

"So, I've good taste, then? Here, take this one. Finn will bring mine out in a bit." I move my basket closer to her. "I've not seen you in since St. Paddy's."

She grabs a chip and pops it in her mouth. Is she humming? Yeah, she's fucking humming...and bouncing in her seat a bit. I can't help the smile that quirks up on one side of my face. "You are correct. I haven't been in since. I think I needed some time to process all that green beer." Her small frown and scrunched-up nose tell me there's something more.

"I never actually introduced myself, I'm Lisbeth. Lis, really." She wipes her fingers on her thigh before reaching out to shake my hand. Just then, Finn drops my food on the bar in front of her.

"Lissy. How are ye?" Finn leans in for a peck on the cheek. "You've met Aidan, then?"

She slides the basket across the bar to me.

"We were just getting to that." She thrusts her hand out again to shake.

The moment our fingers touch, that current runs through me again. Forgoing her hand, I grasp her wrist and pull her toward me. I press my lips together, intending only to brush a chaste kiss on her cheek, but she turns just then. Just a bit, but it's enough that my lips land on the corner of her mouth, and time stills. Her eyes go wide before fluttering shut and I want to stay there, right there for the rest of my life. But fucking Francie chooses that moment to slam his glass on the bar making Lisbeth jump away. I'm pretty sure that was his intent by the murderous look in his eye.

What is his fucking deal? I've seen Finn and Jimmy flirting plenty with patrons and taking kisses far more intimate than that across the bar. She's smiling shyly with her fingertips resting against her lips when I drag my eyes away from Francie. I give her all of my attention, pitching my voice low. "You didn't think I'd let Finn have a kiss and just be satisfied with a handshake for myself, did you?" I turn back to my dinner giving her a moment to think about it.

She takes a long draught from her pint and lets out a contented breath—I want that satisfaction to be because of me. "No. I don't suppose so," she whispers, meeting my eyes in the mirror behind the bar. Mhmm.

"Tell me what you do when you're not here, drinking pints with the help."

She pops her last chip in her mouth and tilts her head back and forth while she chews. "I'm either in school or mixing drinks, myself. But I'll be doing instruction hours in the hospital soon, too."

"All of that? When do you find time for fun?"

She shrugs her right shoulder and wipes her hands dropping her napkin in the empty basket. "I don't really have a lot of free time. I either collapse on the couch with a movie or a book, or I come here with Gracyn, my roommate. She was here with me the other night."

Finn turns resting against the bar and folds his arms across his chest glaring at me. "And where's your Gracyn tonight?"

"She's in Florida for spring break, but I need the hours so..." another shrug as she peers at me over the rim of her glass, "I'm sure she's having enough fun for both of us."

"You didn't want to go?" I take her glass and reach across the bar to refill it. The idea of her lying on a beach, her creamy skin kissed by the sun has me tied in knots.

"I would love to be on the beach, are you kidding me? But I get to take everyone else's shifts this week so that helps a ton. I should be able to cover tuition for my summer classes by the end of this week." Lisbeth gives a quick nod, genuinely excited by this.

"Your parents don't help you?" Her beer becomes her sole

focus as Finn's head shoots up from his phone and Francie glares daggers at me. What the fuck?

"No, I'm doing this on my own. Just me." She says that like it's not any big thing before she snarks, "Plus, I got to have dinner with the help, so..." She pulls out some cash and hands it across to Finn, but I'm not done. I'm not ready for her to go, for this to end.

I reach out taking her hand and turn it over in mine. "Can I take you to dinner? A real one, not bar food. Do you have a night free this week?" The inside of her wrist has the softest and silkiest skin. I brush my thumb along it and feel her pulse ramping up. Her breaths are shallow as she watches my thumb pause and take measure.

"I...um, I have to..." She lets out a soft sigh and looks up into my eyes. "I only have tonight and tomorrow night off. I..." After a quick glance to Francie, she eases her hand away from mine, breaking not only our contact but our connection. I feel the loss of her hand more than just physically.

"I'll be needing your address to pick you up, then." I grab a napkin, a fucking cocktail napkin—how cliché—and a pen from near the taps. I slide them toward her. "And I'll be needing your number as well." I study her profile while she writes out her information. Her skin is pure like porcelain, and her lips are all I'll be thinking about as I try to fall asleep later. The taste of them. The feel of them.

I reach out and let a silky lock of her hair fall through my fingers as she finishes up her mobile number. The smell of her shampoo washes over me and, suddenly, I want to grab a fist full of it and drag her toward me. I want to feel it brush across my chest. I want a lot of things that would earn me all kinds of looks from Francie.

I'll have to talk to Francie—find out what his problem with me is. And get Jimmy to take my shift tomorrow night.

Why does she not have any help from her parents? Where's her support? And why is Francie keeping such a close eye on me?

5

Lis

I feel his gaze on me as I walk across the bar, searing into my back as I leave for home.

I can still feel the way his fingers danced across the inside of my wrist caressing—sending electric heat through my veins.

The way his voice washed over me as we talked of everything and nothing at all. Deep and a little smoky like a good bourbon, I want to drink it in. Talking with him tonight—his focus solely on me—was like I was the most interesting person he'd ever spoken to. Like I was important. I don't know the last time I felt that.

I slide my car up to the curb right in front of my building, grab my bag from the back seat and check for cars before getting out. There's not a lot I like about being all alone this week, but I'm not ever going to complain about padding my checking account or a good parking spot.

Normally Francie watches to make sure I get home safe

but he was acting ten different kinds of twitchy and weird tonight. I pull out my phone as I pop up the steps to my apartment and dial the number for McBride's. "Hey, Finn. It's Lis, can I talk to Francie for a minute?"

"Have to wait your turn. He's having a go at Aidan just now." Finn's obviously enjoying not being on the receiving end of a tirade for a change. I love Finn, but that boy is a mess. "O' course, Aidan might like an interruption. Are you up for swooping in to save your man?"

"What? Why is... Just, yeah. Tell Francie I need to talk to him." I hear harsh words filtering through the noise in the background before Francie jumps Finn's shit for interrupting, tearing into him, until I hear...my name. They get freakishly quiet and my heart pounds against my ribs. The shuffling of the phone, the hiss of static as it changes hands, and muffled warnings make their way through to me.

"What can I do for you, love? You're safe home?" It's not normally awkward when I call Francie, but tonight this is for sure. His words are terse and distracted.

I stumble through telling him I'm fine—that I wasn't murdered in the few blocks home. It suddenly makes sense— the garbled phrases, the tone of what I heard.

I steel myself with a deep breath and launch into it. "I know you're looking out for me, and you know I appreciate it, but..."

"Lisbeth darlin', I'm setting the boy to rights. He'll not be bothering you again, love."

He full-named me.

This is serious.

"Francie, we're going out to dinner tomorrow night. He wasn't bothering me at all. Last week you asked for my thoughts on him, so..."

"No, you're not. No. He's a shift to work tomorrow night so he won't be available." Where the hell is this coming from?

"Is he married?"

"No."

"Is he a murderer?"

"No, Lisbeth." Francie huffs, obviously frustrated with me. "I'm looking out for you and..."

"Is it my heart in general or is Aidan the problem?" My phone pings with a message distracting me from Francie's assurances that it's me he's worried about.

Unknown #: I've switched shifts with Jimmy. Just ignore Francie.

L: Aidan?

Unknown #: Yeah. Just tell him you understand and let him go. I'll take the verbal lashing and see you tomorrow.

Unknown #: 7pm

I stare at my phone trying to think of a response, but I'm at a loss.

Unknown #: Sleep well, love.

I'm finally able to get off the phone after giving Francis the required, *yes, I understand.* With a freshly poured glass of wine, I head in for a long hot soak in the bath. The bubbles will relax me, or maybe the wine will, but there aren't many things that a hot steamy bubble bath won't make better. And while the tub fills with lavender-scented bubbles, I make sure to save Aidan's number to my contacts.

THE NIGHT BARTENDER was supposed to be here an hour and a half ago. His car trouble means I've done all the dinner shift prep, restocked the beer coolers, and I no longer have time to buy something new to wear tonight. With both blenders whirring, a blown keg that needs to be replaced, and the clock ticking down the minutes, I'm about to come unglued.

I'm not normally a bitch, but I just can't today. Can't even.

"Let's get caught up and then you can run." My boss, Jenna, slides behind the bar and grabs a stack of drink orders. "Dumbshit needs to know he can't take advantage of you like this."

I've been working for her since high school, bussing tables until she needed another server. When a spot opened behind the bar, she gave me the chance. I get the new keg tapped and pour out the daiquiris, moving on to the next order up.

A few minutes later, we're caught up and Jenna pushes me out from behind the bar. "Go—I've got this. Have fun, Lissy." She hands me my bag after upending my tip jar into it.

"Thanks, Jenna. You sure this is okay?" She's been so tired lately, I feel really bad leaving her like this.

"I'm good." She stares past me to tonight's bartender ambling through the front door looking like he just got out of bed. The sound of Jenna ripping into him follows as I hop down the stairs, fading as the door shuts behind me.

I HAVEN'T HEARD much from Gracyn since she left for the beach and I need her desperately right now. She's posted a few pictures on her Instagram, but has been pretty quiet—for her. Something's up, but I have a feeling, it's gonna take a bottle of wine to figure it out when she gets back to town this weekend.

I text her really quick, hoping she's available now—Lord knows, she might decide in the middle of my dinner that she needs to talk to me.

L: Hey…you there? I need to borrow clothes.

G: Sure. Whatcha got going?

L: Dinner?

G: Who with?

L: Aidan. From McBride's. Chatted last night. He's sweet.

G: Mhmmm. Make good choices. All of that…

L: Thnx. Talk later?

I check when I get home and again when I get out of the shower but she doesn't text back.

My plans for a glass of wine while I straighten my hair and YouTube makeup tutorials are replaced with half-dried wild waves spilling down my back and a quick swipe of mascara.

I send up a prayer that Gracyn didn't take her black knit swing dress with her as I rifle through her overflowing closet. I have no idea where we're going tonight, but that dress is my favorite and I can dress it up or down easily enough, depending on what Aidan has on.

Fuck, fuck, fuck.

He's going to be here soon.

Finally, in the very back of her closet, I find the dress and pull it over my head while running back to my room for shoes. Taupe ankle boots or spiky heels—I grab both and set them by the front door.

After another coat of mascara, a little blush, and some lip gloss, I step back, trying to see myself as Aidan will. I haven't been on a first date in more than four years, and my nerves are just kicking in to full riot mode. I nearly jump out of my skin when I hear a knock at the door.

I take a deep breath and let it out slowly, trying to calm myself, but my heart slams in my chest as I swing the door open.

Aidan's black hair is still damp from his shower or maybe he took the time to style it. The curve of his lips, the stormy night of his eyes. The scruff on his jaw. I want to stand here and admire him, commit everything to memory—and maybe mess him up just a little.

His crisp white shirt stretches across his shoulders, sleeves rolled up to his elbows, showing the pure strength of his forearms. My eyes travel down his body taking in the way his dress pants fit snugly to his hips and thighs. He's even polished his shoes—totally an odd thing to notice but *Rob would never have bothered with that. He'd have bought new ones.*

Aidan cares how he looks, more than just a change of clothes and spray of cologne.

I get caught staring and feel a hot blush searing my cheeks. I bite at my lip and meet his smiling glance as I try to cover this awkward feeling. "You look great." His smile crinkles the corner of his eyes calming my inner mess.

"Thanks. You're sure, then, or do you want to take another look before we go?" he teases and reaches for the jacket I threw over the back of the couch. I slide my feet into my heels and laugh.

As he helps me slip into my jacket, he runs his fingers lightly down my arms—leaving a trail of goose bumps—until his fingers find the inside of my wrists. His touch there sends tingles through my entire body; it takes everything I have not to shudder. "Shall we go?" he rasps out as he reaches for the door sliding his other hand to my lower back, guiding me out.

6

Aidan

I guide her down the stairs to the walkway in front of her building keeping a hand at her back as much as I can. "Are you okay to walk? It's just a few blocks." I'd made reservations at a café close to where she lives, but those shoes she put on—fuck me.

She smiles and nods, teetering as we start toward the restaurant. I reach for her hand to steady her and tuck it securely into the crook of my elbow. The need to touch her driving me, I clasp my other hand over the top of hers, holding her firmly in place. Her gaze meets mine, followed by a sweet smile and a squeeze to my arm.

She blatantly checked me out when she opened the door to her flat. Her gaze lit every inch of my body, lingering on what she obviously liked. She moves her hand to my bicep. I can't help but flex the muscle; I want to impress her. I want to feel her hands caress me the way her eyes did. She shudders almost imperceptibly as I move my hand to reach for that spot on her wrist again. I rub small circles there with the pad of my thumb, focusing entirely on her reaction, the hitch in her breath. The soft sigh she lets escape.

The café is fine. Dinner's lovely. But Lis? Lis is fucking brilliant.

With the table separating us, it's awkward to reach across to her, and I miss the contact.

"Tell me more, Lisbeth. Why nursing?" The more time I spend with her, the more I want to know what's in her head, her heart. What her dreams are.

"I like to take care of people, help them when they can't do things for themselves. I get to see life in all its forms—beginning through the end. There's something beautiful about that, reverent."

My breath catches in my throat and I roll my lips in between my teeth.

Her fork clatters to the table and she reaches for my hand. "Aidan, are you okay? I'm—did I say something?"

"Erm, no. You're fine." I shake my head, unable to form the words just yet. Do I want to share this? Open up my heart the way I've already asked Lis to do?

Her touch is warm when she reaches her hand to cover mine, soothing me—calming me. I look up and her lips are pressed tightly together, dipping down at the corners. This was supposed to be a nice dinner with a lovely distraction. How did I get to a place where I'm shoving down raw emotions at the same time that I'm wanting to bare my soul?

I clear my throat and stare at nothing across the room. "I'm fine, I just—my brother just passed away. That's...that's why I'm here. In the States, I mean. I had to get away." I blink back the sting in my eyes and force a tight smile to my lips.

"I'm so sorry. What—do you—I'm sorry." Lisbeth wraps

her free hand around mine, grasping it between hers and for the first time since I watched Michael's coffin get lowered into the ground, I feel able to say the words.

"He died very suddenly, diagnosed and then gone in a matter of weeks." How can that be? I don't want to do this, have this huge heavy weight smothering us. "He was thirty-two—far too young to die, but he'd be pissed if he thought he were ruining our evening." It's true, actually. He'd be livid with me with how this is turning out.

The laughter comes out unbidden and Lis looks a little shocked. "He was a smart-arse; I'm sure that comes as a huge surprise." This is what Michael would want, how he would want to be remembered. "The night before he passed I was sitting with him and he said, 'it was hard and fast, and over way too quick' and then he cracked up laughing like a twelve-year-old boy."

Lis smiles broadly and nods her head. She seems to get it. The need to laugh and hold desperately the happy memories. I raise my glass to his honor and finish my whiskey.

"So, you ran away." It's not a question, she says it like a fact.

"I did. But I think I landed well."

We linger over coffee and dessert, conversation turning back to her school and my work—my photography. We share a dense, decadent chocolate cake, and thank fuck she's focused on that, because I can't take my eyes off her. The way her lips slide the gooey sweet chocolate off the fork. The way her tongue darts out to lick at every last bit. The way her eyes flutter closed, lost in the ecstasy of the moment. The moan that escapes her lips. *I want to put that look on her face. I want to own that.*

Christ, I have to calm this shit down or the walk to her door will kill me.

After settling the bill, I pull out her chair and guide her into the soft evening air. The walk back to her flat is leisurely and relaxed. This town is quaint—quiet and safe-feeling. The walkways are lined with trees and the business owners decorate their storefronts. Idyllic, really. The biggest danger to Lis right now is me. My thoughts are anything but pure and wholesome.

At her door, she turns to me. "Thank you. I...this was great. Thank you." Her lips—*fuck*—they soften and lift sweetly at the corners.

"It was my pleasure, Lisbeth. Thank you." I reach my hand up to cup her cheek and lean in for a good night kiss. Chaste. Respectful.

But all my good intentions ignite, the moment my lips touch hers. I slide my hand through her silky hair to the back of her head. She gasps in a breath and parts her lips.

That moment.

That. Right. There.

I slide my tongue along her lips and taste the sweet hint of chocolate. It's overwhelming but not nearly enough. I deepen the kiss, tasting her. Our tongues tangle and fight for control.

My senses return when I hear and feel her moan low in her throat. That noise—the one from the restaurant. The one that she gave the cake, but I wanted for myself. I stop. I have to. Placing a truly chaste kiss on her forehead, I take her keys, opening the door.

"Good night, love." I need to bang my head against the fucking wall and go before I get carried away. I turn and head down the stairs. To safety.

· · ·

MY FLAT IS empty when I get there. I need time and a glass of whiskey to sort myself. Tonight's distraction became an emotional carnival ride.

She's beautiful, and intriguing, and I want nothing more than to spend ridiculous amounts of time with her. Learning her, knowing her. *Christ, the way I want to know her.* The taste of her lips, and the ways they move. Her curves just barely hinted at under that dress she wore tonight. My thoughts are sinful, at best.

Eyes closed, I lay my head back against the cushions of the sofa and let my mind go—just for a minute. I can't stop it. Her chest rising and falling. Her pulse thumping to match mine. The feel of her skin beneath my fingertips. The pale pink flush on her cheeks as it creeps down into the neckline of her dress caressing the tops of her breasts. The featherlight touch as she moves her hands up my chest to land on my shoulders.

Fuck.

The key scrapes in the lock and I reach for one of the throw pillows on the sofa, jamming it down across my crotch and rest my tumbler of whiskey on top. Looking fucking casual, if I do say so. Finn tumbles through the door with a tiny little blond thing. That's just what I need tonight; to hear them through the thin-as-shit walls. His "friend" is completely engrossed in him and hardly acknowledges me, but the laughing grin from Finn speaks volumes. Shoving the pillow aside now that I'm no longer going to embarrass myself, I grab my earbuds and glass, and head up to my loft bedroom.

The squeals and giggles floating up the stairs promise to

make tonight unbearable. I need to invest in noise-canceling headphones. Doesn't matter how loud I crank the volume, I can still hear them, Finn and his pixie. I try my best to ignore them and just fall asleep, but I give up. Before I register what's happening, my hand slides down my stomach to the waistband of my boxer briefs. Between the noises coming from downstairs and my lingering thoughts of Lisbeth, I reach in and grip my cock, stroking firmly. The release is not nearly satisfying—not near as good as what I imagine with Lis.

FRANCIE MEETS me at the door of the bar the next morning ready to tear into me. He was either waiting by the window or heard my piece-of-shit car coming from a mile away.

"The fuck do you think you're doin'?" he bellows, throwing his hands in the air spilling coffee all over the floor. I should have expected this. Talking Jimmy into trading shifts with me had been no big deal, but I hadn't thought about how bad the fallout would be today. I've got to work a full double shift now, I'm stuck here until closing.

"Francie, I took her out to dinner. That's it." I try to speak calmly, like I'm trying to soothe a spooked horse. "I walked her to her door and used my manners—made sure she was safe home and tucked away for the night. What did you think I was going to do to her?" He's being ridiculous.

Huffing a big breath out through his nose, Francie glares. "I've already talked to Lissy. I am well aware that ye behaved the gentleman." *What the fuck?* "But that girl has been through enough. She doesn't need you to work her up, lead her on and break her heart, Aidan. She doesn't need that shite again." He looks devastated, fucking heartbroken for her.

"Francie, what happened with Lisbeth? I know her family is not involved, but something else must have happened to put you in this mode..." I move him toward the bar and grab his coffee cup to refill it for him while I grab some for myself.

We're going to settle this. I need to know what's got him so up in knots. *Fuck, I need to know what I'm dealing with in her.*

I'm clearly invested in this girl—but I'm not prepared for the shite I pull out of Francie over the next hour while I clean and prep McBride's for the busy Thursday night. It takes some prodding and a little Jameson in his coffee, but I think I get it. All of it. The whole shitty story of the fucking bastard that broke her heart.

Francie assures me that I'll not have to deal with the arse and Lisbeth's sister, but, God help me, if I don't feel my heart squeeze. I get it, now—Francie's protection over her, Finn and Jimmy's affection—she's family to them. They're family to her. Blood may be thicker than water, but love is thicker than anything.

7

Lis

That kiss. The sweet touches throughout the night simmered on the walk back to my apartment and then when he kissed me? I thought I was going to melt right there.

Francie has been blowing up my phone most of the night. I ignored it all through dinner, but when it rings as I lean my back against the door, I answer.

"Lisbeth, where've you been?" he fusses and just that quickly, I'm pulled from my happy little bubble. His voice sounds mildly panicked. "What are you doing, love? Tell me you've got your head on straight and you're not gettin' caught up in a boy." He sounds pissed.

"Francie, I'm fine. We had dinner and talked," I soothe, hoping I can calm him down a little. "Aidan walked me home and was an absolute gentleman." Surely that'll put his mind at ease—or not. I talk to him for a good twenty minutes over the background of a full McBride's. The last thing I want is for Aidan to get ripped apart for taking me out.

It's time for me to start dating again. I've been working so hard in school and life to move forward from the devastation that Maryse and Rob left me with.

Like Gracyn said, this might be the perfect distraction.

Aidan is nice, but this isn't where his life is. His family, his career, are all back in Dublin and this is just a temporary reprieve.

Francie finally calms and promises not to lay Aidan out in the morning.

Ending the call, my thoughts go straight back to that kiss. It's all I can think about while doing my thing and getting ready for bed. I return the dress to Gracyn's closet and grab my laptop as I hop into bed. I slide under the covers and get comfy, pulling up a new browser to Google Aidan Kearney. And his photography. I have no idea why he's working in a bar.

I scroll through images of children in third world countries. Images of major political players across the globe. Of celebrities and their families. I scroll through the seemingly endless photographs, stopping when my eyes start to blur. Aidan is not just talented, he might well be famous. The photos he's taken have been published, printed, and shared thousands of times over. He's had his work in every major news outlet, both print and digital.

Then there are pictures of him in a school uniform showing an adorable, much younger version of Aidan. His dark hair flops down over his forehead, but his eyes. His eyes are the same. They are an absolutely stunning clear dark blue like the evening sky as the moon chases the sun across it. There is a cute little girl sitting with him. Her blond piggy tails are lopsided, but her bright green eyes are all smiles for

Aidan. I don't even think when I crop her out and save the picture to my desktop.

I fall asleep thinking of him, about why a relationship with him won't work. We're in such different places looking for much different things.

WITH MOST OF the staff being on spring break, I've worked back-to-back shifts Thursday, Friday, and Saturday this week and I'm absolutely exhausted. But I made the rest of my tuition for summer session and a little extra.

I drag ass home after closing up the bistro late Saturday night. I need a shower so bad right now and then to just crawl into bed. I want to wash away the grease and sweat. And, I really, *really* want the hot water all to myself, just one last time before Gracyn gets back.

I thought she was getting home tomorrow, but the lights are on and the sound of water running hits me as I throw my keys on the table by the door. "G, you here?" Instead of waiting for an answer, I crack open a bottle of wine and pour us each a glass. I have a feeling we're going to need it to get the dirt from this past week out of Gracyn.

"Hey, is that you?" she yells as she slides into her room and shuts the door leaving a trail of wet footprints behind her. "Go shower—I know you feel gross. I'll open some wine for when you're done."

"Way ahead of you." It's like she knows that she has no choice but to spill her shit. I grab my shorts and a thermal tee, and pray for just a little hot water.

"Oh. I think I might have used all the hot water, so..." And there it is, reason 4,852 that I need to graduate early and start making real money. Our place is so small and so old, we're never guaranteed enough hot water for both of us.

I rush through my tepid shower to find Gracyn curled up in the corner of the couch. "Why are you home early?" She looks up from refilling her glass with this look on her face that I can't quite place. Sad, maybe, but not quite. "Are you okay? I hardly heard from you this week." She's already shaking her head before I can finish the question.

"Let's talk about you. How was your date with...what's his name again? Tell me about your week." She's in full-on avoidance and I give her the squinty eyes as she downs half her glass of wine.

"Aidan." I'll give her a little space before I press. "It was great. We talked over beers Wednesday night and he...he pulled me in for that kiss you seemed to think I needed. Francie about lost his shit over that and then we talked about you being away and me having to stay here and work, and school and his—" I pause to take a breath from my crazy and Gracyn looks really sad. "G, talk to me. I'll give you every detail later, but, honey, you need to tell me what happened. Is it...? Do we need to call the police? Do I have to kick someone's ass?" She's staring into her glass with an intensity I rarely see on her. "Gracyn, talk to me. I'm really starting to worry."

With a huge sigh, she refills both of our glasses and finally looks up at me. "I...I met someone." I try to school my features, but I feel my eyes growing wide. Gracyn has sworn up and down that she will not get serious with anyone until after she graduates. She never really wants to talk about why, but she's stuck to it for the past two and a half years. I give her the go-ahead nod so she'll keep talking.

"He's in a band that was playing at one of the beach bars

and," she forces a huff of air out through her nose, "it's just shitty timing. He's in a band, for God's sake, did I mention that? He's in a band." She goes back to staring down her wine and I struggle, not knowing what to say.

Gracyn's studying to be an accountant. She's supposed to take over her dad's accounting firm, so a guy in a band is pretty far outside her wheelhouse. This doesn't fit to Mr. George's ideals at all, but I feel like there's more to it.

"Tell me why this one is a big deal." She glares at me over the top of her wine glass and I shrug, deflecting her hard look. "What's he like?" I draw out the *he*, hoping she'll at least give me a name.

"His name's Gavin, and he's different, not like..." She shakes her head, seeming to need to pull herself together. "God, he's so interesting—well read, crazy smart..." She draws her brows together and gets lost inside her brain.

"Where's the bad part, G?" This girl has been my rock, and it kills me to see her struggling like this.

She pinches at her lower lip and blinks several times before continuing. "We spent hours upon days talking on the beach—arguing over books and getting to know all the crazy, stupid little things about each other. He hates pickles, and loves documentaries." She looks so far away from this place —this moment.

"And then I came home and he moved on to his next spring break gig with his band. The end."

"But you got his number, right?" The look on her face tells me everything I don't want to hear. "G, you did, didn't you? Exchanged numbers—email? Facebook?"

"We deleted each other's contact info before I left. You know how this goes, the timing was shitty and that's the end of it." I can't believe her. "Now, tell me about Aidan."

8

Aidan

She comes in a couple hours after I open for the day. It's been weeks since we had dinner. Since I left her at her door with just that kiss. It's been playing on a loop in my fucking mind.

School is her priority, she was clear on that. Very clear. And I respect that and her need to devote time and energy to her studies. I waited a full week before I texted her, other than the one I sent the next morning telling her how much I enjoyed our evening. But she didn't respond. Since then, I've spent a lot of time talking myself out of pursuing her. A lot of really good reasons to let this thing go. I'm not long for this small town.

The photo shoots I've picked up over the past couple weeks have gotten me noticed again by the right people. Maybe it's too soon to get back to it? It's been less than six months since I stepped away from my camera, from my career. My family—Michael and his wife— were so much

47

more important at the time, but if I wait any longer, it'll be that much harder to get back to it. I can't lose momentum again.

But, this girl.

She settles in at the corner of the bar, dropping her bag on the chair next to her. The push and pull of her is bloody confusing. I make my way over to her, wiping the bar as I go. "Wasn't sure I'd see you again. You weren't avoiding me, then, were you?" *Christ.* Where the fuck did that come from?

"Sorry. It's been crazy. I..." She sighs pointing to the Guinness tap, her head tilting to the left just a little. "I had tons of work this week and spent every last minute in the hospital. I'm exhausted. I don't know if I'm gonna make it."

Hospital? "Are you all right?" I reach across the bar for her wrist, my thumb automatically caressing the tender skin that I love. I've completely forgotten all about *letting things go.*

"No. I'm fine, it was for school. I had clinical hours I had to do, but they assigned me nights." She takes a long pull from her pint. "I know I'll have to work them when I start for real, but I don't know how I'll make it. My days and nights are so screwed up."

I watch a yawn roll over her and take control of her entire body. "And I have to work at the bar tonight." Her wrist slides from my hand as she pulls her shoulders back. She sweeps her hair up off her neck and arches her back, pushing her chest out toward me.

I can't think. All I can do is stand here staring at her, my eyes raking down the graceful line of her neck—across her delicate collarbone, to the swell of her tits straining under the confines of her top. *Jesus.* I want to trace that line with my tongue. I want to taste her skin—touch, feel, nip at every part of her. She has no idea what she does to me—making me want things I have no business wanting.

Bracing myself on the bar, knuckles white from gripping so hard, I dig deep to find some semblance of control. I clear my throat, interrupting the sensual show in front of me. Lis looks suddenly embarrassed, like she just now realizes her effect on me.

"How long does your crazy schedule last?" I ask. "Will it be like that for weeks? Months?" I don't like the idea of her so tired, so worn out. But really, I'm selfish—I want to know if I can see more of her.

She shivers as she pulls her computer out of her bag. "This rotation is done for now. I'll have to do another over the summer and again in the fall. I'm just so tired," she manages to get out as another yawn takes over—her skin pebbling up with chill bumps. "Sorry, I can't seem to stop that—is it cold in here? I'm freezing."

I grab a couple mugs and pour us each a cup of coffee. The sweet contented smile that spreads its way across her face as she wraps her hands around the porcelain is intoxicating. I could fucking get lost in that. "Lisbeth, what can I do for you? Can you not take the night off—sleep a little?" She just shakes her head, wrapping herself more tightly around the warm mug. The tension is starting to leave her body and she looks like she might fall asleep on the bar. "You need to go home and take a nap, love." God how I would love to join her, though she really needs to sleep and if I were there...

She flicks her eyes up to the clock above the bar and grimaces. "I have to submit my clinical notes by one o'clock. Do you mind if I do it here? And can I have some fries?" She's grabbing for her coffee more than her pint at this point. I refill her mug and head to the kitchen to make her some lunch—she needs more than a basket of chips to keep her going.

There's not a lot I can do to help, but I can feed her, maybe keep her warm. She's stopped typing and is practically falling asleep with her cheek resting on the heal of her hand and her eyes glazing over. I slide her laptop out of the way, and set down her plate. I grab my jacket from behind the bar and gently place my hand between her shoulders. She mumbles, "...'m awake..." as she sits up and scrubs her hand up and down her face. She was clearly not awake.

I wrap her in my jacket, rubbing her arms to warm her up. "I thought you could use more than just a snack, love." Pulling her hair free of the collar, I caress the side of her neck, lingering just behind her ear. I don't know what's come over me, but I want to lose myself in this spot.

She stills, holding her breath a moment before releasing a shaky breath. But instead of leaning into me, she pulls away.

"Th-thank you."

Nodding, I step back behind the bar to give her some space. "Sure. Let me know what else I can get for you." Not what I wanted. I rattled her, and maybe even scared her off.

I busy myself stocking the bar for the evening, lost a little in my head. Is she pulling back because of that arsehole? The bastard that fucked her sister? It seems different, more than that. Maybe it's me.

I clear her plate and refill her coffee while she works. It's just been the two of us here this whole time, and it's been *fucking torture*. I spend as much time as I can in the kitchen and stockroom, cleaning counters that are already spotless. Straightening liquor bottles that I've already alphabetized. Am I avoiding her? Hiding from this pull I feel?

I hear her putting her computer away, zipping up her bag.

I need to do something, say something to make the awkwardness go away. "Are you finished, then?"

She meets my eyes, as she slides off the barstool. I dump her pint glass into the sink and wipe down the already clean bar. "I think so. I got everything sent to my professors so we'll see. What do I owe you?" she asks as she digs through her bag for her wallet.

"Not a thing." She moves both of her eyebrows up and opens her mouth to protest. "This one's on me." I chuck the bar rag over my shoulder and cross my arms over my chest, hoping I'm giving out that there's no room for negotiation. She blows a lock of hair out of her eyes and just stares. She really does not do well with others caring for her.

"I can't let you do that. I feel so much better than when I walked in here earlier. Please let me pay you, Aidan."

I glance at my watch and look her straight in the eye. I'm pushing this a little, probably more than necessary, but she's dead on her feet. The need to take care of her drives me. When she starts to fidget, I lean toward her. "Go home and rest. Let me just do this for you. We'll figure out a way for you to pay me back later."

Her wheels are spinning and I can see the battle she's waging inside. "Okay. Thank you." She pinches her brows together and screws her mouth up on one side. Another deep breath and she relaxes as she lets it go. She gives me a quick nod and turns to leave. I watch as she hefts her bag higher on her shoulder and heads out the door—still wrapped in my jacket.

9

Lis

I am so glad I stopped at McBride's on the way home. We have nothing beyond a bottle of wine and stale crackers in our kitchen. I half wish that Aidan wasn't there though. I've done a pretty good job of avoiding him. I know I got scared. Talking with Gracyn about her trip reminded me that I need to stay focused. I have so much riding on school. Graduating early. Making this work. But he took care of me. I don't really know what to do with that.

I learned really early on that depending on people leads to nothing but disappointment. My mom flaked out right after she divorced my dad. She needed to work on her—at least, that's what she claimed. Really, she was pretty much done with being an adult and even though I was only seventeen, she decided I was old enough to manage paying the bills, going to the grocery store, cooking and cleaning. After all, she had raised me. *Right.* My dad drank away all of his money and my mother just didn't have anything left for me after paying my sister's tuition. I was used to Maryse being the priority. It had been going on for as long as I could remember.

I know I'm not good at having people help me. I can give without batting an eye. Doesn't matter what it is, if someone needs help, I'm on it. Accepting it? Yeah, no. It had me rattled, or maybe falling asleep on a bar mid-day did that.

I move to take off my jacket and realize, it's not mine. It was warm when I left the house last night so I just had my scrubs on. This is all Aidan—spicy, masculine. I hang it on the back of my desk chair and head back in to take a shower and wash away the hospital. I love what I do, but there's a lot of gross stuff I deal with there and I do not want to bring it into my bed while napping.

The hot water feels amazing, soothing my sore and tired muscles. I fall into bed and wait. As tired as I am, I just feel restless and disconnected. Like I'm too exposed. I drag myself out of bed and put his jacket back on. I wrap it around me and crawl back under the covers surrounded by Aidan. After checking my alarm, I let sleep wash over me.

I COULD HAVE SLEPT for days, but by the time I get to work, I almost feel human. I dump my bag and Aidan's coat in the back room and check the bar stock. Filling napkins and straws. Cutting up fruit. Checking the kegs and listening to the hustle and buzz of the restaurant on a Friday night.

Jenna pulls out a chair and sits at the end of the bar. "Hey. How'd your hospital thing go this week?"

"It was good. I didn't love working nights. No...that's not true. I actually loved the quiet hush of the hospital at night, but my body and brain are so confused right now." Out of habit, I pour a glass of her favorite wine and set it in front of her. She eyes the deep crimson liquid and slides it back toward me, resting a hand on her belly. "But the people. Jenna, I love it. I love helping them and making sure they're comfortable and settled and the...all of it. I love all of it." I sigh and offer her a huge smile. She knows my dream—my nature—and how hard I've worked to get here.

"Sweetie, you will make the best nurse. The absolute best." She winks at me. "I'll let you change my bedpan any day." I love this woman. She and Tony just found out they are having a baby and if everything goes the way it's supposed to, I'll be graduated and waiting on the results of my boards by her due date in January. I would love to be there when she delivers.

I look at the wine I poured and it clicks that my pregnant boss can't enjoy her favorite drink for months yet. I really am tired. I grab a new glass and fill it with ice, a couple limes, a splash of cranberry juice, and soda water. Jenna laughs as she takes a long drink and looking longingly at the wine.

"I do miss a glass of wine. Tell me what else is going on. I feel like I haven't seen you in forever. You still seeing that guy?"

I pick at my words, trying to sort out how I feel. "We went out to dinner, that's all. I don't really have time. I need to get through this year and pass my boards. Then...I'll think about it." It's like I'm constantly trying to talk myself out of wanting to spend more time with Aidan.

She's looking past me, over my shoulder, smiling at a customer.

I paste on my smile and turn to greet...Aidan. How much of that did he hear? "Hey. What are you doing here?" My heart skips erratically as I place a cocktail napkin on the bar in front of him.

"Thought I'd have you tend to my needs for a change." His smirk is ridiculously sexy. I feel flutters deep in my belly. "I'll have a whiskey, neat. And a menu." I hand him a menu and turn to get his drink. Jenna's having a full, silent conversation with me, one I'm trying desperately to ignore. I do catch the look she gives me when I grab for the house whiskey. She shakes her head, looks directly at the good stuff and nods, smiling her wicked little smile.

She and Gracyn have obviously talked about who I'm dating. Not dating—one date. And drinks and food at McBride's. And today—how he took care of me. Dammit. I grab the bottle of Basil Hayden's and a heavy crystal glass. Jenna gave me the go-ahead, whether she realizes it or not, so I pour him a generous glass. I fill a small pitcher with distilled water, placing it on a small plate with fresh lime wedges and mint. Jenna's quiet laugh barely reaches me as she grabs her drink and heads back to her office. There's no way in hell I'm getting away with avoiding the dating discussion with her now.

I place the tumbler in front of him and the small plate off to the side, turning it so the limes and mint are toward him. Presentation is everything—or maybe I'm putting way more thought and effort into this than is necessary—since I'm not interested, and I'm *so* focused on school. *Right.*

I take his dinner order and excuse myself to the kitchen to grab his salad and a breadboard. Tony yells as I'm on my way out, "Is this what Jenna ordered? Christ, she's killing me with these pregnant cravings. She's never had a rare steak in her life." I lose the rest of his rant to the flare of the grill and his mumbling.

"No. She went back to her office, that's for a..."

"For a special diner at the bar, Tony." Jenna elbows me as she scoots past to grab a bowl of soup. "Lis is trying to impress someone." She winks at me with a big goofy grin on her face. I just turn and walk away. Nothing I say is going to stop the inevitable teasing.

My heart flutters as I set Aidan's place at the bar and serve his salad and bread. "What are you doing here, for real? I... I'm sorry I left with your jacket earlier. I have it in the back, let me go grab it for you." I take a step back, but he reaches for my hand and stops me.

"Erm—don't worry about it. I'm away this weekend. I've got to go into the city for a meeting. Do you want to go with me?"

"I can't." I really want to. "I have to work and get ready for finals, I have a ton of studying to do." Why am I so disappointed? I have no problem telling everyone else that I'm not interested and I need to focus. I just can't seem to convince myself. "I'll be done in three weeks, maybe we could go then?" *What the fuck?* My mouth and my brain are so not communicating.

"Absolutely. We'll go when you're done." His gaze locks with mine and I feel those fluttery tingles again. It's like he can see deep into me. It's uncomfortable—I don't know if I like it.

I turn away to fill drink orders for the servers and a few other patrons at the bar, trying to give myself some space. I'm just so aware of him. I can feel his gaze on me. As I duck under the bar top to grab his dinner from the kitchen, I hit my damn head and muffle a curse. The soft laugh from Aidan doesn't escape me and my cheeks catch fire.

I set his plate in front of him, and clear away the others. "Is there anything else I can get for you? Another drink?"

He gives me a quiet *mhmmm* as he cuts into his steak.

"Does everything look okay?"

He watches as I pour him a fresh whiskey. "Things couldn't look any better."

I snap my attention up to meet his hooded gaze. My whole body heats up. Desire rushing through me. "I...uh... okay. I'll let the chef know."

He has me so off balance and flustered. I know I'm running away again, but I let the hostess know the bar is unattended for a bit, and run to the restroom. Bracing my hands on the counter, I stare at my reflection. For the love of God, I look panicked.

He's just being kind—I'm just a distraction. I wash my hands, letting the cool water run over my wrists hoping it'll help to calm me. He's getting to me.

My mini-breakdown lasts longer than it should and when I get back to the bar, he's gone.

Just gone. His glass is empty. Plates neatly stacked. Gone.

I fill the drink orders that have accumulated while I was busy falling apart in the bathroom for no reason, and check on the rest of the customers at the bar. When I clear Aidan's plates, I find a hundred-dollar bill and a note on a cocktail napkin. I clear his tab and tuck the ridiculous tip in my back pocket. No way in hell am I keeping that. With a quick glance to see that everyone at the bar's glasses are full, I lean against the register and focus on the note.

Lisbeth,

    I enjoyed taking care of you this morning and wanted to see you again. I'm sorry I'm making you uncomfortable. That's not my intent. I'll leave you be for the remainder of your term so you can study and make grades. But I've let your boss know that you need the weekend after term end off work. Don't bother trying to change it—she agrees fully that you need a break. Study hard. Do well. And I'll see you in three weeks' time. Hang on to my jacket as long as you need.

xx

Aidan

10

Aidan

I t's time. The last three weeks of her term are over and I've
got our trip to NYC planned. Gracyn has been brilliant,
feeding me details on when Lisbeth's last exam is, letting me
know what time to be here. Waiting.

The day is gorgeous and it gets even better as I watch her
walk toward her building. All her focus on her phone, brows
pinched together and nose wrinkled. I want to photograph
her. She is art in motion. And she's not paying attention at all
to her surroundings, just about tripping over me sitting on
her steps.

"Shit. You scared me." Her hand flies up to her chest as
she startles. "What are you doing here?"

I can't help the grin that spreads across my face. "How
was your exam?" I hand her a steaming cup of coffee and
stand to let her by.

"Good. I'm done—for this semester." I watch as she rolls

her shoulders shaking off the stress of the term and adjusts her ruck. Every movement captivates me. She is stunning.

"Mmm...thank you for this. That final started way too early." She raises the coffee to her lips and inhales a long pull from the cup. "Oh my God, this is so good." She's wrapped around her coffee like it's going to save her life. The tension visibly leaves her body as the caffeine settles in.

Following her inside the flat, I take her bag and set it by the front door. "We have a few minutes, if you want to grab your bag. I think Gracyn put everything you'll need for the day in there." Her expression is beautifully confused.

She sets her coffee on the hall table and props a hand on her hip. "What do you mean?"

"Love, I told you weeks ago we were going to the city today to celebrate your term end. You're done now, yeah?" She nods tightly, like I'm an eejit since we just fucking discussed this. "Where's your confusion, then?" I step closer to her. "Grab what you need," I lean in and pluck the coffee from her hand, "and let's go." I look her straight in the eye as I take a drink from her cup, loving that my lips rest where hers were only minutes ago. I smile and turn, heading out the door—grabbing her keys on the way to make my point.

THE CITY IS HUMMING with activity, a drastic change from the quiet calm of the train ride in. We practically had the train car to ourselves and the solitude combined with the movement of the train and clack of the tracks lulled Lisbeth to sleep. Her head dipped to my shoulder as the car swayed on the rails. The scent of her hair enveloped and soothed me and I savored the feel of her body against mine. It was heaven.

As we exit Grand Central Station, I stop and grab a hot pretzel and a couple bottles of water. "Is there anything specific that you want to do today? Museums? Shops? A show?"

She shakes her head when I point to the mustard accompanying our paper-wrapped pretzel.

I hand Lisbeth a bottle of water, and place my hand at her back, guiding her down the crowded sidewalk.

"Nothing specific, I just really like it here. The people watching is out of this world—where else can you see Elmo, Cinderella, and the Naked Cowboy in the same place?" We head north toward Central Park, weaving through the throngs of people and sharing our pretzel.

"I have a friend from Dublin, here." I look to see her reaction. "He asked to meet for a drink a little later on, is that alright?"

"Of course, are you kidding me? I can hang out in the park, or whatever, take as much time as you need—I can just…" She's so sweet.

"Jimmy's down here too. He had to visit his gran this morning but said he'd meet us for dinner so you've someone to talk to while I catch up with Liam." I've waited far too long to spend this time with Lis, I don't want to spend even a single minute away from her.

We continue on along some of the smaller paths and come out at a small white gazebo and huge rock that juts out into the lake at the center of the park. There's a boathouse along here somewhere, but the view from this rock is gorgeous and we are remarkably alone.

It amazes me that in a city of this size, two people can find a private moment at all, let alone in such a public place. I watch as she scrambles up the rock. I should have gone ahead of her and helped her up, but the view from behind her is worth my breach of chivalry. I climb up after her and set myself down on the top of the rock.

Turning with a sweet smile over her shoulder, she lowers herself down next to me. "This is one of my all-time favorite places. I love it here." She practically whispers, "It's so serene. I saw a marriage proposal last time I was down here." She looks toward the arched bridge wistfully. "It was the most beautiful thing I've ever seen."

I run my hand down her back, unable to refrain from touching her. Grasping her hand, I pull her in close, her back to my front. Her body melting into mine. She untwines our hands, instead running her fingers lightly up and down my arm. "Tell me what was beautiful about it. Was there a rowboat? Champagne and great declarations of love? Tell me you heard him quoting Oscar Wilde."

"No. Nothing that elaborate. Just a simple proposal. At the center of that arched bridge." She nods off to our left. She's quiet a moment and obviously touched by the memory. "They weren't dressed up, they weren't doing anything fancy, just enjoying a day together completely alone, surrounded by a ton of people. He paused just shy of the top of the arch, pulled her around to face him, holding both her hands in his." She meets my stare and smirks. "No Wilde was harmed or abused in the overture. He just got down on one knee and asked." She looks back at the bridge—seeming lost in the memory. "She said '*yes*,' and he pulled a small box from his pocket. It was a normal, nothing day that became the start of their forever."

It hit me then how simple she is. Not simple. Uncomplicated in her wants and desires. I'm the one making things complicated for her.

I'd heard what she told her boss the night I had dinner at her bar. I got it the first time she told me she had a plan and needs to stick to it. I just can't stop myself from wanting to be with her. This is becoming more than a distraction to me— much more.

I hold her hand, touch her back, some kind of contact for our walk through Central Park and the little zoo that's there. The time passes far too quickly and we need to get on to meet up with Jimmy and Liam at McCoy's.

I need to talk to Liam. I need to know what's going on at home.

11

Lis

Aidan's been touching me in some small way all day.
And though I'm not used to being on the receiving end
of so much attention, I don't hate it. I don't hate it at all.
Weeks ago, it made me really self-conscious—exposed and
on edge. But, now I think I like it.

It was reassuring, having his touch as we walked through
Central Park and the zoo. It had been so much a part of our
day that it totally takes me by surprise when he drops my
hand and puts a little extra space between us as we walk into
the pub where we're meeting Jimmy for dinner. I try not to
bristle, but it just doesn't feel right.

"I'll be right back, I'm going to run to the restroom." I've
felt off kilter since practically tripping over Aidan outside my
building this morning.

What are we doing?

Aidan is at the bar, deep in conversation with someone

but Jimmy's at a booth near the back of the pub. I move to slide into the seat across from him, but he pats the seat next to him. "Sit here. If he's gonna be a daft fool, we can work on making him realize it. Come 'ere."

I perch on the edge of my seat and reach for a menu. "What do you mean?"

"I saw him. Dropped your hand and took a step away. Fuckin' stupid arse..." I miss what he mumbles after that as the pub erupts in cheers at a game up on the screens around the bar. Jimmy snaps his focus to the game and launches into a tirade on Gaelic football and the team that just scored. "... it's like rugby but fewer rules, yeah? The players are tougher, harder—thicker skulls." I nod along, not really paying attention, my mind picking the day apart. "...played back in Dublin."

"Wait. What?" I drag my gaze from the screen to Aidan. This is not where my focus is. I can't see Aidan in the short shorts, no protective gear, with ruddy cheeks and sweaty hair fighting for an oversized football. "But he's a photographer. They would crush him." As fit as he is, Aidan is small compared to the guys in this game.

"Concerned for him?" Jimmy smirks. "He played for his school—he was the big one on the field then, yeah." He leans in sliding a pint glass toward me.

I push him back and taste what he ordered me. "What is this?"

"That, love, is a snakebite. Treat it with respect, or we'll be carrying you to the train." He laughs at me while checking to see where Aidan is. He's no longer at the bar, they've moved to a small table by the door. He looks pissed, really angry about something.

65

Jimmy tries to pull my attention away from what's becoming a pretty heated discussion. He signals to the waitress and turns to me. "Are we celebrating tonight?"

"Celebrating what?" The waitress sets a couple shots on the table and waits while Jimmy orders some appetizers. I down the shot of Jameson and look back toward Aidan "What is he so upset about? Do you know?"

"Erm, you'll have to take that up with your man." Jimmy signals for another round of shots and puts his arm around me pulling me closer. The waitress unloads plates piled full of nachos and potato skins. Our table is ridiculously full with all the food, fresh pints, and more shots. Aidan looks over and his expression goes from curious to pissed when he takes in the drinks and empty shot glasses in front of us. Or maybe it's how close Jimmy's leaning in to me.

"Jimmy." Our faces are closer than I realized. "What are you doing?"

He reaches across me, enveloping me in his grasp as he grabs the ketchup. "I told you. We're going to show him what he's fuckin' with." He sits back and looks straight at Aidan with an eyebrow about lodged in his hairline. Challenging him.

I feel even more off balance than I did when we walked in here. The shots, the things coming out of Jimmy's mouth and the steely glare Aidan's throwing this way. I grab the two shots that were just deposited at our table and down them one after the other, immediately realizing my mistake.

The alcohol burns its way through my veins, making my head swim and my cheeks heat up. When Aidan finally tears his attention away from me, I feel like I can breathe again. I excuse myself to the restroom, needing some space to think.

I lock the door behind me and fall back against it. What am I doing? The back and forth in my head is driving me insane. No matter how hard I try, no matter how busy I make myself with school and work, I end up thinking about him constantly. I crave him. His wit, the way he cares for me—his touch.

Rob is my benchmark. Ours is the only real relationship I've had and that was a mess. I've never done the casual hookup thing—can't imagine a one-night stand. Emotionally, it's not me, but adding in my clinical knowledge, makes it a hard no.

This thing with Aidan falls somewhere in the gray area. There's definitely an end point. He's here for an extended visit, not to make a life. I know I'm not ready to jump into dating or anything serious, the draw to him is very real. I can spend time with him—date him—knowing that it will end. It all makes perfect sense bumping through my whiskey-addled brain.

He can be my distraction.

The bumping turns to pounding and I realize it's not in my brain, but someone needing the restroom. The pub filled up while I was hiding out, and there's a line five people deep. And Aidan is at the table with Jimmy. Heads bent together in a heated discussion, mirroring the scene between Aidan and Lance? Lucas? before I escaped into the restroom.

The conversation blatantly dies as I return to the table. Jimmy's turned his back to the brick wall with his legs stretched across the seat, and nods toward the spot next to Aidan.

Aidan reaches for my hand, guiding me down to sit with him. "That took a lot longer than I thought it would. I'm sorry." His thumb rubs my inner wrist sending electric heat coursing through my body.

I'm at the tipping point, where I either should stop drinking and take a nap or just fully commit to feeling awful tomorrow. "We...we had some things to straighten out, Liam and I. I'm sorry for the time it took. But you and Jimmy—you were alright, yeah?" There's a spiky edge to his question, something else that I can't quite read.

"Yup." My rational thoughts blur into a fuzzy haze, my pulse speeding up under the lazy circles he's tracing on my wrist. I reach for Aidan's tumbler of whiskey and drain it in one gulp. I just shut my brain off, letting go of my tightly ordered thoughts and become a happy little mess.

Aidan

I got well and truly stuck in the conversation with Liam. I had agreed to meet him—really, he strong-armed me into it—while he was in town, but this is not at all where I want to be.

I left Dublin to get away from the drama and to try and grieve my brother's death. On my own. In my own way. Michael was too fucking young to die. And now his widow has more shite on her plate than anyone should.

Liam had gone 'round to check in on Lorna, and because burying her husband at twenty-six was not enough, she just learned she's fallen pregnant. The hits just keep on coming.

While I thought this would be a quick meetup, I've spent far longer with Liam than I had planned, watching as Jimmy and Lisbeth drink and laugh—watching him move closer to her. That shite's not okay.

I can feel my blood heating as I tense, staring daggers

through him. I'm not concerned he's making a move on her. I just wish it were me cozied up to her.

"Are you fuckin' listening to me?" Shite. I am—but not really. "Lorna's not okay. She's really struggling. I think you need to talk to her. Maybe come home."

"I'll talk to her. But Christ, Liam, I can't come home just now. I—"

He follows my line of sight and drops his pint glass to the table. "Yeah, mate. Sure." Liam huffs out a judgmental breath, shaking his head. "Aidan, have your fun here, yeah? But you've family at home that need you. She's having a baby. She just buried her husband. You were best fucking friends and the one helping her deal with all that and then you just fuckin' left—" Liam's good and hacked off at me for leaving Dublin just days after Michael's funeral. "She depended on you. And now she needs you more than ever—and you're over here, fuckin' about." He's practically spitting the words at me now and Lisbeth is watching us.

Fucking hell.

I lean in toward Liam, my voice calm and low. "I will talk to Lorna. I'll let you know when I've spoken with her. And what we're gonna do." I push back from the table and stand. "It was good to see you, Liam." I clap him on the back and turn, ready to put this all behind me for today and get back to Lis.

I watch Lis walk away as I move toward the table in the back. She seems to have this need to escape when things start to overwhelm her. Like she just needs to wrap her head around the situation on her own before she can face it.

I slide into the seat across from Jimmy, my thoughts swirling around in my head. I ran from the overwhelming emotion of losing my brother and left my best friend in the process, and now I'm not ready to go back. Eyes trained on the door of the loo, I swirl the whiskey 'round my glass wishing that my thoughts could order themselves the same way.

"Are you fuckin' listening to me?"

"What?" No. I've not heard a damn thing Jimmy has said.

"The fuck are you doin'? You're stupid—droppin' her hand and blowing her off. Francie saw that, he'd fuckin' lay you out..." Jimmy's ripping into me.

I lean in and make sure I've got his attention so I can catch him up on Lorna and the baby.

"Don't you fuckin' ruin shite with Lis, man. You need to come clean. You need to tell her what's goin' on." Jimmy emphasizes his point by pounding his shot glass on the tabletop.

"I know, just...let me talk to Lorna first, figure out what to do there. I...*chssss*—" I break off mid rant as Lisbeth comes back to the table.

I don't want to do this now. I've wasted enough of the evening and I want to take it back, spend it with this girl—not thoughts of my brother's pregnant widow.

THE TRAIN RIDE back home was a mess and I feel nothing but relief that I have these two safely tucked away at McBride's. I tried—truly tried—to talk them into calling it a night but they're dead set on drinking each other under the table.

I end up helping Finn behind the bar since Jimmy's in no shape to work his shift. It's not all that busy tonight, but that and his inebriation give me the leverage I need to swap shifts and have tomorrow free to spend with Lis.

She's going to feel like shite as it is, so I water down her drinks and try to get her to eat something. "What is it with you and food? We should just go have a picnic—that's totally what we should do." She slams both palms down on the bar to make her point. "We should go to...that place on the river...that mansion?" The place is beautiful. It's a historic mansion with gorgeous grounds and gardens. I drove through there a while back and have had it pegged as a place to go and shoot—to get creative with my photography.

"Maybe we should get you home soon so we can take advantage of..."

She cuts me off with another slam to the bar top. "There will be no taking advantage of m-me tonight. Nope. Sorry, not gonna happen." She's adorable and trying so hard to look offended and serious...and not off her tits.

"No feckin' takin' advantage of your girl. You treated 'er like shite today and you canna do tha...and ye nade ter be 'onest wit 'er..." Jimmy's far gone and making no fucking sense anymore. I can hardly understand his slurs—hopefully Lisbeth will miss what he's getting at, as well. But I slide him another pint to distract the bastard from spilling about Lorna.

Jesus, I need to call her first thing in the morning and talk with her.

"Love. We need to take advantage of the beautiful day tomorrow." Though, Christ, if I'm honest with myself, I'd love to take advantage of her. "Let's get you safe home and to bed, and we'll go on that picnic tomorrow." Jimmy glares at me, just now figuring out that I distracted him with a beer. I hold his stare and slide him another pint. "We'll talk later, yeah?"

As I help Lisbeth toward the door, I turn to Finn. "I'm

taking her home now—and Jimmy's got my shift tomorrow. You good?"

Finn looks up from his phone. "I am. You taking Jimmy home wit' you?"

Shaking my head, I laugh and silently tell him *no.*

12

Lis

My head is a splitting, fuzzy mess. I cover my eyes to keep the bright sunlight from killing me, as I feel around for my phone. Why? Why did I do this to myself? Why did I drink so much? After rummaging through my sheets and blankets, I finally find my phone stuck to the back of my thigh—Jesus. I peel it off and swipe the screen awake squinting to check the time. Thank God, it's only ten o'clock. I close my eyes as gently as I can, not wanting to face the world yet.

I know Aidan brought me home and Gracyn helped him tuck me into bed, with a glass of water and a bottle of ibuprofen. Probably, I should feel worse than I do, but I pull my duvet up and snuggle in to sleep this misery away. *I'm never drinking again.* Who doesn't think that at a time like this? Just as I'm drifting off to sleep, my phone buzzes with a text.

A: I'll be there in an hour.

L: Why would you do that?

A: This was your idea.

L: OK. What was?

A: Our picnic at the mansion. I'll bring the food. Drink your water and hop in the shower. You'll feel better.

L: I doubt it.

Reluctantly, I drag myself out of bed and have to sit right back down. Good God, just how much did I drink last night? *Way too much.* I take a couple sips of water and wait for my stomach to accept or reject what I'm putting in it. Somewhat satisfied that the water is not going to make a reappearance, I shuffle to the bathroom. I start the shower before even chancing a look at the mess in the mirror. Mhmmm—ratty auburn hair, raccoon eyes.

I strip out of my clothes and step into the steam, letting the hot water wash over me. My body shudders, actually shudders, in appreciation and I find a small bit of hope that I'll live and not resent the hell out of life today. I stay in the shower far longer than strictly necessary and come out feeling pretty close to human. Not human enough that I deal with blow drying my hair. Instead I lazily twist it into a loose braid, where it leaves a wet spot as it lies on my tank top. I swipe on a little mascara and brush my teeth twice.

Absently, I glance at my phone to check the time, and grab my sandals and the biggest, darkest pair of sunglasses I can find.

"Gracyn?" The sound of my knuckles against the wood sends a fresh flash of pain through my skull.

"Yeah? You feeling okay?" she rasps, her voice laced with either tears or sleep.

I scoff at her question as I crack her door open, holding up her sunglasses. "Not great, can I borrow these?" She is exactly where I want to be—in bed—in the dark, not headed out into the world with a hangover. "How am I going to do this? I don't know that I'm gonna make it today." My eyes close and I lean my head against the doorframe—the cool wood offering a touch of relief to my aching head.

"Lissy, you'll be fine. Go get another glass of water. You drank the one he left you last night, right?" This conversation is usually the other way around. Me taking care of her. I know the routine, I just don't want to move. "Go drink another, take something for your headache and pray he brings you something good to eat."

My feet make their way to the kitchen even though my head is still wishing it was soaking in the cool, smooth wood. In the kitchen, I move to fill a water bottle and take some ibuprofen. My phone buzzes just as I'm tipping the little brown pills into my hand. Of course, it makes me jump, spilling the perfectly round painkillers across the counter with each of them bobbling and tinkling as they spin around.

I lean my forehead on the cabinet in front of me and answer. "Hello?"

His voice is soft. "I'm here. Are you ready to go, or do you need a minute yet?"

"I'm ready. I..." I sigh and gather up the pills I dropped, popping a few of them in my mouth. "I just need to clean up my spill. Do I need to grab anything?" I swallow the pills just as they start to dissolve on my tongue with that acidic burn.

"Erm, yeah, actually. I forgot to grab a blanket. Do you have one we can use?" Bless him, his voice is still soft and low.

"I'll find something and be right out." I check my closet and grab the flat sheet from my extra set. It's just going to have to be good enough. "Bye, Gracyn. Thanks." There's no response, she's probably fallen back to sleep.

Sunglasses. Water bottle. Sheet. Keys. Deep, bracing breath and I head out to see Aidan leaning against the passenger side of his car. He looks at me with just a touch of pity and a beautiful smile.

"Good morning, love," he murmurs as he leans in and presses his lips to my cheek right by my ear. "You look beautiful. Let me take this." He puts the sheet in the back seat of his car and opens the passenger door for me.

AIDAN'S quiet while we walk toward the back side of the historic mansion. I've toured it tons of times and while the mansion is beautiful, the grounds are unreal. This place was built as a summer home for a railroad tycoon during the Golden Age with servants' quarters, a carriage house, and formal gardens. It's magical. My happy place.

In dire need of a little shade, I steer him toward my favorite spot. It's a little niche tucked into some trees—perfect for a hammock and a good book. Sadly, I'm pretty sure the park service would frown on my efforts if I tried to put one up. Instead, I spread the sheet out where the grass is soft and fewer people are around to spoil the peacefulness. And it's idyllic back here. Really perfect.

"This is lovely." Aidan squints toward the sun. "We'll be good here? I've Irish skin, yeah? I don't want to burn and freckle..." He turns his smirk to me and chuckles softly.

Now, I totally want to see his cheeks turn red. And I can't help but stare at the fine smattering of freckles high on his cheekbones and across the bridge of his nose. "No, I think your delicate complexion will be fine." I'm starting to feel a little icky again. "Can we eat? I think I have a bad case of..." I scrunch up my nose and shake my head a little reaching for my water bottle. I really should have known better.

Aidan sets the bag on the grass and pulls me down to the middle of the sheet. "Lisbeth, don't try out-drinking Jimmy again. Love, he's Irish..." God, I was an idiot to think I could hang with him. "And he's years of experience on you."

I groan as Aidan unpacks sandwiches and fruit, knowing I need to eat, but the lurch in my stomach from the leftover alcohol is a lot to handle right now. I grab my water and let the cool liquid roll down my throat, saying a silent prayer. "You learned your lesson, then? No more showing off—trying to prove yourself?"

I mumble a quiet *no* as he unwraps my sandwich and hands it to me. God, it's perfect. Aidan's amazing. He keeps doing these little things, taking care of me. Making sure I have what I need.

"What? Why are you laughing at me?" Food finally sounds like a good idea to me. He can laugh all he wants, this is the stuff that love is made of.

"Lisbeth. I don't think I've ever seen someone so thoroughly enjoy a fuckin' turkey sandwich. You've hearts in your eyes."

13

Aidan

I brush a lock of auburn hair back off Lis' cheek, tracing the soft lines of her lips. Her nose twitches and she reaches up to brush away the tickle. Christ, she's beautiful all rumpled from sleep. I can't help but smile softly at her as she comes awake.

"Did you sleep well?"

"Mmm... I fell asleep?" She rolls to her back and wipes at her eyes. I reach over and gently dust an eyelash away from her cheek.

"Love, you've been out for an hour or so. You drove everyone else away with your sweet snoring." Sitting up, she looks around us, eyes wide and darting around, pink staining her cheeks. Most of the others are gone, but it had nothing to do with her.

Only a handful of people are spread across the lawn. We pack up the trash and remnants of our food quietly. Watching a couple kids playing with their mum.

There's a path near where we're sitting leading away from the house. An older couple passes by, holding hands as they stroll toward the car park. Lis leans into me and quietly asks, "How long do you think they've been married?"

"What makes you think they're married?" I lean in closer. "Maybe they meet here for their weekly tryst." Her face—Jesus, the look on her is priceless.

She pulls away, and stares at me, her mouth forming that perfect little "O." "Aidan, they've got to be in their seventies—really? They're married and have kids and probably a ton of grandkids." She gets a good smack in on my arm and I grudgingly release my hold. She looks suddenly shy and a little unsure as she asks, "Do you...um, want to go see the gardens?" She looks around like she's trying to find a place to escape to.

We're going to have to talk about that.

We have a lot of shite we need to talk about, but not today. It can wait for another day. Lorna didn't answer my call this morning, so it's best if I wait to talk about that bit.

The path leads to terraced gardens. I catch the sweet heady scent of the flowers well before the riot of colors surround us. The gentle breeze carries the fragrance through the tunnel of the trees. I stop to pull my camera out of the case as Lis walks on ahead. The sunlight dapples through the trees casting her in the most beautiful green and golden glow.

"Lisbeth, will you stop a moment?" I snap several frames just as she turns to look back at me. Her smile soft and her eyes go from questioning to sparkling in a heartbeat.

Lis hops down the steps as she leads us deeper into the gardens. The color is breathtaking. I stutter to a stop when we round a corner—graced with the sight of a gazebo at the far end of a reflecting pool. The light. The sun dipping lower in the sky; we're coming up on the golden hour. The time when the sun's rays are pure magic. I live for light like this.

She glides along the edge of the pool toward the gazebo, arms out to the sides for balance. There's a statue of a woman at the far end. Grecian? Roman? It hardly matters. It's a beautiful day and I have a subject I can't wait to shoot.

She stops in front of the statue and gazes up at it, taking in its form.

Click click click

The shutter counts out quietly. Lis turns and grins at me. "Can you imitate her pose?" Her right arm goes up and bends so that her hand is just behind her head. Looking back at the statue, Lis mimes gathering flowing robes and pops her left foot back just a touch so her shoe rests on the toe. "Tilt your head—to the right. Look down a little, toward the center of the pool."

Click click click

This light. This is one of those moments. I don't usually do artistic portraits. I shoot the news, humanitarian pieces, photos that oftentimes evoke hard emotions. That's my career. But every now and then, God hands you a moment—a subject—that's too good to waste.

Click click click

I need my other camera. Digital is good. I love the instant feedback with a digital camera, but there is something undeniably magical about film. Old school. It's more of a challenge. Film forces you to focus on the subject as opposed to watching the screen. It's more of an art.

I stoop down to grab my old camera body and glance up at her as I affix the lens. The sheet she brought for our picnic catches my eye. Pulling it out of the satchel, I unfold it as I approach her. She drops her arms and shifts toward me.

"Do you think we can use this? Wrap it around you like her robes?" I ask her.

She takes the sheet from me and turns to study the statue. Gathering the material, draping it around one shoulder, and tucking it into place, she does a brilliant job imitating the look.

I adjust the sheet as it flows across her chest and bunches over her left arm. After coaxing her back into the statue's pose, I drag my hand down the underside of her raised arm. I tilt her chin, making minor adjustments as I hold her gaze. Scooping her hair forward over her shoulder, my fingers twisting through the silky burnished locks, I lean in so my lips graze her ear. "Breathe." She releases her breath and closes her eyes. She's as affected by this moment as I am.

I jog back to my spot, anxious to frame the shot. It's beautiful, but— "Can you push your top down your shoulders a bit? Just so it doesn't show around the sheet?"

Mesmerized, I watch as she does that thing girls do. That thing where they can slip out of a bra without exposing themselves? Yeah, that. She shimmies her tank top and bra off her shoulders. Fucking witchcraft. She holds my eyes as she raises her arm and gets back into position. *Christ, now I'm the one not breathing.*

Click click click
Click click click

We haven't seen anyone else since we've been in this part of the garden. The sky is turning the most beautiful soft golden color as the sun moves further west.

Click click click

"Erm...the sun's filtering through the sheet. It's...it's back-lighting your shorts. Really taking away from the stunning artistry of the shot." I smirk as she raises her eyebrow at me. I know I'm pushing my luck, but it really is taking away from what this shot could be.

She cocks her head and reaches into her "robes." God, how does she maneuver without dropping that thing? I can't move my eyes as I watch her unbutton her shorts and wiggle them down her legs.

Breathe.

Breathe.

Damn, I have to keep reminding myself to do that simple task.

Click click click

I shoot more film as she gets herself back into the pose.

Breathtaking. Absolutely, fucking breathtaking. The soft rays of the sun highlight her curves and set her auburn hair to flame. The effect is unreal. She looks like a goddess.

Click click click

I work my way through the rest of the film, capturing subtle shifts in her expression and changes in the light as it slowly fades. I don't know if she's listening for the shutter click—that's no longer there—or if she somehow senses that the moment has passed, but she raises her eyes to mine and time stands still.

I put down the camera and move toward her.

I can't stop myself.

My hand goes around the back of her neck, fingers weaving into her hair. Neither one of us takes a breath for that moment. That moment just before our lips brush, ghosting across each other. It's a split second that lasts for days. I press closer, kissing her again, suddenly all too aware of her lack of real clothing. Her lips are soft and yielding. She tastes faintly of strawberries and wine. The kiss is getting ready to take on a momentum of its own when I force myself to pull back just a bit.

"I should...we..." She shifts, and hugs the sheet closer to her body shivering a little. The sun is setting and the air is rapidly cooling. "The grounds close at dusk. We should probably get going."

I pull in a deep breath and step back while running my fingers through my hair. "Erm, yeah. Right. I'll, uh...pack up my cameras while you..." I wave my hands at her and the sheet, unable to find words that make any sense.

I HOLD her hand as we walk through the grounds back to the car park. I want to touch her. Maybe it's the intimacy of the moment. Maybe I don't want her to pull away again. Maybe I've become completely intoxicated by her, but the reflecting pool changed something in me. Maybe in her too.

I walk her around to the passenger side of the car and help her in, not letting go of her hand until I have to. What. The. Fuck? Lis shifts nervously, giving me the side eye as I settle in the driver's seat and turn down the radio. "So, are you going to let me see?"

"See what?" I want to hear her ask.

"The pictures. I want to see what you got. What I look like."

I sit and smirk at her for as long as it takes to make her a little uncomfortable. I think I like her a little rattled.

"What? Can I see them?"

"Well that's the thing. A moment like that needs to be treated special. Treated and captured in a way that sets it apart from all the rest."

She scrunches her nose up at me as I pull out onto the

main road heading to her flat. "You'll have to wait for the proof sheet."

"What? Just give me the camera, I'll scroll through and scrap the shitty ones before you doctor them up with filters and magic." The scent of her hair floats around me as she turns, trying to reach the ruck in the back with my equipment. My skin tingles and raises chill bumps where the strands brush faintly across my arm.

"I switched cameras. This afternoon could only be done justice with film. I'll need to develop them at the dark room. I should have the proof sheet tomorrow—maybe later tonight."

Lis huffs out her frustration right there.

"Are you cranky, then? Need to get you home so you can take another nap, or go to bed early, yeah?"

"I have to work tonight." She drops her head back and closes her eyes. "Jenna texted me—the other bartender called in sick. Bastard is probably just hungover." This girl works hard. Too hard.

I pull up to her building and hop out to get her door. Not sure if I'm being a gentleman, full of shite, or just have to touch her again, but as she steps out of the car, I wrap my left hand around her neck and pull her to me. It's still there. That magic from earlier. I brush my lips across hers, hating that I have to let her go for the evening. "Be safe at work, yeah."

She nods, licks her lips, and makes her way inside.

I set off for the photo lab straight away.

14

Lis

"Hey, what time are you working tonight?" Gracyn really needs to get a handle on her volume control.

"Seven to close. You wanna shush a little?" Easing out a deep breath, I close my eyes willing myself to grab another water and some more ibuprofen. I'm definitely feeling better, but I need sleep.

"Still have a headache? You're looking all wobbly and woozy—sun too much for you today?" She's obviously feeling perkier than she was this morning, and there's no escaping her now. I shrug and shuffle down the hall to my room to change for my shift.

"Are you working tonight, too? You wanna ride in together?" *Please, please let her say yes.* If she drives, maybe I can catch a quick nap. And make it through the weekend without having to put more gas in my car.

No lie, this week is going to kill me. I have rent, books for my summer courses, and a million other bills to pay for. My tiny financial cushion from spring break is officially gone.

"I think I'll drive, though." She looks at me with her lips curled up in a smirk. "You still look like shit."

My phone buzzes while I put some makeup on and try to tame my windblown hair.

A: Hey-I got darkroom time tonight. I can come by when I'm done.

L: How long will it take to process all the photos?

A: Christ, far too long. I'll just get the thumbnails done. Come by for a drink.

I can't tonight. I just can't. The past two days have been some kind of crazy and intense. I need a minute to think about this afternoon. About what passed between us.

Pouring drinks and mixing cocktails will give me just the right amount of monotony to work through my thoughts and feelings without having to face them directly.

L: Can we meet up tomorrow? It's going to take everything I have to make it through tonight with my head still pounding.

A: Right. I'll try to get time in the morning. We can hook up whenever and then I can make some prints.

L: Is that a spectator sport?

A: ...?

L: Can I watch you work?

A: I'll text you a time.

His last response takes a lot longer than the others. I don't have time or energy to try and figure out why. Gracyn's pushing me out the door and I have to force my brain to switch gears to get through the night.

Sadly, my plan for work taking my mind off Aidan and the past couple days, totally backfires. It's really slow for a

Saturday night and I have way too much time on my hands. He's all I can think about and Jenna's not even here to distract me. *Why the hell did I need to come in tonight?* My mind is spinning. I really like him. I have fun every time we're together and he's so sweet to me—opening doors and always making sure I'm okay—I should try to trust him. Give him a real chance. Maybe he won't let me down.

When the night is finally over, I shoot Gracyn a grin. "Nope, not drinking tonight. I'm going home, crawling into bed, and sleeping yesterday off."

"Yeah, I kinda figured," she chuckles. "So, you haven't told me anything about the past two days with Aidan. I mean, obviously you got shitty yesterday, but what's going on with you guys?"

We grab our bags and walk out the back door.

She's pushing for info. She's been really off since spring break and I haven't wanted to bug her. "I don't know. I'm scared." I hate admitting that, but my fear is honest.

"Lis, you have to try eventually. You know that, right?"

Of course, I know that. It's all I've thought about tonight. "I do. It's just..." God, this is hard. "...I can't do it again. My heart can't handle the idea of breaking again so soon." I try to hold my tears back, but they just have to break free. Swiping at my cheeks, I try to pull myself together. Getting emotional goes hand in hand with being tired and I'm so there.

Gracyn hands me a tissue along with the start of an epic pep talk. "Lissy, he's been nothing but kind and considerate. You need to give the boy a chance. He fought Francie, has taken you out, respects your commitment to school and took care of your drunk ass without taking advantage of you— because let me tell you—he so could have taken whatever he wanted last night. You asked him to, multiple times. But he tucked you into bed, made sure you took something for your headache and that you had water. You don't want to compare, and I get that, but Rob wouldn't have done any of that, even on his best day. Aidan's different." She's totally right. "Tell me about today. What did you guys do?"

Sighing, I stare out the window. "He took me to the mansion for a picnic. Packed the most amazing food, and…"

"What?"

"I swear he watched me sleep for a couple hours—not in a creepy way, but just really sweet. And then we went for a walk to the reflecting pool."

"Dude. That's your favorite place. Did he know?"

"I don't know. I think I was babbling about it last night at McBride's." I can't believe I'm spilling this. "And he brought his camera. He…he took pictures of me." I drop that on her as I get out of the car and pray she leaves it alone.

"He what?"

"He took some pictures of me in the garden. He's a photographer, so, you know. It's no big deal, just…" I shrug as I open our door. And my phone pings. "It was nothing. You can have the bathroom first, just hurry. I need to be done with today."

Gracyn does her thing and is out the door in record time. She seems like she's getting back to her normal self—her before-spring-break self. I don't know what changed with her today. I'm just relieved to hear the lock click and finally be alone.

I take the longest, hottest shower I can stand. I scrub my hair, condition it twice, shave my legs and let the lavender scent calm and soothe me. The thick lotion I slather on after toweling off feels like heaven. Pulling on my shorts and tank, I hear my phone ping. Again. I totally forgot that I got a text earlier. And, evidently a couple more while I was in the shower.

A: I've got the proof sheet done. Want me to come by?

A: You still there?

A: The place looks dead. Did you close early?

A: Christ. Could you check your phone?

The dots start up again. He's getting a little cranky; I'm not the only one who needs a good night sleep.

L: Give me a sec. I just got out of the shower.

That was stupid. Why did I text him that?

A: Are you needing help?

L: Thanks for the offer. I'm good.

My phone starts vibrating as soon as I hit send. Shit. "Hello..."

"Well?" The smoky timber of his voice sends a shiver down my spine.

"Well, what?" My teeth dig into the side of my lower lip as I try to hide my physical response to just his words.

"Are you wanting me to come by or are you free tomorrow mornin'? I've the dark room at ten o'clock for a couple hours." I can hear bar noises muffled in the background.

"Um, I'm free tomorrow, all day. You sound like you're busy anyway. I'll just meet you there." I try to stifle my yawn, but am not at all successful.

"Yeah, I came to the bar to grab a bite to eat and ended up working for Jimmy. You might've given him more of a run for his money than he let on. He's lookin' a bit peaked and asked me to stay for him." His chuckle is low and deep, rumbling straight through me. He definitely affects me more than I am ready to admit. "You sound like you're ready for sleep yourself? I'll text the address and see you in the morning, yeah?"

I yawn again. "Uh-huh. I'll see you tomorrow."

89

"Sleep well, love."

It's been ages since the last time I was in this part of town. I pass the building three times before I text Aidan that I'm here. A steel door creaks open down the alley and Aidan steps out. The sun is behind him with rays streaming down around him, highlighting his silhouette. He is breathtaking.

I slide through between his body and the doorframe, brushing up against him slightly. "'Scuse me."

The whole building stinks like chemicals—rotten eggs. It does nothing to enhance the 1970s plastic and linoleum decor. I wrinkle up my nose taking in the room. "This is... nice... How'd you find this place?"

Aidan huffs out an amused chuckle and reaches for my hand. "I asked at the college—I hoped they would let me use theirs, but this'll do. Not many people have a need for the labs now. But I learned the old ways when I was in school."

I raise my eyebrow at him—he's not that much older than me, right?

"Come with me, I'll show you the 'magic.'"

It's kind of creepy moving through the empty building, past offices, and storage rooms. We are very much alone in here. Aidan soothes me with his warm hand—stroking my fingers with his thumb and squeezing me a little as we enter the darkroom. I check my watch. "What time did you get here?" The red light is on and there are shallow trays lined up on the work surface. It's a crazy, organized chaos.

Aidan quietly closes the door behind us and leads me over to a table with a folder and a small box. "Just before you. I mixed up some chemicals and got things ready." He puts one hand on my shoulder and leans into me a little grabbing the box. "Do you want to look and see what we've got?"

The room feels almost cold after coming in from the glaring sun and I'm suddenly very aware of his warmth at my back. I shiver when he straightens, opening the box.

"It's cool in here. Are you okay?" His warm breath on my ear sends another shiver through me.

"Um...yeah. I'm good. Let me see." I grab at the proof sheet, again feeling Aidan lean into me. He slides the sheet out of my reach and holds it away from me.

"You're eager, then." He smirks. Pressing his left hand into my lower back, he slips around to my side. He holds his hand there for a beat longer than he needs to, but not nearly long enough. Something changes, and he shifts his eyes from mine. Pulling back from me, he mumbles, "Well, erm... Right. Let's just get this set." He starts moving around, putting distance between us. Slipping the proofs under some weird magnifying thing—adjusting knobs, and buttons, and lights.

Is he nervous? This man has been touching me in some small way since I got here and now he's stepping away, keeping clear of me. He was all flirty on the phone last night. He's...I don't know. Trying to give me space?

"Can I see now?" We've killed half an hour with this little dance. It's obvious Aidan is stuck in his head. Maybe he's nervous? Scared to show me the images.

He blows out a big breath pursing his lips, and steps back. "Erm—you can. Just look through at the contact sheet and, erm...let me know when you're ready for the next one. We'll just..."

I'm a little freaked by this viewing thing he's been messing with. It's intimidating, but the image that greets me is nothing short of amazing. "Wow. That's..." I'm completely speechless.

"They get better," Aidan whispers as he reaches over and adjusts the sheet so the next frame comes into view, his confidence coming back.

After a few awkward minutes of sliding the frames through slowly and clumsily, we start to fall into a rhythm, relaxing into each other. Aidan gets a little lost in his craft and forgets whatever it was that made him put distance between us earlier.

Each frame is better than the next. His artistic eye is seriously well developed. The light created a halo effect as it streamed through the arbor. Illuminating the subject's hair and the sheet that's wrapped and draped around her form. He's clearly decided which ones he wants to print. I want to see them all—it doesn't register that it's me in the pictures. It never even crosses my mind.

I move back a bit, just watching and listening. I could do this for hours, it's beautiful. I know I asked for the magic of making the prints, but I kind of get lost myself. It's dark and quiet. And as gorgeous as the shots are that we've looked at, Aidan in the flesh is a site worth appreciating. Maybe he would let me take some pictures of him.

I watch him fall into a kind of artistic abyss. He's lost in the poetry of his movements, and the lilting melody of his voice washes over me as he explains what he's doing. I'm absolutely captivated by him. I'm lost in him, lost to him.

15

_____

Aidan

She's not paying attention to what I'm doing anymore. I can feel her gaze on me. I'm ready to dazzle her. *Christ.* Who thinks shite like that? It's like I was fluffing my feathers trying to impress her.

I don't know what the fuck made me so jittery earlier. I loved holding her hand, touching her when she first got here. When I pressed my body up against hers and her arse pressed back into me—her arse in that little skirt she's wearing—Jesus, Mary, and Joseph. I swear, I heard the fucking angels sing. Yeah. That's what did it. I can't be thinking of that here. Not the place for it. And space—I need to remember to give her some space.

I print the three photos we picked. No filters, no flair. Just the simplest process. She looks like I just presented her with the most amazing prize. Yeah—just fucking wait until she sees what I can do. I start the process over with the first photo. This one is my absolute favorite. I focus her image, fade, and blur around her. Highlight and exaggerate the beams of light streaming through the arbor. They point to her like a beacon, drawing your eye to her.

She's moving closer, intrigued. The magic—the fucking magic is working. I put the print through the final wash, giving her just a hint of what will be a beautiful piece hanging in my loft. I'll be spending a lot of time staring at this one. I hang it to dry, turned so she can't see the finished product. I want that moment to be one I can savor and I need to print a few others.

I take a deep breath as she approaches me, breathing in her sweet scent.

"Can you show me what you did with that? How...how did you blur the outside? How did you get it all focused like that?"

I feel her body pressed against me again. *Christ.* Is she moving fucking closer to me? I start the process for the next photo.

She's close.

Getting closer.

Asking me questions. I've got her attention again. And of course, I want to fucking take advantage of it.

The processing, I can do in my sleep. I go to autopilot and just get the prints done, murmuring the explanation as I go. She's excited, captivated, watching this happen. I hang this print next to the first to dry, turning, and she's right there. Right fucking there. "I'll be needin' to wash my hands. The chemicals, they're bad." I brush against her as I pass and wash up quickly. She's looking at the first print—staring at it. The wonder in her eyes stirs something deep inside me.

She makes this breathy sound as she moves from one photo to the next. Fuck's sake, I can feel that sigh. I feel it deep within me tightening every single muscle. It's like I've lost control over my hands. They're in her hair before it registers what I'm doing. Her gaze lifts up to meet mine.

The light is low and she is stunning.

Time stands still as I move a hair's breadth closer to her. She blinks in slow motion, like we're muddling through the mire.

I feel her breath on my lips. Feel it feather across me. I lean in that last little bit until our lips brush and that spark is too much to resist. I don't want to stop.

I grasp the hair at the nape of her neck and drag her closer to me. My tongue sweeps out along her soft lips, back and forth until she opens for me, and I taste her.

God, she tastes sweeter than she did yesterday. Sweeter than I have words for.

Stepping in, I guide her, direct her, move her against the wall. This is a bad idea. *So bad.* This is not the time or place. Shifting to step away, I feel her move with me. She's almost dancing with me, giving in to me. I press her back into the wall, fingers twined through her hair as I run my other hand down her cheek, caressing her neck, stopping on the swell of her breast. Holding her there. Pressed between my body and the wall.

My head is telling me to stop.

My heart? My heart wants to hear nothing of it.

She slides her hands down my arms, and behind my back, grazing the waistband of my trousers—my skin tingling from the heat of her touch. Dragging my nose along her jawline, I plant small open mouth kisses from that spot by her ear—that spot—down her neck to where it meets her shoulder. I could get lost in the line of her collarbone. That delicate bone has to be one of the sexiest spots on a woman.

I run my hand around her waist skimming up under the bottom edge of her t-shirt. She gasps a sweet breath when I brush my fingers up the soft skin at her side. Spreading out my hand, my fingers wrap around her back and my thumb caresses the underside of her tit. I'm trying—but when she runs her hands up under my shirt and digs her fingers into my back, I lose what little grasp I have on my control. I make short work of her bra clasp and palm her left breast while I tug at her shirt to get that shite out of my way. Something clatters as it lands behind me—I couldn't care less what I just fucking spilled. I wrap my lips around her nipple and pull it between my teeth.

Her gasps and moans are music to my fucking ears. I need her lips, I need to taste her, I need to own every one of those sounds. Grabbing her arse, I lift her up, her legs wrapping around my hips. She grips me tightly as I carry her over to the work surface—clearing the solution trays to the floor, not giving a shit what's there. I don't think my cock can get any harder as she rakes her fingers through my hair, pulling on it as I grind into her. I lean in setting her down, a hand to her chest I push her to lie back. The low light casts shadows across her, accentuating her curves—her peaks and valleys. As much as I appreciate the art of the moment, I need to touch every inch of her.

"Aidan..." It comes out as a breathy moan. She tugs at my shirt as I reach behind me and drag it off—adding it to the pile of cast-off clothing behind me. She has me fucking captivated. The feel of her nails scraping across my shoulders and down my back has me shaking. "Please..."

I'll do anything for her. "Please what, love? What do you need?"

She practically purrs as I run my hands down her body,

skimming over her curves to the sides of that flirty little skirt. This fucking thing has been driving me insane. I slide my hand down her knickers, teasing her as much as myself—light skimming touches. I want to draw this out. I want to explore every inch of her, worship her, make her mine. I run my thumb up and down her core feeling how her body reacts to my touch, caressing her and circling her clit through the fabric. My fingers slip under the fabric of her knickers. *Christ, she's wet.*

Sliding my thumb up to circle her bundle of nerves increasing pressure as her breathing picks up and she starts panting out my name.

"Aidan...God, Aidan..." One finger circles her, and dips in—two fingers. "...Aidan..." She is stunning like this. My left hand firmly holding her in place, my right pumping, stroking, driving her higher...closer. "...Aidan..." It's fucking amazing hearing my name on her breath. She bucks her hips with the first pass of my tongue. "...Aidan..." she keens with the second pass. And when I wrap my lips around her clit sucking hard, her back arches and she fucking comes apart—pulsing around my fingers, heels digging into my back, my other hand clutched to her chest.

She. Fucking. Comes. Undone.

I kiss along her inner thighs as she calms, sliding my fingers from her, and putting her knickers right. Her gaze meets mine as I stand and suck my fingers into my mouth, tasting her, licking them clean.

16

Lis

He drags his fingers from his mouth and I have to look away. *No one has ever...done that to me before.*

"Done what—which part?"

I snap my eyes back to his. They're dark and hooded.

"I didn't think I said that out loud. Sorry." I push myself up to sitting and smooth my skirt back down over my thighs. Aidan steps in. His erection straining against his zipper.

"Answer me, love. What has no one ever done to you? Licked you?" He pulls me to the edge of the table pressing his hard cock to me. I can't help the shudder—or the quick intake of breath. "Made you come?" Leaning even closer, he brushes his lips against me as his words rumble low in my ear, he presses me tightly to him. "Made you worship his name?" He's biting and sucking on my earlobe, distracting me. "Tell me." The shell of my ear is on fire as his tongue traces it.

"All of it." I can barely speak. Drawing in a deep breath,

his chest expands against mine and he dives for my mouth. Devouring me. *Oh. My. G*—Jerking his head back, Aidan holds me tightly—shielding me from the door at the other end of the room. "Someone's here?" Panic bleeds through.

"They won't come straight in. The light outside—whoever it is knows the darkroom's being used."

I'm panicking and he's cocking an eyebrow and smirking like this is funny.

"I'll see what they want. Maybe we should...fuck..." Grabbing his shirt and tugging it on, he hands me mine. Pausing at the door, he makes sure I'm dressed. He adjusts himself and takes in the mess of trays and negatives on the floor, "Don't touch anythin'. I'll be right back."

Murmurs float through the door, I can't make out what they are saying, but I hear Aidan's laugh and his hand on the doorknob. He slides back in smiling and shaking his head. "The darkroom's been double booked. I told the guy we had a chemical spill and needed to clean up—he, uh, wanted to share time. Not fuckin' gonna happen." Aidan throws away the ruined negatives, gathers the prints he made and hands me his bag. We clean up as quickly as we can and leave. Thank God, the other photographer is nowhere to be seen.

IT'S like a different world outside than when I got here. The sun that was beating down earlier has been replaced with clouds and the wind is whipping off the river. My hand slaps down to grab hold of my skirt trying to keep it in place. Aidan reaches out taking his bag from me. "Much as I'd love to have my hands on your arse again, I'll let you get hold of that. I don't want to think of anyone else seeing your knickers." He slings the bag over his shoulder and settles his hand on the small of my back. Well, really, it's on my ass. "What should we do with the rest of our day?"

The rumble from my stomach answers for me. "I guess I'm hungry. Want to go grab a bite to eat?"

The look he shoots me is full of mischief and satisfied pride.

"Already ate, love."

I'd smack him, but this skirt will be gone if I try.

"Hmmm...Aidan, I'm going to go to the bistro and get lunch. Would you like to join me there?" My voice is so sugary sweet and my smile is as plastic as it can be. Fumbling with my skirt and my keys, trying to stay decent, I struggle with unlocking my car door.

I feel his warmth behind me just as he reaches around to take my keys. As soon as I give them up, he presses me into the side of my car, pinning me there with his chest against my back, hips against my ass. Maybe, I don't really need lunch. My stomach rumbles again and I drop my chin to my chest laughing. Sex or starvation?

"I'll follow you there. We'd best get you fed—don't want your strength waning." He presses into me one last time before opening the door. Staying close, he shields me as I slip into my driver's seat. "Wait for me when you get there. I'll help keep your honor intact." With a wink, he closes my door and heads further down the street to his car.

Watching him, the way he moves, the way he carries himself makes my heart skip a beat. He's so full of confidence and grace. His khaki pants wrap his ass perfectly, and his t-shirt? That shirt is stretched tight across his broad shoulders and is clinging to his arms. There's a shadow, just barely hinted at beneath the fabric on the left side, high on his shoulder blade. I caught a glimpse of the tattoo in the darkroom—just that it was there. I can't imagine ever getting a tattoo. I don't know that there is anything I would want to permanently mark myself with, but I want to know what he has. And why he got it.

GRACYN DROPS the menus at our table with a basket of garlic bread and a couple glasses of water. "What have you guys been up to this morning? Anything exciting?" She bumps me with her hip and plops down in the booth next to me. Aidan huffs out a chuckle while I pull my lower lip between my teeth and cock my head to the side. Looking back and forth between us, her smile takes over her face. "I'm guessing there's a good story in there somewhere." Aidan's eyes sparkle, the skin crinkling at the corners. "And I guess I'll have to wait and get it from you later, Lis. What can I get for you today?"

"I'll have the chicken parmigiana sandwich. Fries, and seltzer with fruit. Please."

Gracyn looks up at Aidan, waiting for his order. "I'll have the same, with the fried mushrooms for an appetizer. Guess I'm still hungry, after all." He winks. He fucking winks at me with Gracyn right there.

"Got it. I'll put this in and be right back with your drinks."

My face flames red and I duck my head away rummaging through my purse for absolutely nothing. I could just die right now.

And, of course, my dear friend misses nothing. "We'll talk later." She tickles my back as she skips away from our table.

After lunch, we grab a couple picture frames from the store and head to Aidan's apartment to look through the few pictures we were able to print before we got distracted.

17

_____

Aidan

Jesus. Having at Lis in the darkroom was not what I fucking planned, but I'll be damned if I'm going to feel bad about it. I just want her more now. Our weekend of no work ended with me taking on Finn's shift Sunday and Lis at home—not mine, hers. I want more.

My thoughts were that she'd have a lot more free time with her term having ended, but it's like her spring holiday all over again. Every available minute is spent working for the two solid weeks before Lis starts in with her summer term. I have never seen anyone so driven.

I pick up several photo shoots while she's working and manage to sell some of my journalistic pieces to a few news outlets in the city. My career is getting back on track, but I've spent far too little time with Lisbeth.

And I've not heard from Lorna—at all.

No texts. No calls.

Nothing.

I walk into Lis' bar and settle in an empty spot at the end. She's mixing drinks for tables in the dining room, while smiling and chatting up the people at the bar. It's busy enough in here to afford me the luxury of watching her. I take her in, every move, every smile.

Last time I was here, we were still just friends. Just an innocent thing. Now, I can't get her out of my mind. The look of her, the sounds she makes—the taste of her. Beyond that, I just like her. The little things. The corner of her lower lip between her teeth when she's concentrating. The way one eye all but closes when she smiles really big. Her quiet determination. She's amazing.

"Hey," she says with that smile. The one that pinches her eye shut. "What can I get you?"

I prop my elbows on the bar and speak quietly. "I'll have a whiskey, yeah?"

When she leans in to hear my words, I take hold of her hand and my thumb slides to her inner wrist. That spot calls to me. Her skin is so soft there—so smooth. And the smell of her perfume is fucking intoxicating. She sighs and leans just a little bit closer. Seeking a kiss. Just a quick one, but I'm over the moon that she does that.

"Do you want dinner too, or are you just here for the whiskey?"

"The whiskey is fine, a steak would be great, but I'm here for the company. I've missed you."

Another smile and she pulls away, fixing my drink, checking the others at the bar.

"How was your class today?" I ask when she comes back down to my end of the bar. We've not spoken much since she started her summer term three days ago—we've had maybe seven texts in the last three days.

Lisbeth's face totally shifts, her shoulders slumping, and her lower lip goes between her teeth. I want to be the one nibbling them. "We had a quiz today. I didn't do well at all." She pops down a bit to pull a pint for the old guy sitting a few seats over. "I might need to drop it and just graduate next May with everyone else." She tries to hide the stress and worry behind a weak smile.

"It's one quiz. You've got time to make your grades. Why are they giving exams two days in anyway?"

"The class is accelerated, like really accelerated. And it's Advanced Anatomy—a ton of memorization. I should probably drop before it's too late." She grabs a napkin rolled around utensils and places it in front of me with the salt and pepper shakers.

"If you drop this class, you have to push off your graduation?" She bites at her lip again and nods. "Why would it be easier in the fall? Why take it later?" She puts so much pressure on herself to do well. To do it on her own.

"The semester is longer, so I'd have more time to memorize the body systems—and I'd have my study group. They're all taking it then and we can quiz each other—flashcards, that kind of thing." She moves down the bar checking her patrons, filling drink orders for the dining room.

The smell of steak and mushroom risotto fills the air around me making my mouth water, and Gracyn slides a plate in front of me.

"How're you doing tonight? My girl there has been a bear the last couple weeks." She stares me down, hand propped on her hip, attitude in full effect. "You know anything about that?"

"Jesus, Gracyn. Lighten up. I told you it has nothing to do with Aidan." Lis' hands go to the long loose braid hanging over her shoulder, fingers twisting and twirling at the soft curl at the end.

"I'm tired and this class is going to kill me." Turning to me, Lis asks, "Is your steak cooked alright?"

"Fucking perfect." It's red in the center and perfectly seared on the outside. I cut a piece and scoop up some of the risotto, turning the fork to Lisbeth.

I'm awestruck watching her lips wrap around the fork, hearing that moan low in the back of her throat. She's fucking made that noise for me—beautiful. I adjust my cock and look up to find both girls' eyes on mine.

Gracyn raises her brow and points her finger in my face. "Don't you hurt my friend. Don't you dare...or you won't need to do that ever again." She waves a hand toward my crotch and walks away.

"So, your class...would it help to have someone quiz you on your facts?"

She tilts her head from side to side like she's thinking about it.

"Maybe?" And the lip again.

Between her teeth.

I reach up and pull it free with my thumb. "I would love to help you study. I'm fairly sure I'm capable of quizzing you. When is your next exam?"

With that, her whole demeanor changes.

"I have another quiz Friday. And I only have until the middle of next week to drop this class and get my money back. Aidan..." Elbows on the bar, she puts her face in her hands. The stress is rolling off of her. "What am I going to do? I've worked so hard. I need to graduate in December. I just need to be done. I'm exhausted. I'm gonna cry if I have to extend this whole thing another semester." Hands rub down her face as she looks up at me, worry pinching at the corners of her eyes.

"Lisbeth, let me help you, please? I want to help. What's your week look like?"

"I just talked to Jenna and took the rest of the week off. Gracyn's going to cover for me here, so other than my class, I'll be studying."

18

Lis

I can't let this one stupid class set me back a whole semester. I've worked so hard and for far too long.

Last night, Jenna told me not to worry about my shifts for the rest of the week. She grabbed cash from the register and tried to give me a "summer bonus" to offset my lost income, but I tucked it back in the drawer with a quickly scribbled *Thank You* before I left for the night.

Aidan kept me company for most of the evening, talking between customers, sharing his dinner with me and trying to ease my worries over this class. I've got to make this work—got to pass this and then the next one in the series next month.

I used to love summer classes—being able to concentrate on one class at a time, immerse myself in the material and just get it done. In theory, it's great, but I may have to just suck it up and push off graduation.

I set my coffee on the corner of my desk making sure to pack away my notes and the review packet for Friday's test.

Aidan told Francie he needed the next couple of days off to help me study. Francie even pulled both Jimmy and Finn into work making sure the guys' apartment is quiet and I can concentrate.

The sun beats down on my shoulders replacing the chill from the classroom as I walk out to my car. I grabbed everything I need to spend the next several hours shoving as much information into my brain as I can. Aidan is really sweet offering to help me, but I fully expect him to get bored after a while. This way, I can go straight to the library or coffee shop and keep studying when he's had enough.

I pull up to his loft with my coffee refilled and the hot wind whipping through the car windows. After parking, I wrap my hair up in a messy bun high on the back of my head, and swap my sunglasses for real ones.

As I lean in the passenger side to grab my bag and coffee cup, my skin tingles and I feel his gaze on me. I should have taken the time to tie my hair back before the wind on the drive over made it such a mess. Should have put more effort into how I look. *I'm here to study. That's all.*

Straightening up, I reach to pull my bag higher on my shoulder but feel the weight lifted from me—literally and figuratively.

"Let me take that." Aidan grabs my leather tote bag and closes the car door. I'm backed up against the hot metal and pinned in place by him. "You ready to learn my body?"

"Wh-what?" The tingles I felt moments ago turn into a full riot of chills along my arms and neck.

"I figure you'll have to map the terms you're learnin', yeah?" What is he doing to me? "It's anatomy we're studying?" I can barely manage a nod. "I'll let you use me anyway you need in order to get your grades. I'm at your mercy."

Holy hell.

Aidan steps back with that smirk on his face, the one that says he knows he's got my heart racing. He pulls me toward the steps and guides me inside.

My brain finally kicks into gear and I stop short. "You know I'm here to study, right? For a test?"

His low chuckle goes right through to my core. "Of course, love. Whatever you need." He drops my bag on the small table in the kitchen and grabs some sandwiches out of the fridge. "I thought you might like some lunch before we start, but we can get straight to it if you prefer."

Is he talking about studying or did he think this was going in a different direction? I'm so confused right now.

"I..." I'm not opposed to the idea of sleeping with Aidan— feeling more of what he gave me in the darkroom. I've thought about it a lot. A lot. "...Aidan, I have to study. I..." I've avoided his eyes through this whole exchange and need to take a deep breath before I chance it. Releasing it slowly, I lift my eyes to find him laughing at me?

"Lisbeth, I promised to help you study. Relax, eat and we'll make the flashcards and get your terms memorized."

"You're a shit," I huff out at him as he chuckles at me and grabs us a couple glasses of water. "It's just...this is really important and I...I..." I couldn't tell if he was serious, if he wants me, or just *that*.

But I can't say it. My heart squeezes a little at the thought of a relationship, of taking this further. I'm petrified of being cast aside.

Again.

"Lisbeth, stop. I'm sorry if I crossed a line." All joking is gone, his expression soft.

I hand him a stack of flashcards I made early this morning before class and he patiently quizzes me for the next several hours, but I can't help thinking about it. *That line.*

Eventually, we stop and grab some dinner close by. I need a break—out of his apartment. I'm starting to make mistakes and getting answers wrong.

After burgers and a couple beers we walk slowly back to Aidan's loft. The fresh air caressing my skin as it clears the fuzz from my brain. Since he's been quizzing me on muscle groups, I run through them as he trails the back of his fingers down my arm—*trapezius-spine of scapula-deltoid-brachialis-brachioradialis-flexor retinaculum.*

"Good on you." He's got that spot on my wrist again, rubbing soft circles with his thumb.

"Did I say those out loud?"

"You did, and you got them all perfect. I think the flexor retinaculum is one of my favorite spots on you." He raises my hand and places a sweet kiss on the inside of my wrist.

We make our way up the stairs to the door. Aidan unlocks it, but holds me there—pressing his front into my back. His hand slides across my belly, pulling me tight to him, his lips skating across the back of my neck. "Though, I'm fond of this spot as well."

My skin tightens with anticipation and desire. I've spent every one of the nights since the darkroom thinking about this. I was surprised, and kind of disappointed, that it seemed like a onetime thing. Aidan hadn't made any further attempts; didn't try at all.

We spent time together, but maybe we were always around other people. Gracyn at our place, Finn or Jimmy here.

"Let's go study, love. We've a lot left to cover."

And just like that, I'm back to confused and frustrated. Which has me answering questions wrong again and getting pissed.

"I think I'm getting dumber."

We're on the couch with the fucking flash cards and I can't seem to get anything correct. The flash of his camera snaps my attention from my puddle of self-doubt.

"What are you doing?"

"Getting creative with your studies. The curve of your trapezius wrapping 'round to your collarbone is gorgeous." Turning the camera, he shows me the image.

Captured in black and white, is my pale neck, exposed and open to him by the tilt of my head and the strap of my tank that's slipped down my arm.

"Maybe I should be taking pictures of you." His lips are right there when I turn my head. Right fucking there.

"Maybe you should use me like I offered earlier. Practical applications, yeah?" He's so close. And not smiling anymore. Heat and desire are flushing my chest and burning through me.

He leans forward placing his camera on the coffee table and I run my nail down the exposed muscles in his arm. He stills sucking in a breath.

Grabbing at something from the table, Aidan straightens and pierces me with his dark gaze. "Take this," he rasps as he hands me a pen and reaches behind his head. He pulls his shirt off, leaning back into the arm of the couch. "Mark me. Label the muscles." His voice is low and husky.

I shift closer. This is such a good idea—and such a bad one.

The pen cap pops as I pull it free. He's laid out for me, his breathing slow and deep. His eyes flash darkly from the pen in my hand to my eyes, to my lips. I know I'm biting the bottom one, trying so hard not to shake as I move the tip of the pen to the skin at the base of his neck. He's not a bulky gym rat, but he is well defined. *Really* well defined. He holds his breath as I drag the pen across his skin outlining the muscles of his chest. *Holy shit.* His nipples harden and his skin pebbles up.

"Lisbeth," my name rasps across his lips, "name them. Now."

Barely making contact, I feather my fingertips across his skin, naming each of the muscles, circling his nipple, scraping the skin there with my nails.

Heaving out a harsh breath, he grabs my wrist. Neither of us move. We're stuck here, searching, deciding, reading each other. I know he can feel my pulse is racing. With my hand held firmly in his grasp, he sits up and pulls me closer.

"Lisbeth." He breathes my name across my lips.

I full-on shiver as he pulls me so I'm straddling him.

With one hand wrapped around my wrist and the other on my hip, Aidan shifts me closer still. All thoughts I'd had that he didn't want me fly away as he moves his hips again, grinding his cock against me.

Finally—*finally*—our lips connect, his tongue sweeping along my bottom one. Pushing his way in, he licks my top lip and deepens the kiss, exploring me, devouring me. Ripping my breath away. He places my hands around his neck and grabs me by the backs of my thighs, standing like it's no effort at all.

His lips never leave mine as he carries me up the stairs to his loft bedroom.

Turning, he sits on the bed, pulling me with him. He

slides his hands up my sides, taking my shirt with them, pushing my arms over my head as he launches my tank to the floor. His hands land on my hips and squeeze—just a little—before trailing heat back up my sides to my breasts. They tighten and tingle as his thumbs caress the sides driving me crazy with need before his fingers trail up, pulling the straps of my bra down my arms—pinning them to my sides. Not really trapped, but Aidan stops, holding me there.

"Lisbeth? This okay?" My name rasping across his lips steals my breath away.

All I can do is nod, my fingers tremble as they seek out his plump lower lip. I want this. I'm scared, but I want this.

Reaching behind me, Aidan unhooks my bra and adds it to my tank on the floor. He leans in, whispering, "Gorgeous," against my skin. I barely catch the word as he kisses across my breast—licking, scraping his teeth along my skin— pebbling my nipples to hard almost painful peaks. Twining my hands in his silky black hair, I gasp at the scrape of his stubble on my sensitive skin.

He pulls back checking my eyes. Okay with what he sees, he slides his hands around to unbutton my shorts, his finger-tips trailing along the top of my panties.

I'm surprised, shocked, when he pushes me off him, my feet landing on the floor. I barely keep my balance as I reach for the button, certain he's changed his mind. Pushing my hands away, he hooks his inside the waistband of my shorts.

"Do you want me to stop? 'Cause I don't want to, not in the least," he rasps as he presses open-mouthed kisses from one hip to the other.

"Don't." I squirm, his kisses tickle as they fuel the need and desire coursing through me. He starts to pull away. "No,

Aidan. Don't stop." The words come out on a breath, and I press my hands to his shoulders.

His thumbs dig into the waist of my panties, shoving them and my shorts over my hips until they fall to the floor. Pulling me with him, he moves back to the middle of his bed. His lips gliding up my torso to the underside of my boobs.

I feel exposed as he lies back, his gaze taking in all of me before he meets my eyes again.

"Lisbeth, this is all you. This goes at your pace, love. As fast or slow as you want—or stop when you say."

My heart skips a beat. He knows me and how much this means to me. He has been so considerate of me. Telling me I have control, when I know deep inside who's really in charge —and that's okay with me.

I drag my fingers down his torso and reach between us. Popping the button on his shorts, the zipper spreading wide, I run a fingertip along his boxer briefs, circling the dot of moisture at the tip of his cock. He's hard—really fucking hard.

Gasping, I fall forward as he bucks his hips, my hands landing hard on his chest. He shoves his shorts and briefs down, his cock exposed. Thumbs press in at my knees, spreading them wider before sliding up the inside of my thighs.

Once again, he pauses silently asking permission— waiting for the dip of my chin before touching me. He slides his thumb from my opening to my peak, spreading my arousal. Circling my clit changing the pressure as he does, bringing me right to the edge. Heart racing, my eyes wide.

He stretches to the side, grabbing a condom from the drawer next to his bed, ripping the package open with his teeth. I whimper when he takes his hand away from me to roll it down his length. The whimper turns to a gasp as he grabs my hips and slides me back and forth over the hard length of his dick. He had me so close before, it takes nothing to set me on edge again.

Aidan relaxes his grip on my hips, giving control back over to me. Letting me make the next move.

Leaning forward, I lift my hips and reach between us, positioning his cock and sliding slowly down his length. I rest my hands heavily on his chest, his wrap around my hips—fingers pressing into my flesh—supporting me, holding me.

His jaw clenches, muscles ticking. Neither of us move, savoring the moment, allowing us both to adjust. *Holy shit.* I release a trembling breath through pursed lips, closing my eyes and feeling all of him.

"Look at me, Lisbeth. Open your eyes—I need to see you."

He holds himself back until my eyes, soft and glassy, drift open to meet his heated gaze. Only then, when he's got that contact, does he start to move—sliding out and thrusting in, the drag of his cock pushes me again. Pushes me back to the edge I've already been on too many times. It takes nothing for me to get close—close, but not quite.

He whispers, murmurs, tells me he's got me. "That's it, love. Let go..." I'm so close. I can feel my pussy grip him—tightening, squeezing his cock. I just can't quite get there. I don't know what to do, how to move, how to make this happen.

"Help me, Aidan. I...can't...please..." My heart slams in my chest, on the edge of exploding

He pulls me down to him—chest to chest—moving me, taking the control he had the whole time. The change is all that I need—the change gives me the pressure, the friction I need.

To. Come. Undone.

19

Aidan

And there it is.

The look on her face, the sounds that she makes, the moment she falls apart, it's all I'll ever need again. And I follow her. Every muscle in my body tightens, contracts, and then relaxes as we both shudder, panting to catch our breath.

After tossing the condom into the bin, I slide back in bed and wrap myself around her. Her hand in mine, both of them pressed firmly to my heart. This feels like more.

More than a shag, more than a fling.

Just more.

The moment she gave herself over to me, needed me and asked for, pleaded for my help, something changed. Lisbeth has been burned and burned badly, but in that moment of putting her needs and desires first, something shifted.

She trusted me.

And I want to cherish and honor this.

Feeling her heart beat and listening to her soft, even

breaths, I lose myself to a sleep I've not slept since arriving in Beekman Hills.

Several hours later, I only just register the sounds of the boys coming home from the pub. I can hear everything in this fucking loft and usually they're louder than a pack of wild dogs when they come in after work.

Lis' things strewn about, and my fucking shirt on the floor down there must not be lost on Finn and Jimmy. The volume drops and other than a few whispers and a quiet chuckle, I hear little else.

The thought crosses my mind, with her body pressed up against me, to wake her and have her. Have her again. But as much as I can hear them downstairs, they can hear every move I make up here. This thing we have between us is not something I'm willing to share. I won't do that to her, she's mine.

Trust.

I wake with Lisbeth's head in the crook of my shoulder and a hand on her hip. My other hand, though. It's resting on my chest—with hers pressed firmly between it and my heart. Like she owns it. Like it's hers. I lie there relishing this for as long as I can. My body screaming for another go. To explore every curve, hear every sigh, every moan. And like a bucket of cold water, those thoughts are washed away. Those sounds are just for me. Mine. I'll not take advantage and share that with anyone, especially the two arseholes sleeping below us.

Sliding from the warmth of her body, I grab my jeans and head downstairs for coffee. As it brews, I look through the fridge taking note that there's still bacon and eggs. I'll make

Lis breakfast when she wakes and then dive right in—to studying, helping her.

I grab my phone and steaming cuppa, stepping out onto our minuscule deck. Three texts and a missed call. Mostly work—photography inquiries, but there's one from Lorna.

Lorna: Hey. Sorry for not getting back to you before now. Can we talk? Soon? xx

Aidan: Yeah. I'm committed to something for a couple days...I'll call.

Aidan: Sunday?

Lorna: Yeah. Good.

She's yet to tell me about the baby. We're going to need more than a quick chat for this.

Liam's seen her a couple times since we talked, but I can't figure why she's been avoiding me. It's got to be tearing her up. They had been trying for a family before my brother's diagnosis. Jesus. I still can't believe how quickly he went. Fucking cancer.

"You look like you have the weight of the world on your shoulders." Her soft voice washes over me as Lis ghosts her fingers lightly down my spine, a trail of goose bumps showing in its wake. She presses a small kiss to the Celtic cross on my shoulder. I reach behind me, grabbing her hand from where it rests low on my back and pull her into my arms.

"Hmmm... Just thinking of some things going on in Dublin." This moment doesn't need to be ruined by my brother's death. I'll tell her later, when she's not worried about her studies. Leaning in and taking the kiss I want—need—the topic is laid to rest.

"Coffee's ready. We can get back to your studies after breakfast," I murmur, bringing her hand to my lips to press a soft kiss to her knuckles.

Inside the kitchen, I push her up against the counter, trapping her. Molding my body to hers, as close as I can, feeling every curve. I take a final kiss and tear myself away from her to hide adjusting my cock. The last thing I want is for her to think that's all I'm after.

The moment I turn to hand her a cup of coffee, she meets me with a warm cloth, rubbing away the ink trails from my shoulder and chest. She's so gentle with me. Trading coffee for the cloth, I rub at the marks and have them just about taken care of when Jimmy stumbles out of his room to plop down at the table. In his fucking boxers.

"Making the eggs? There tea or just feckin' coffee?" I want to smack him upside the head, but he at least gets us back on track. "Mornin', Lis."

And, of course—fucking of course—Finn shows his face only when the smell of bacon fills the flat. Grabbing his plate, he pulls a chair up next to Lis. "You the reason I couldn't sleep?"

"What? No..." Lisbeth stutters as her neck flushes pink.

"Thought that was you I heard screamin' all night." Finn winks, thinking he's being funny, but Lis is uncomfortable and I'll be kickin' his arse soon. I'll kill him.

"Finn." Jimmy lifts his head from the table, shooting him a warning.

"I'm going to go...um..." Her words get lost in the embarrassment swirling around her as she escapes up to my loft.

"Christ, Finn. Are you fuckin' stupid? Why would you do that?" I growl, hands clenched, muscles quivering. "She —*fuck*—no fuckin' class. Might want to look at yourself—see why you're not near as slick with the girls as you think you are. Fuckin' arsehole." I pace the length of the small kitchen trying to keep calm. "Out. I need you out of the flat today."

"Jimmy's on at the bar, I've all day to hang out wit' you." Finn grins, oblivious of just how close I am to throwing him out of the flat right now.

"No. Out," I grit out as I turn my back to them. "Get the fuck out, and don't come back 'til tomorrow. Fuckin' bastard. Don't think I won't kick your sorry arse." Their grumbles follow me as I launch my body up the stairs, taking them two at a time. Finn will feel bad and apologize once Jimmy gets it through his thick skull what he did to fuck up, but for now, I can't be near him.

Crawling across the bed to her, I wrap my fingers around her wrists and I settle myself in front of her. "Lisbeth. Don't let him..."

"It's fine. I'm fine. Maybe I should just go. Study at my place."

"He's goin'." I rub circles with my thumbs—caressing that spot—bring one wrist and then the other to my lips, planting a soft kiss on each. "He'll be gone all day. Stay. Please. Jimmy's goin' to work. We'll study and get you sorted. Please—let me do this. Let me help you."

"Your accent changes depending on what's happening." The smile creeps up her lips.

"What?"

"It does. When you're mad," she leans in, "when you're drinking," her warm hands slide up my legs, "and when you're..." She squeezes high on my thighs, her thumbs pressing in right by my cock.

"When I'm what?" Every time she moves, the subtle scent of her perfume teases me.

"When..." Her eyes go straight for my crotch, making my cock twitch.

"When I fuck ye?" I want to push her back and bury

myself in her for the rest of the day. I want to hear my name on her lips. I want to make her scream, the way Finn was talking about. I want her to forget he said that shit. "They're still downstairs, love. Much as I want to, I don't want to share you. Not with them here to listen."

We're wrapped up in each other's breaths, hands twined through her hair, pulling her in. My lips sweep across hers; she darts her tongue out, licking my bottom one. Fuck. Her name comes out on a groan as she palms my cock, and rakes her teeth across my lip. Biting me. Squeezing me. She's pushing this. She knows we're not totally alone and she's still going. Working me up, making me hard.

The sound of the shower starting fills the loft as the front door slams. I pitch forward, shoving her into the mattress, silently pulling at her clothes and we spend the rest of the day completely wrapped up in each other. Finn stays away and Jimmy must find someone to go home from the bar with.

The flat is ours alone.

We spend hours studying for her exam until she knows her material inside and out. When Lis finishes packing away her books and papers late in the evening, I set her bag by the front door.

I grasp her hand and lead her back up to my room and study the subject I've been yearning for all day. *Her*. What makes her sigh, gasp, and tremble. What makes her blush and beg for more.

HER TEST IS early Friday and I wake to the mattress shifting as she tries to leave. Wrapping my hand around her hip, I pull her back to me. "Aidan, I need to go." God, I don't like the feeling of her leaving my bed.

"Just five more minutes." I drag her so she's lying almost on top of me, her heart aligned perfectly with mine—beating with mine.

"I have to go home and clean up—change before my test," she murmurs into my chest dragging her fingers across my stomach. "And I don't want the weirdness from yesterday, again. I didn't mean to spend the night—"

"They didn't come back, either of them. Take a shower here. I'll get you coffee and something to eat on your way." Squeezing her tight to me, pressing a kiss to the top of her head, I untangle us and leave the only place I want to spend my day.

After Lis leaves with a bagel in one hand and her coffee in the other, I try calling Lorna but get nothing. No answer. Nothing Saturday. Nothing Sunday. Late in the day Monday, just as I catch Lis' eye through the window of the bistro, Lorna phones. The tears are heavy in her voice and there is no way—no way—I can have this conversation in a bar. Closing my eyes, I back away just barely registering Lis' expression as I turn and head to my car for what can only be a heart-wrenchingly emotional conversation.

"Aidan—please come home."

20

Lis

I walk out of my test exhausted and emotionally spent. I feel really good about the test itself, but I'm wiped out and I have to work all weekend to make up for the days I spent studying. Maybe, though. Maybe I'll get through this.

Maybe.

The weekend passes in a blur of sleep and hours upon hours spent mixing drinks. Aidan left for a shoot and will be away for a few days. It's built-in space. The space I usually crave to get my head on straight and in the right place. And I don't want it. Sex changes everything, but I'm feeling like it's a good change and I find myself wishing time away.

Grades for Friday's test won't be posted until tonight, but I still feel really confident that I did well. Anything above a B and I'll stick it out for the summer session. The bistro is slow and I settle in to study. Aidan is meeting me here for dinner and then, who knows. I know this is scary territory. I've opened my heart to him. I've let him in.

Jenna pulls me out of my textbook. "Lis." She nods toward the front window. "You waiting for someone?"

"Who is Lissy waiting for?" It's so slow in here tonight that Tony's left the kitchen to his sous chef and is having dinner with Jenna. I don't know if it counts as a date if you own the restaurant and cooked your own entrees, but that's what they're doing.

I bring Tony another beer and look out the window watching Aidan cross the street toward the bistro. Toward me. "Who's that?" Tony's gaze going from me to the man who's wiggled his way past my barriers. The man who takes days off from work to help me. The man who's made me feel important.

My smile spreads across my face, when he finally looks up and his eyes meet mine. I lean my body toward the window—feeling the pull to him—when his steps falter. Pulling his phone from his pocket, he stares at the screen for a beat. That same look he had last week washes over his features. The look like he's holding things together, but just barely. His shoulders rise with tension as he stops and puts the phone to his ear. Closing his eyes, he pushes the air from his body like he can push whatever news he's getting away with it.

My stomach twisting, I slink into a chair at Jenna and Tony's table and watch as Aidan pivots on his heel, turning back to cross the street. With nothing more than a small wave thrown my way, he disappears around the corner.

Aidan

"Aidan, I'm...I'm pregnant." Even knowing the words are coming doesn't prepare me for the level of devastation in her voice. "I'm... I don't know what to do." Lorna's words are nearly drowned out by her tears.

"Lorna, love, shhh...it's okay." It's okay. It's good, really.

Weaving through people, I make my way back to my car and lean up against the side, clinging to the hope that I can sort this quickly and get back to Lis.

"It's not, Aidan. I can't do this alone. This was supposed to happen with Michael, not by myself. I'm all alone." She's sobbing, now. Unable to catch her breath, she hiccups through the miles and my heart breaks all over again.

Resigning myself to the fact that I'm not spending my time with Lis tonight, I get in the car and head home, hoping the flat is empty or at least quiet. It might be time to think about getting my own place.

"Lorna, you're not alone. You've your parents and mine. You've family and people who love you within arm's reach. And now—now you have a piece of Mick too. This is what you wanted. What you both hoped and prayed for. Shhh... you're alright." Hearing her devastation through the phone and not being there to make her a cup of tea, hold her hand while she cries, is so much harder than I thought it would be.

We'd spent the two weeks from Michael's diagnosis to his death in a shocked version of that. Holding on while letting go. I'd been scheduled to leave on assignment when he'd called and asked me to come over. The whole thing was unreal. Cancer sucks.

"Lorna...Lorna," Not sure she can even hear me through her tears, I call to her softly, trying to soothe her, trying to calm her. It's late in Dublin. There's a good possibility she'll end up crying herself to sleep. And then what? *Christ.*

I'd needed the space, distance, from his death to get over

the shock. To grieve. But I'd not thought or planned for this. This may well be too much to talk through on the phone.

Heading straight through the flat to the kitchen, I pause to stare out the window. The neighbor's kids play in their garden. Heart heavy in my chest, I reach for a beer, opt for a whiskey, and go sit out on the deck. The warm humid air even feels sad wrapped around me.

"Will you talk to me? I need you to talk to me, just like before, like we did a couple months ago. Teacht anois." *Come now.*

"...I miss him so much..." There. We're making progress. "Aidan, what am I going to do?"

"Lorna, you're going to have a baby. A piece of Michael, a piece of his heart to hold close to you for the rest of your life. You don't ever have to give him up, now." Lord, don't let that compound the sadness. "Tell me the good stuff. You've been to the doctor, yeah?"

My hand goes to the back of my neck, squeezing as I wait for her to say yes. To let me know she's at least done this— Christ, she's got to be four? Five months along? I don't know.

"When are you due?"

Lorna sighs. "November...the end of the month." She sniffs, but her voice is starting to sound stronger. "I heard the baby's heartbeat, and all I could think is that Michael should be with me. God, he'd be beside himself."

It feels like hours that we talk. About everything, about nothing, about my brother's baby and how she's going to be just fine. She needs to talk to both sets of grandparents—I can't believe she's not told them yet.

"Lorna, you need to take care of yourself. Think about how excited they'll be."

"I know. I think maybe...I wasn't ready for the excitement

part? I don't want to be sad about such an amazing gift, but... it's bittersweet, yeah? And I'm surrounded by him, but he's not here. It's...I don't know. Maybe I need to move."

She is surrounded by him. I tried to help her clear some of his things away after the funeral, but it was too soon. I didn't make it a week before leaving Dublin. Trying to run from the grief.

"You need a holiday, maybe. Go shopping in London. Spend a few days at the beach. Visit a spa. Is that kind of thing okay for you to do?"

Finally, she lets out a laugh. It's small and sad, but it's a move in the right direction. "Yeah. I can do those things. I just feel like I should save every penny—I don't know. And alone? That kind of thing's not fun alone, Aidan."

"Don't worry about the money. I'll send it to you. Take a girlfriend. Take one of our sisters—Christ, there's enough of them to choose from."

We were both from big families, but Lorna and I had been close. Close in age, growing up together we were always running about. At their wedding, I was both the best man and the man of honor.

The last of my whiskey slides down my throat as my thoughts turn to my niece or nephew. "Will you find out whether it's a boy or a girl?"

"I will. Next month, I think. You could...you could go with me? I miss you, Aidan. Are...are you coming home soon?"

No. Maybe.

Her question asks for answers that I can't give her right now.

"I don't know. I'm doing well here. I'm settled." Torn. I'm absolutely torn. I ran away from Dublin and now—now there's a reason for me to stay here. "I'll send you some money. Go somewhere—take care of you and we'll talk soon, yeah?"

Fucking hell.

I log on to my bank account and send a good chunk of money to Lorna. Enough for a holiday and some extra to help ease the expense of setting up for a baby—or to help ease my conscience. I want to stay. I want to see what this is with Lisbeth. I want a chance at the happiness my brother and Lorna had—just no tragic ending.

Jimmy eases out the door and joins me with the bottle of whiskey resting at his side. "Was that Lorna, then?" He pours a good measure for each of us. "She tell you, finally?"

"She did."

The street light illuminates the amber liquid as I swirl it around my glass. Legs stretched out in front of me, I lean my head back against the side of the building and close my eyes. Jimmy lowers himself down next to me and waits. Patiently. He nods and sips his whiskey as I fill him in on all that Lorna and I talked about.

"What are you goin' to do?" He shifts his eyes from the faint smattering of stars barely visible above us to my face. Gaging where my head is. "Are you leaving? Goin' back home?"

The question sucks just as bad the second time I'm asked it tonight. "I don't know."

Aidan

"Aidan, I'm...I'm pregnant." Even knowing the words are coming doesn't prepare me for the level of devastation in her voice. "I'm... I don't know what to do." Lorna's words are nearly drowned out by her tears.

"Lorna, love, shhh...it's okay." It's okay. It's good, really.

Weaving through people, I make my way back to my car and lean up against the side, clinging to the hope that I can sort this quickly and get back to Lis.

"It's not, Aidan. I can't do this alone. This was supposed to happen with Michael, not by myself. I'm all alone." She's sobbing, now. Unable to catch her breath, she hiccups through the miles and my heart breaks all over again.

Resigning myself to the fact that I'm not spending my time with Lis tonight, I get in the car and head home, hoping the flat is empty or at least quiet. It might be time to think about getting my own place.

"Lorna, you're not alone. You've your parents and mine. You've family and people who love you within arm's reach. And now—now you have a piece of Mick too. This is what you wanted. What you both hoped and prayed for. Shhh... you're alright." Hearing her devastation through the phone and not being there to make her a cup of tea, hold her hand while she cries, is so much harder than I thought it would be.

We'd spent the two weeks from Michael's diagnosis to his death in a shocked version of that. Holding on while letting go. I'd been scheduled to leave on assignment when he'd called and asked me to come over. The whole thing was unreal. Cancer sucks.

"Lorna...Lorna," Not sure she can even hear me through her tears, I call to her softly, trying to soothe her, trying to calm her. It's late in Dublin. There's a good possibility she'll end up crying herself to sleep. And then what? *Christ.*

I'd needed the space, distance, from his death to get over the shock. To grieve. But I'd not thought or planned for this. This may well be too much to talk through on the phone.

Heading straight through the flat to the kitchen, I pause

to stare out the window. The neighbor's kids play in their garden. Heart heavy in my chest, I reach for a beer, opt for a whiskey, and go sit out on the deck. The warm humid air even feels sad wrapped around me.

"Will you talk to me? I need you to talk to me, just like before, like we did a couple months ago. Teacht anois." *Come now.*

"...I miss him so much..." There. We're making progress. "Aidan, what am I going to do?"

"Lorna, you're going to have a baby. A piece of Michael, a piece of his heart to hold close to you for the rest of your life. You don't ever have to give him up, now." Lord, don't let that compound the sadness. "Tell me the good stuff. You've been to the doctor, yeah?"

My hand goes to the back of my neck, squeezing as I wait for her to say yes. To let me know she's at least done this—Christ, she's got to be four? Five months along? I don't know.

"When are you due?"

Lorna sighs. "November...the end of the month." She sniffs, but her voice is starting to sound stronger. "I heard the baby's heartbeat, and all I could think is that Michael should be with me. God, he'd be beside himself."

It feels like hours that we talk. About everything, about nothing, about my brother's baby and how she's going to be just fine. She needs to talk to both sets of grandparents—I can't believe she's not told them yet.

"Lorna, you need to take care of yourself. Think about how excited they'll be."

"I know. I think maybe...I wasn't ready for the excitement part? I don't want to be sad about such an amazing gift, but... it's bittersweet, yeah? And I'm surrounded by him, but he's not here. It's...I don't know. Maybe I need to move."

She is surrounded by him. I tried to help her clear some of his things away after the funeral, but it was too soon. I didn't make it a week before leaving Dublin. Trying to run from the grief.

"You need a holiday, maybe. Go shopping in London. Spend a few days at the beach. Visit a spa. Is that kind of thing okay for you to do?"

Finally, she lets out a laugh. It's small and sad, but it's a move in the right direction. "Yeah. I can do those things. I just feel like I should save every penny—I don't know. And alone? That kind of thing's not fun alone, Aidan."

"Don't worry about the money. I'll send it to you. Take a girlfriend. Take one of our sisters—Christ, there's enough of them to choose from."

We were both from big families, but Lorna and I had been close. Close in age, growing up together we were always running about. At their wedding, I was both the best man and the man of honor.

The last of my whiskey slides down my throat as my thoughts turn to my niece or nephew. "Will you find out whether it's a boy or a girl?"

"I will. Next month, I think. You could...you could go with me? I miss you, Aidan. Are...are you coming home soon?"

No. Maybe.

Her question asks for answers that I can't give her right now.

"I don't know. I'm doing well here. I'm settled." Torn. I'm absolutely torn. I ran away from Dublin and now—now there's a reason for me to stay here. "I'll send you some money. Go somewhere—take care of you and we'll talk soon, yeah?"

Fucking hell.

I log on to my bank account and send a good chunk of money to Lorna. Enough for a holiday and some extra to help ease the expense of setting up for a baby—or to help ease my conscience. I want to stay. I want to see what this is with Lisbeth. I want a chance at the happiness my brother and Lorna had—just no tragic ending.

Jimmy eases out the door and joins me with the bottle of whiskey resting at his side. "Was that Lorna, then?" He pours a good measure for each of us. "She tell you, finally?"

"She did."

The street light illuminates the amber liquid as I swirl it around my glass. Legs stretched out in front of me, I lean my head back against the side of the building and close my eyes. Jimmy lowers himself down next to me and waits. Patiently. He nods and sips his whiskey as I fill him in on all that Lorna and I talked about.

"What are you goin' to do?" He shifts his eyes from the faint smattering of stars barely visible above us to my face. Gaging where my head is. "Are you leaving? Goin' back home?"

The question sucks just as bad the second time I'm asked it tonight. "I don't know."

21

Lis

Gracyn is burrowed into the end of the couch with a glass of wine watching shit TV when I get home. "Hey. How'd it go today?"

"Not yet. Give me a minute?" I go straight to my room and ditch my clothes for jammies. Wrapping my hair in the messiest of all buns, I make a beeline for the glasses and bring the rest of the open bottle of wine to the living room. "Okay. I'm ready."

"You get the grade on your test yet?" Gracyn peers at me over the top of her glass.

"Nope. Hand me your laptop." The look on Aidan's face as he answered his phone earlier is replaced with the memories of ink marking his skin and the look in his eyes as he broke through my barriers. I log into my university account and take a big gulp of wine. "Ready?"

"Yeah. Go." Gracyn buzzes, almost as tense over my

grades as she is over hers. "What do you need to stick with it this summer?" She's practically bouncing with nerves.

"Anything over a B, and I should be okay. I just..." Gracyn jumps and almost spills her wine when I screech. *Almost.* "I got an A—holy shit." I bite my lip trying to suppress the huge smile that wants to take over my face. "G, I'm gonna make it. Oh my God, I'm gonna do this." Eyes huge, I split the rest of the bottle between our glasses.

"Yeah, you are. I never doubted you," she says with all the sincerity in the world. I'm the one with all the doubts and fears of failure.

I set her laptop on the coffee table and let out a huge sigh of relief, nestling myself into the arm of the couch and shoving my feet under the throw blanket she's got wrapped around her.

"And what about Aidan? Things are good there?"

The first thing that pops into my mind is the call he got—the frustration and concern etched across his face. He hasn't responded to my text, yet.

"I think, yeah. I haven't seen him since Friday, but yeah. He was incredible helping me...study?" I didn't mean for that to come out as a question. "He takes care of me. Makes me feel like I'm a priority to him. I think my trust—my comfort? —is important to him."

I grab my phone from the table and send him another message before dropping my phone in my lap.

"Yeah?" I know for sure that she's concerned for me, but her questioning it makes my glass pause on my lips. "What's the plan there? Is he staying, Lis? In the States? Or is he going back to Ireland?"

I check my phone for a message I know isn't there, lower my glass, my gaze falling to the loose thread in the blanket.

"I don't know. We haven't really talked about that. It's been all about me—my needs—my..."

"Don't you think you should find out—before it's too late?"

Deep breath in, I tilt my head back against the side of the couch.

"Lis?"

The air rushes out of my lungs. Thoughts are racing through my head. Pinging around inside my brain. "This is just a distraction, remember? It was your idea," I whisper.

"I...just don't want you to get hurt. Talk to him. Don't set yourself up for heartache again."

My eyes drop from the ceiling meeting hers in an intense stare.

Gracyn raises her hand, palm out while she rationalizes. "Not that I think for a minute he's going to go fuck Maryse behind your back, but what's he doing here? Where is his head? You need to talk to him. Soon."

"Yeah, I know." Not much about tonight's sitting well with me. "What about you, G? You gonna sit there and tell me I need to protect my heart, when..."

She cuts me off with a snort. "Dude, really? I've got your fucking back—I'm just looking out for you."

"When you've been *off* since spring break, Gracyn." Not good. I don't want to do this with her. I hate fighting. "What's up with your shit?" Trading my wine glass for her laptop, I open Facebook and search her timeline.

"What are you doing? Stop, Lis." Her feet push at me and I have to grab at the computer to stop it from hitting the floor.

"Look Gavin up, do a search. Have you looked for him at all?" The heat rolling off her glare is scorching. "I love you, and you know I appreciate you looking out for me, but what about you? For the love of God, G—what's the deal? It's been months and I still find you staring at his picture on your phone, but you won't look for him? Contact him?" It's totally ridiculous that I'm getting this pissed.

Deflecting? Probably, yes.

"What if he's in the area? What if he's thinking about you as much as you're thinking about him?" She's blinking way too fast for that to be anything other than tears she's fighting. "Gracyn. What's the name of his band?"

"*The UnBroken.*" She practically whispers it. "But I don't want to know. The timing's bad."

"The timing is only bad because you won't let it be anything else. I care about you too, you know. And you've been moping for months." There are a ton of posts on Facebook for the band—they're tagged all over Instagram—all over. "G, they were just here last week. They were the band that played the college summer series. Did you know?" She refuses to make eye contact with me. She absolutely knew. "You knew he was here and you took all my hours last week."

"You needed the time off to study. This class is important to you." I don't know what to even say to that.

"Don't you dare twist this and make it about me. You know someone else could've worked the bar. Using me as an excuse makes you sound like my mom—and you don't want that—I know you don't." My mother has been manipulating shit my entire life. Anything to make Maryse look good. "Gracyn, I love you, but that's just wrong. I'm...I'm going to bed. I can't...forget it." The air in the apartment seems to have shifted. The tension is high and I'm pissed.

Of all the fucking things to do, twisting my needs to suit her wants and fears is too much. And she knows it. She's seen my mom pull that shit and Gracyn's been the one to scrape me off the floor from the aftermath. Literally.

Done with today. I'm done with it. The morning hasn't improved my mood. The fight with my friend reminded me why I'm not good at accepting help. I never thought this shit would happen with Gracyn.

Never.

"Lis, I'm sorry, okay? What...what do I need to do? How can I apologize?" She knows. She fucking knows that she can't twist things and use me as an excuse to get what she wants—or avoid what she thinks she doesn't.

I've got Gavin's tour schedule saved to my phone. They come anywhere close to this area again and I'm dragging her ass to the show. That'll help.

"Dammit, Lis, stop. Just...I knew I would end up there if I didn't have somewhere else I had to be." Her voice drops and she slumps into a seat at the kitchen table. "I needed to work that night as much as you needed the time off."

"Why not talk to me, though? What the hell? I don't understand." I throw my hands up in the air, before letting them fall to my sides.

"I know. I...you have so much going on and...listen to me, just for a minute." Her fingers twist through her hair, frustration rolling off her in waves. "If anyone gets how important this class is for you, staying on schedule to graduate early, it's me. I know. I get it—I've been with you through all of your family shit. I'm sorry I didn't tell you he was here and that I needed to be busy. I just...I will. Okay? Next time, I will." She finally raises her head and looks at me. "I just need some time."

"Gracyn, you're scaring me. Tell me what happened?"

"Not yet. Not now, but I promise to tell you everything.

Soon." And with that, she leaves. No makeup, not put together. Just grabs her keys and leaves. Tears already streaming down her face.

This is so not right. It seems like every time things start looking like they're all going to line up and life is going to move forward without drama, something shakes loose. We'll be okay. It just goes to show that disappointment is lurking.

This is the most we've talked in weeks. We just haven't crossed paths—which is odd. I can honestly say I've not been avoiding her. I really hate conflict and the shitty feelings that never seem to dissipate, and talking is the only way I know to make things better. But she's been steering clear of me.

I dump the rest of the coffee into my go-cup and grab my bags. I'm going straight from class to work today, like I have been for most of the summer, and then hopefully to Aidan's.

Things have been going really well, other than with my dear sweet friend, and it scares the shit out of me. I don't want to think about the next thing to go wrong, but I feel like the snowball has started down the mountain.

MY KNUCKLES barely land on the door, when it flies open and Aidan steps into me. He wraps his hands around my cheeks pulling me in close and kisses me like he hasn't seen me in ages. I'm completely consumed by him as he kisses my breath away.

He pulls back and with his lips ghosting over mine, he whispers, "Christ, I missed you. What are you doing to me?" Aidan's forehead rests against mine as I breathe in the faint scent of stale beer, sweat and him.

"Come in, then. I was just waiting to take a shower until you got here."

He scoops my bag off my shoulder and pulls me through the door.

"Pretty presumptuous," I laugh when he turns to look at me, cheeks flushed and brows pinned to his hairline.

"Not what I meant, but if you're offerin', I won't deny you." His sparkling eyes contrast with the low, gravelly timbre of his voice.

Before a response has a chance to form in my head, the door swings open again, narrowly missing my backside. Finn and a couple guys from the pub stumble in, smirk hitching up on the left side of his mouth.

"Am I intererruptin'?" He looks back and forth between us knowing full and well that he might be.

"Nope. I just got here." I take my bag from Aidan's hand and stalk to the stairs. "Aidan, why don't you shower first? I'll go after you." And up the stairs I trot to the sound of snickering and mumbles.

FRESHLY SHOWERED, damp hair piled on my head, I walk through the apartment quickly, avoiding the furtive looks from the guys sprawled across the couch. Aidan is out on the small deck with a couple icy glasses of water for us and the noise blissfully dies as I pull the door shut behind me.

"Guess we're not watching a movie?"

Aidan huffs out a laugh and hands me a glass. "We're not. Sorry, it's pretty crowded here at times." He's leaning against the railing, arms crossed over his bare chest, shorts slung low on his hips. His gaze settles the four, loud man-children who took over the couch and TV.

With a decisive nod, Aidan straightens up and ducks inside grabbing a pillow and a light blanket from the basket by the couch. "Here, take my glass—" He leans over the railing and chucks the stuff he grabbed to the deck of the apartment below us.

"What are you doing?" I snort out a laugh and watch him scale down the ladder that runs down the side of the deck. "Aidan?"

"Hand down the glasses and come on." He reaches up and takes our drinks.

Shimmying down the ladder, I step onto his neighbor's deck. Aidan throws the pillow on a hammock spread between the deck supports. "Aidan, we can't just use his hammock," I laugh. The guy who lives here is nice, but this is a bit presumptuous.

"Help me with this. We'll spread this out and lie on top of it." He hands me the blanket and opens up the netting. "He's out of town this weekend. Asked me to watch for a package delivery." He climbs into the hammock and reaches for me, pulling me in. I yelp as it sways from my weight dropping in. Aidan chuckles, adjusting me so I'm half on top of him.

"He told me I was welcome to use his deck if I needed to get away from the boys. They get to be a bit much sometimes. And you're the one I want to spend my alone time with." He trails his fingers down my arm as the breeze blows gently across us.

"This is perfect." I yawn, resting my hand over his heart. "Tell me about your tattoo—the cross." I've wondered since catching a glimpse of it in the darkroom. I've seen it plenty since. Traced it with my fingertip. Studied the intricate knots, the heart, and hands. The crown.

"I got it in honor of Michael." He places his hand over mine and slides it down so his thumb finds the inside of my wrist. "His passing."

The shift is subtle, but it's there. I can feel the tension, like there's more to say, but he's not quite ready. I get it.

"I'm sorry. So sorry." I place a soft kiss to his warm lips and press my hand to his heart, and the tension eases away. My eyes are heavy and everything about this moment feels right. I feel a connection to him that I haven't truly known before. Our breaths match—our heartbeats in sync.

As I drift off, I hear Aidan murmur, "*Codladh sahm*—sleep well."

22

Aidan

I lie here in the hammock with Lis' hand pressed to my heart once again. It's fitting, her hand resting there. She owns me.

I've been waiting for the question about my cross—she's spent a fair amount of time staring at it, tracing it. And it hits me. Right now—in this moment—my heart is cocooned safely between Michael's memory and Lisbeth's presence. The beats evenly match up to the rhythm of hers.

As exposed as we are, swinging in a hammock on my neighbor's deck, I can't imagine feeling closer to her—more in tune to her. It feels a lot like love, and I want to stay here. Not just here in this moment, but here—in the States. Thoughts of what I need to do in order to stay here start swirling through my brain. I'll need to sort my visa to start, an apartment of my own. To talk to Lis and tell her the rest of the story. I just don't know how.

The hammock is a romantic idea, and certainly better

than the sauna of my room, but I want more. I need to have a space for just us. For us to be together, maybe live together. The thought washes over me as the soft breeze ruffles her hair, blowing wisps of it across my chest and I relax into sleep, feeling like I have a plan, a purpose, and someone to share it with. Not someone, Lisbeth.

MORNING COMES WAY TOO EARLY, the sun streaming through the trees barely filtering it before it hits my eyes. This is how I want to wake up on the regular. Wrapped up in this woman, feels like the definition of *home*.

There's no way I can pull myself out of this thing without waking her. Instead, I squeeze her and tickle my hand from her hip, up to her waist and back down until she starts squirming.

"Why? Why would you wake a person like that?" she grumbles while planting her hands on my chest and pushing up. Her hair is a wild mess, her cheek is red where it was pressed against my skin all night, and she couldn't be more beautiful.

"I couldn't wait to see you. It was selfish." My smile stretches wide across my face as I slide my hand up her arm and try to tame her wild hair away from her face.

Much as I love this moment, I need to get things moving. "Come on, love. Let's go back upstairs." I swat her arse and try to sit up, but the hammock sucks me back in. The motion making us swing way too hard, the ropes creaking as we rock.

After another failed attempt and both of us almost falling out on our heads, we're out of the damn thing and back up on my deck.

"What's the plan today?"

"Go get dressed, we're going to get you some coffee and breakfast. I like you better when you're fed and properly caffeinated." I drop a kiss on her forehead and head up to my loft to grab my laptop and get ready for the day.

Lis

We round the corner to the diner, the bell jingling, and find a booth toward the back. I slide in and Aidan scoots in next to me. "Uh... What are you doing? Something wrong with that side over there?" I smile and nod at the other side of the table. "You know Gracyn and I make fun of people for doing this at the bistro. Right?"

"I do. You've both shared that with me many times, but we have to work on our to-do list, for today, yeah?" He pulls his laptop from his bag as the waitress comes to the table, coffee pot in hand. Bless her. I flip my cup on its saucer and push it toward her eagerly.

"What can I getcha?"

I dump in a dollop of creamer and inhale a healthy dose of the life-giving liquid. I look up to order and both the waitress and Aidan are staring at me. I might have groaned as I drank half my cup down. The waitress refills my cup for me while we order a mountain of food and Aidan pulls up a website for apartments in the area. "So, your plan?"

"Right. It's time for me to look at a different living arrangement. And I would love for you to help me. Would you look with me?" He turns his very serious eyes to mine and holds his breath.

"Okay. I can tag along. Do you know where you want to look?" I lean into his shoulder and wrap my free hand around his arm, for a better view of the screen. Yup, *just* for a better view of the screen.

"What do you think? You've lived here longer, I'll trust your guidance."

"Okay." We haven't really had the talk yet about how long he's staying. I bite my bottom lip and lean back to get a better look at his face. I'm taking Gracyn's words to heart and much as it makes me feel squishy, I ask, "Are you looking for something short term? Month-to-month?"

The air stills as I wait, searching his face. I want him to say he's staying. I do. I really do, but this is scary as shit. There's no way I could ever ask him to stay, so feeling him out is the safest for my heart. With the rest of his family still in Dublin, he has no reason to stay.

"Erm. Maybe three months to start. Just to make sure the location works." That tells me nothing. "Or maybe an Airbnb. That would make more sense since they're already furnished."

I pull back, dropping my hands to my lap, wiping sweaty palms on my shorts.

"So, just for an extended vacation, or...?"

"Lisbeth. Truly, I don't have any furniture, it would be smart to move into something furnished."

Our food arrives and we scroll through the site between bites. This is so far out of my comfort zone. Asking questions of someone, trusting them not to hurt me. And true to everything he has shown me, Aidan senses it, my nerves.

By the time we're done, we have forty minutes to make it to the first appointment.

Aidan

We spend most of the day trekking around town looking at different flats. Nice ones with no furniture, crappy ones with too much furniture and the stink of cats that will last far longer than the building will be standing. And a few that would be just about perfect.

Lis points out the things she likes and doesn't in each of them and I file that information away as quite important. I want her to like the place I get. I want her with me.

"I have a test to study for, again. It's the last one before my final and then I have like three weeks off before clinical rotations start. Do you want to order food and come hang out with me? And watch me study?"

"Much as I would love to watch—or help you study," God I love the blush that creeps up her neck at that, "I have some calls to return for work, for photography. And, I don't want to distract you." Her thoughts have gone straight to our first study session.

I park behind her car, really not wanting to let her go, but knowing I have to. Much as I would love to spend the evening with her, with nowhere to go and nothing to do but watch her work, I know I need to say no.

I press my lips tight together and step out of the car, rounding the front to open her door.

"So, you don't want to come over?" She leans into me wrapping her arms around my waist and tilts her head up. Her wide eyes bouncing back and forth between mine.

"I want nothing more than to come over—and over, and over." I push my smile as wide as I can while running my mind through all things I'd love to do with her—to her.

She smacks my chest, laughing while pushing away from

me. I open the door to her car and tuck her inside. "I know this—school— takes priority right now. Your test is tomorrow?"

"Yeah, and my final Wednesday. But, then I have time. I can breathe for a bit—I can be all yours." Her hand hovers above her eyes, blocking the few rays of sun as I angle my body to shield her. It's the smile that squinches her eye almost closed.

"Can we do dinner after your final? Maybe make some plans for that *all mine* idea?" I'm already making plans and lists and more plans.

"Yup. That'll give me something to look forward to. Is there an incentive for grades? A sliding scale, maybe, better rewards for better grades?" It takes nothing for her to wink since her eye is about shut already, but it's adorable when she does it. She darts her gaze to the sky, mentally running through her schedule. "Wednesday?"

"That works. Study hard and I'll check in with you." I lean in her open window for the kiss that will have to get me through the longest stretch we've spent apart in weeks. Hands wrapped in her hair as she strains to get closer to me. It's not near enough, but I let her go. And bound up to my flat to put my plans in motion.

23

Lis

Relief washes over me as I walk my final exam to the front of the classroom. I'm almost done. I made it through this set of classes and it starts to settle in just how close I am to graduating. Oh. My. God.

My drive home is full of windblown, wild hair and blaring music. This feeling, there's not much better. I drop my bag under the table by the door and chuck my keys into the dish. I'm exhausted.

Gracyn promised to help me get ready for dinner tonight, but I can't resist crawling into my bed for a little bit. I close my eyes and commit to this nap.

"Hey. You need to wake up, Lis." Gracyn jolts me from a dead sleep. I sit up, throwing the covers off and rub the sleep from my eyes.

"What time is it?" My phone lights up with a couple missed calls and a voicemail.

"Yeah, I tried calling to let you know I'd be a little late, but you didn't answer. Go, jump in the shower and hurry." There's no point in arguing or pointing out that there's plenty of time. Gracyn has a look in mind, and I am at her mercy.

This thing with Aidan has grown, changed. He's found his way into my heart as much as that scares me. This date tonight is different. It doesn't just feel like a simple dinner out, it feels like more.

As soon as the shower is warm enough, I get to it. Our hot water situation has gotten worse over the past couple months and I have a very limited amount of time before I freeze. Shampoo, shave, shower gel. It doesn't take long for the water to cool, so I wrap up and think about moving to a nicer place once I graduate.

"You ready for me?"

"Does it matter? You're coming in regardless." Gracyn lost all modesty living in the dorms her first year of college. Sharing a community bathroom with fifty girls gave her that as well as the desire to move out as soon as the semester was done. I, however, had put up with digs from my mom and Maryse about my ass that was too big, my boobs being too much—my mom even suggested liposuction. So, I'm used to covering up as much as possible. I grab my robe and throw my towel around my hair.

Once my hair is dry, my body is moisturized and my toes are painted, Gracyn pushes me out to her room. "Tonight's big? This date?"

"It feels that way. I mean, we're celebrating the end of my summer classes. G, I'm gonna make it. I'm going to graduate; the hospital wants me. I'm gonna be okay. I won't have to struggle anymore. We can move to an apartment with two bathrooms, and hot water."

"What about Aidan? Didn't you guys look at places over

the weekend?" Gracyn still hasn't talked to me about Gavin, and we've been kind of dancing around each other. Her helping me get ready for a date would have been nothing before, but now it feels like a big deal "Close your eyes, Lis—thanks. So, you talked to him, right? About what this is, how long he's staying?"

"A little? Not really. We looked at some furnished places, three-month leases, that kind of thing, so he'll be here into the fall." I shrug, not wanting to give this more weight than it already has. "But his whole family is in Dublin, G. His parents and his brothers and sisters. He's got nieces and nephews there. This, I mean, I don't know. I think I'm falling in love with him, but what if I do? What if I fall completely, head over heels, can't live without him in love and he goes home? What if he decides I'm not enough and he leaves me too? I don't know that I'll survive." It feels safe talking about all of this with my eyes closed, like I'm in my own little bubble.

"Lis," Gracyn sighs as she pulls my hair back over my shoulders, curling it as she goes, "look at me. You can't go through life so guarded. Rob, your sister, even your parents have been shit, but that doesn't mean you stop trying. And it sure as hell doesn't mean that Aidan is like them. Ask him tonight, just ask him. You're not making demands, but if you're worried about your heart, and you have every fucking right to be, then ask the question. Knowing where things stand is the only way, you can't *ostrich* this anymore."

"God, you're right. I hate it."

A few curls tumble down the side of my neck as she works her way through the rest, pinning my hair low at the back of my head.

"I don't hate it that you're right, I hate that I'm so stupidly scared of getting cast off again, that I get all tongue tied and nervous."

I reach up to pull at one of the loose curls, but Gracyn takes my hand, squeezing it gently. Her voice going soft. "You have nothing to worry about. Have you seen how he looks at you? Have you seen the fire in those stormy blues? That boy has it bad for you, Lis. Do what you have to do, ask what you need to ask and know that you are enough. You really are.

"Okay, let's get you dressed now." Gracyn pushes me out of the chair toward my room. "So he can think of undressing you all through dinner."

The dress she has laid out for me is unreal. "Where did you get this, Gracyn?" I know this dress.

"Do you remember trying it on? When we went shopping for the party at my dad's firm, and you were trying for funsies? I went back a couple weeks ago and it was still there." She's waiting for me to blow up, because this dress cost almost half of my rent. "Just stop. It was the only one left and on the clearance rack. Obviously, this was meant to be so just put it on."

I slip into the navy fabric, settling it just off my shoulders. It takes a little wiggle to get it over my hips, but once I do, the side zips right up.

With a deep breath, and tears threatening, I look up blinking. "Gracyn, what..."

"I said stop. It's not that big a deal. Here, put your shoes on." She hands me my maroon patent leather peep toe heels and drops my phone, keys, and lip gloss into her clutch. "You look amazing. Lis. Absolutely amazing." She's like my very own fairy godmother.

"I don't know what to say, Gracyn. Thank you..." Three knocks at the door and my head whips around.

"Go get him, Lis." I turn to open the door and hear her mumble something that sounds a lot like, *we'll see if he can leave the fucking country after he sees this.*

Aidan

The door opens and my heart stops. It stops and I can't breathe. I brace my hand on the doorjamb, and pray that I remember how to breathe before I pass out.

More than beautiful—far beyond gorgeous. She is devastating in her navy dress hugging every one of her luscious curves like they're a fucking gift just for me. With her hair pinned up, I trace the line of her neck to her bared shoulders and suck in a lungful of air. The dress wraps around her— caressing her chest, accentuating her narrow waist, molding to her hips. Just her calves peek out from below, but her shoes. Sexy-as-fuck dark red heels that I want to feel on my back with her legs wrapped tightly around my hips. *Dear God.*

Before I can find appropriate words to compliment Lisbeth, Gracyn pops her head around the corner.

"That's the reaction I was going for." She hands Lis a small purse and whispers in her ear. Her smile and the blush that runs up her neck is almost too much for me. "Have fun, kids. Make good choices."

I hope. I hope she chooses *Yes.*

24

Aidan

The candlelight plays with the few tendrils of auburn curls that have escaped her pins. I can't take my eyes off the exposed slope of her neck. It's absolute poetry. As she studies the menu, I take my time studying her. Her eyes look brighter than usual against the dark makeup; her lips are a bold red, the bottom one caught between her teeth as if this is her biggest decision of the night.

Maybe it is.

Maybe she won't have to think about the answer at all when I ask her to live with me.

She lowers her menu and takes a sip of her wine. I reach for her free hand and pull it closer to me. My thumb over her knuckles, finger rubbing light circles on her wrist. "You look truly beautiful, Lisbeth."

She smiles sweetly over the rim of her wine glass. "Thank you." The waiter comes, takes our orders, and clears the menus, granting me the space to grasp both of her hands between us. "Is everything okay?" Her brows pinch together when she asks.

Jesus, I'm nervous. "It is. Just about perfect, yeah. Your classes went well so you're set to graduate and be done after this term?" It's taking everything I have in me not to blurt it out, and to wait for after dinner. I want to do this right—make sure she knows how much she means to me. Because she means so much.

"God, yeah. I can't believe I'm almost there, almost done. It finally feels real, you know? Thank you for everything you've done to help me. I know we got side-tracked a couple times, but in all seriousness, I would never have made it through these two classes without you." The flickering candle dances in her eyes. I could get lost in their depths. Jesus, they're beautiful.

"Anything you need, love. I told you that." The words want to spill off my tongue. "Lisbeth, I—"

The waiter brings our food just then and the interruption gives me the break I need to find the strength, the resolve to hold off from acting a fool. I want to ask when we're alone—in case she says *no*.

Lis thanks the waiter and waits a beat. Just a moment until he's clear of our table. "You what? What were you going to say?" I've lost all ability to focus on my answer as I watch the fork slide through her lips. My God, this woman. "Aidan? What were you saying?"

"Tell me. Which was your favorite flat of the ones we looked at?" I know I'm stalling, but I have to know that I made the right decision.

"Uh...not the cat place." She wrinkles her nose adorably.

"No," I chuckle. "Not that bloody flat. Not at all." I'm

fidgety, and I know it. I want her in my life, every single day. "Tell me your favorite. The one you liked best."

"Why do you want to know, Aidan?" I love that she's asking. I love the challenge that bleeds through her question. She sets her fork down and clasps her hands together on the edge of the table, leaning toward me, and I decide this is the moment.

"Lisbeth, love. I want you to like where I live. I want you to want to be there. With me." I don't put my fork down. Instead, I turn it toward her and watch as she parts her lips for me. I watch as she wraps them around what I've offered her.

Locking my gaze on her, I wait. Wait for the questions, the answers—wait for what will either make my heart sing or weep.

I had a speech prepared—flowery, lovely words—but patience is not in my arsenal tonight. The small box in my pocket becomes an unbearable weight. And knowing full and well that she's going to freak out, I pull it out and take the ring from its velvet nest.

Her eyes go wide and her fingers shake as she lifts them to her lips. Those lips that I want to capture. "Aidan...I...we..." Pink is tingeing her cheeks; her pulse looks like it's beating frantically at her throat.

"Lisbeth, I would love nothing more than to wake up to you every day. I want you to help me choose a place to live because I want you there with me." Her gaze bounces between mine and the ring in my hand.

"Aidan, I..."

"Do you know what this is? Do you know the significance of the Claddagh?" Slowly, she shakes her head. "Love, loyalty, and friendship. 'With these hands, I give you my heart, and crown it with love.'" My words whisper their way out, quietly enough that she leans closer to me. I reach my left hand across the table with my palm facing up.

"Where and how it's worn shows the true significance. Can I have your hand?" So slowly, she places her right hand in my palm. "On your right hand, with the point of the heart pointing toward your own means you're in a relationship—a committed relationship. It lets the world know that your heart belongs to someone. Will you wear it that way?"

She swallows and nods her head with a barely audible *yes*. "Are you...does this mean you're staying?" The fact that she questions that kills me.

"I plan to, yes. Lisbeth, I would love nothing more than to move you in with me and switch that ring to your other hand." I place a kiss over the ring where it sits on her right hand, and then press my lips to the empty ring finger of her left hand. "I know that this is big. I know that I'm asking a lot of you and I'm asking it quickly. It scares the shite out of me that we've only known each other four months, but I love you, Lis. I don't want to let you go. I want you with me."

I hold my breath, waiting.

I can't let the silence be. She hasn't said anything yet, hasn't responded, hasn't made a noise at all.

"It's down to two places. The smaller flat that overlooks the river is plenty big for me. But I feel like you were drawn to the townhouse closer to town—with the funky kitchen and the garden in the back. There's room for a hammock."

I glance up at her hoping for a sign, some indication of what she's thinking.

"The one with the claw foot tub? The brick walls and wood floors?" Is it a good thing that her eyes are shining like that? I want to believe that it is.

"Yes, that one. Both are available right away. I can move next week, as soon as I get back from the city. The townhouse is just a three-month lease, but the flat is available for longer."

"Which one do you want?" she asks.

"Lis, I don't know how to say it any clearer. It doesn't matter to me. I'll have space, separation from the boys in either place. They're good guys, I appreciate them letting me crash with them, but I'm ready to get out of there. The only thing that matters to me is that you want to be there."

Her breath comes out in a trembling whoosh. Not at all what I was hoping for. "Can—can I think on it?" *Fuck.*

I clench my jaw, grinding my molars against each other. Nodding my head, accepting the utter disappointment at her reaction, I force a smile to my lips. It's fake as shite, but I hope it at least comes across as something better than a grimace.

"Of course."

"It's not *no*. I just, this is big. It's really big. I was with Rob for four years and living together never came up. It just..."

"Lisbeth, don't. Don't put me in the same category as that —as him. That's not fair or right."

Her gaze jumps to finally meet mine.

"I'm not. I'm just, God this is—I don't know." My heart has done its time on the amusement park rides tonight—up and down. Slowed to almost stillness and then thumping through my chest. "Let me try again, I'm not explaining this well," she starts. "I have stuck to a really strict, disciplined plan for the past three years. The only reason I'm here, within sight of graduating early is because of that plan. Focus and a handful of people who, for some reason, believe in me and support me when my own family can't be bothered, have gotten me here."

I know all of these things. I do.

"And I have to talk to Gracyn."

What the hell? I fight not to bristle at her rejection, devastated that she needs her friend to help her with this decision.

"Surely, she likes me enough, yeah?" I huff out a small laugh as I push my hair away from my face. I lean back in my seat searching for some sign that this isn't over.

Did I read too much into this? Maybe.

Lis

"Aidan, I'm not looking for anyone's approval or permission to do this. Yes, it's a big deal and I guess I wasn't sure about us." The hurt pinches his face and mars his features.

"I'm sorry. I shouldn't have pushed for this. It's too soon." His cheeks are flushed and his eyes are glistening as he looks away.

"Please just listen to me. Please?" A slow nod lets me know he's listening. I wait for him to turn back to me before continuing. "I wasn't sure about you—about whether you would stay. I've been petrified, wanting to ask you, but so afraid of the answer. So afraid that this is more to me than it is to you." My hand flutters back and forth between us, but settles over my heart.

"Lisbeth, I will love you regardless of whether you choose to move in with me. That's not going to change."

"You're giving up a lot if you stay here, and..."

"Lis, there is no place I'd rather be. I want to be here, with you. Or somewhere else, but only if you're there too." He leans across the table, reaching for my hand.

"Your family is all in Dublin. What about them? What about your parents and siblings? What about your nieces and nephews? You're willing to give up seeing them whenever you want? You're willing to give that up for me?"

"I'm not giving anyone up. I will see them plenty; every time I travel to the UK for an assignment, and I can't wait for them to meet you, Lis. I want you in my life, and your life is here." His voice drops to almost a whisper. "What else is holding you back? What does Gracyn have to do with this?"

No matter how I say this now, it's going to sound ridiculous. After that huge declaration, I feel completely foolish.

"I can't just leave her without a roommate. I need to give her time, help her find a new roommate or something. We've lived together for more than two years. I can't just run off and dump the other half of our rent on her. She's done too much for me to ever treat her like that. Can I say *yes, soon*?"

He stares at me for what feels like an eternity. I'm not sure Aidan has any idea how much it just took for me to do that, to stand up for myself. To open myself up and argue—push for what *I* need.

The relief is overwhelming as he nods. "Yeah. Yeah, I can do *soon*." He settles our bill and we leave the restaurant hand in hand.

I don't think either of us expected the evening to end this way.

25

Aidan

The bed is far too big to be mine. The air is too cool and quiet to be my flat. And the throbbing in my head is far too severe to be just the drinks I had at dinner last night.

The restaurant.

I peel my eyes open and try to take stock. Not in my flat. I rub my hands down my face and reach deep for the memories. I know for sure I had not planned on waking here alone.

Dinner.

My phone pings somewhere nearby, and the sound rips through my head. I look around again and see it on the floor. It's halfway across the room, past the jumbled pile of my clothes. Christ, what the fuck happened last night?

Lisbeth.

Maybe the whole fucking thing was nothing but a bad dream. Maybe she's decided. Maybe she's ready.

My stomach churns as I push myself up and sit at the

edge of the bed. With elbows on my knees, I take deep breaths until the waves calm. I stumble to the loo, not sure whether to pray that I purge this shit or not. I splash cold water on my face and then rest my hand on the back of my neck.

I rifle through my clothes and pull on my briefs and trousers. Slow steady movements, nothing jerky to upset my tenuous hold on the situation. Hope crinkles at the edge of my heart as I grab my phone. The screen is cracked and there are glass chips on the carpet from an empty whiskey bottle. No wonder I feel like shite.

Nausea and disappointment roll through me. My plan was to wake wrapped up in the woman I love. To finally have some true privacy with her. To celebrate taking our relationship to the next level, moving in together. To touch and talk and kiss and love her.

I toss my fucked phone on the mattress and pull on the rest of my clothes. Throw the evidence of my misery away. I probably should have left the bottle on the floor with the shards of glass, but I can't. Instead, I clean up as best as I can and leave.

THE AIR in the flat is enough to drive me back out into the world. I couldn't stay at the hotel—that was to be with Lisbeth.

I sure as shit can't stand to be here. It's just another reminder of how much I want to move out.

I shed my clothes and step into the shower. I let the scorching spray rain down on me for as long as I can stand it. Sadly, it does little to improve my mood.

The hell with this. I can't hang around here. I need to move, do something. Be somewhere else. It's not yet ten o'clock, but I throw on shorts and a t-shirt.

As I pound on Finn's door, I run a hand through my hair. "Hey, you awake?" I hear the faint sound of bed springs creaking and moans coming through the door. Jesus. "Right. I've got the bar today. You—you just carry on." The words fade as they leave my mouth. That should be me. My reality this morning. Instead, my heart hurts, my head is pounding and I'm heading to work.

It's ridiculous that I'm actually glad the pub is a fucking mess from last night. I lock the door behind me and flip on lights, just illuminating the bar. Only the bare minimum I need to see. I've spent far too much time in my head this morning and need a fucking escape.

As the mop bucket fills, I put all the chairs up on tables, stools up on the bar and crank the music. And pop some ibuprofen and pour myself a pint.

To say I'm focused on the shit task of scrubbing the floor would be an understatement. Scrubbing, mopping, changing out the water. I'm washing up the last section when I see the back door open.

"I thought Finn was openin' today. Didn't you switch wit' him? Take today off?" Francie yells above the music as he takes in the state of the pub. "Jesus, would you turn that down, I can't think wit' it goin' like that."

"That's the point." I reach past the taps and lower the volume to a workable level. I finish up the floor, ignoring the rest of the shite he's asked me. "You wanna start putting the chairs down and I'll get the tables wiped before you unlock the door." I heft the bucket and head out back to dump it. I decide to wash the bucket and thoroughly clean the mop while I'm out there. *Shite should be done right the first time.*

"Yeah, it should but why don't you leave the poor mop alone and come inside. 'Ave a pint wit' me and tell me what's troubling you." Again, I'm so far in my head, I never heard Francie come out. "Come on, Aidan."

He nods to a barstool and slides me a fresh pint. "You took Lissy out last night, yeah?"

"Yeah."

He stands there, like the barman he is, folded arms resting on his belly, hip against the bar. He's had years of practice and will wait me out. I plant my elbows on the bar and scrub my hands over my face. Somehow with the music at a normal volume, my head hurts worse than it did before.

I take a long pull from my glass and heave the breath I'm holding out my nose. The longer I keep my mouth shut, the better. I don't want to deal with what I'm feeling, let alone talk about.

"Out wit' it, lad. Let's go. Did you fuck things up wit' my Lissy? I told you, you weren't to get involved if you were just goin' to mess around." He's all arsed up now.

"I didn't fuck it up. I don't think."

It's under his breath, but I catch something that sounds a lot like *and that's the fucking problem.*

"I can't do this. I'm a cliché, sitting here." I shove my barstool back catching it just before it hits the floor. "You sit, old man, and I'll prep the bar."

I grab a clean rag and attack the bar top. I scrub at nothing, moving just for the sake of moving. Tension is thick in the air. Francie watching me, waiting for me to stop muttering to myself. He moves 'round the bar meticulously straightening all the barstools

"Son, you're going to wipe the varnish off the thing." His voice is much softer this go around and that's what does me in. Bracing myself against the bar, arms wide, I drop my head and suck in a big breath.

"I don't know where I went wrong."

"Did you have a row? Have things gone arseways wit' the pair of you?"

"No, we didn't fight. I told her I loved her and asked her to move in with me." The words physically hurt to speak. Hearing myself say them out loud makes it all too real. I grab my glass and drain it in one go. And because this day can't go any further into the jacks, the keg blows as I'm refilling my pint, spraying the dark sticky beer all over me.

"Fuck." I slap the tap shut with a lot more force than it deserves. I rip the empty keg out like the whole thing is personal. And of course, the fresh keg I need is buried in the cooler under cases of bottled beer and other shite.

I tear through the cooler, stacking cases of beer, boxes of mixers, and bottles of liquor. I know I'm just a hair shy of breaking everything I touch. When I finally get a path cleared, I heft the fresh keg onto my shoulder landing it a lot harder than is necessary. The bruise will be a great reminder of this day I'd love to forget.

"I heard you back there, Aidan. Take a breath—think before ye go throwing that keg around, now."

"FRANCIE, I...Jesus, this is hard. I love her. I want to stay here —be with her—build a life. I thought I was doing that." Now that I've opened my mouth, there's no stopping the tide that comes spilling out.

"We went together, last weekend. Looked at a million bloody flats. I appreciate the loft." I give him a pointed look, making sure he knows I mean it. "But I need some space. I need some privacy and some fucking sleep. Do you have any idea how loud those two are? Finn with his flavor of the week, and Jimmy...Jimmy's just fucking loud when he's—"

Francie cuts me off with a sharp slap of the bar. Pointing his finger at me. "I don't want to know any of that, yeah?"

"Yeah, and neither do I. I've got a good five years on them and I'm past that, done with it." Francie chuckles and shakes his head. "What?"

He leans forward on the bar, emphasizing his point. "Sure you're older than them. Those boys are the same age as Lisbeth."

I stop dead in my tracks. Paralyzed by that bit of information. I think I already knew it on some subconscious level, but she seems so much older, more mature than them. "Christ, I...it's easy to forget that. She's got her shit so together, so capable. I forget she's that young." Maybe I did fuck this up.

"So. You asked her to live wit' you and she said no?"

"She said she needed time. Needed to think about it and talk to Gracyn." I lift the keg into position and tap it, standing back as I purge the line. I fill Francie's pint, flip on the rest of the lights, and unlock the door.

He watches me, lips screwed up in a half smile, nodding his head. "That's not no, then." As hard as he's pushed me away from her, Francie seems almost hopeful. The door opens and the noise of the street trickles in, glancing up I toss a *hiya* at the couple, waiting for the rest of Francie's thoughts on this. "Our Lissy's a smart girl. One of the best. She'll take her time, yeah, but make the right decision—the right one for both of you."

The guy that just came in huffs out a disgusted snort as the girl he's with moves toward Francie. "So, where is my little sister? She's not answering my calls."

26

Lis

I feel like I didn't sleep at all last night. There were too many thoughts racing through my head for me to relax and fall asleep. I sat for a long time looking at the ring he'd given me. It looks nothing like the Claddagh that Francie's worn for as long as I've known him. This is so much more.

I twist it around my finger—around and around—sliding it off.

"Hey, you up?" The smell of fresh coffee wafts into my room as Gracyn knocks and cracks the door. "I didn't expect to see you back here this morning. Everything okay?"

I slide up toward the headboard as she hands me a mug and settles in next to me. "I'm okay." I fumble with the mug and trying to get my ring back on before I drop it in my covers.

"What the hell is that?" Gracyn grabs my hand and pulls me toward her, spilling coffee on my white duvet. It's not a typical Claddagh—not like any that I've seen before. There's a red stone in the shape of a heart, my birthstone maybe. And the silvery blackish metal that makes up the rest of the ring has small diamonds set in the crown. "Lis—"

"I know. I kind of freaked out a little when he gave it to me. But it's not an engagement ring, obviously." I can't take my eyes off of it.

"But it could be, right? It means different things on different hands and which way the crown faces? God, it's gorgeous." She pulls it closer and spins it around my finger sliding it off again. The sun streaming through the window hits the stones, scattering dots of light and color across the wall. "So why? Why are you here? Why did this date end with me drinking coffee in bed with you? Instead of eating a bowl of cold cereal on the couch by myself?"

I set my cup down on the table next to my bed and take my ring from Gracyn, turning it over in my hand. I have been all over the place thinking about last night. Thinking about what Aidan said, what he asked. That he's staying for me —for us.

As the words tumble out of my mouth, I run my feet up and down the sheets. "He asked me to move in with him. He said he's staying and he loves me. He asked me to move in with him." My nose scrunches up as I grit my teeth waiting for her reaction. Really, I want to not lose my shit.

Saying it out loud feels different. It makes my heart flutter and I can't sit still. My knee starts bouncing and I chance a peek at her face.

"Oh, Lissy, that's good, right? Are you gonna do it? Move?" Her wide eyes search my face.

"I told him I'd say *yes* soon."

"Not an appropriate answer to that question, Lis. Why didn't you just say yes? Not because of Rob?"

I bop my head back and forth. "Yes and no. But mostly because of you?"

"Nope. Nuh uh, not okay. Did we not just have a big thing about me not using you as an excuse to avoid life? You can't use me that way either, Lis."

"So not the same thing. I just—you've done so much for me, G. I can't just walk away and leave you here alone. Dump the rest of the rent on you, that's not fair. I told him I needed to talk to you and make a plan. That's what we do, right? We make plans and stick to them?" I pin her with a glare. "Isn't that why you walked away from Gavin? Because of plans and rules?"

"Not now." The edge in her voice cuts right into me. "We'll deal with that another day."

"Because it's not in the plan?" Snotty comebacks, I can do with Gracyn. Only Gracyn. "When are you going to talk to me about him?"

"Not today." End of story. She climbs off my bed and that subject is closed. "So, I start looking for another roommate. No big deal." Those last three words, she tosses over her shoulder as she walks out of my room.

"Are you mad? I don't have to move in with him yet..." I grab my cup and follow her out to the kitchen.

"Yeah, I am." She slams the milk carton on the counter and stares at me. Her shoulders droop as she releases a tense sigh. "Lis, be selfish, just this once. What does your heart tell you? What do you want? Because it looked a hell of a lot like excitement right when you told me. But you're holding your-self back. Is it for you—because you're not sure—or because of something else?"

"I am excited. I don't think I realized how much, though, until I heard myself say the words. It's scary, and exciting and not at all what was in my plan book. You know—*you know*— I have to take a step back and think. I can't make decisions on the spot, not big ones. And this is big—really fucking big." I drop down into a seat at the counter. "I want to. It's crazy and probably wrong and absolutely one of the scariest things I can think of, but I want to do this. I love him and I want to wake up with him, every day. But that doesn't change us, and I'm not leaving you hanging."

My heart flutters when I realize what I just said. What I just admitted to myself for the first time.

Slowly Gracyn's lips lift and spread into a big snarky smile. "Well, then. I'm going to go start looking for a new roommate and you should get dressed and tell Aidan it's happening." She shoves me toward the hall. "Just know, you're not going to look near as hot as you did last night. I bet he's devastated thinking about those heels and where he wanted them last night."

THE VOLUME of voices coming through the door doesn't match the lack of crowd. It's still early and there's only a handful, a really small one, of cars parked outside McBride's. But the voice booming from the bar, nearly explodes as I step inside. And crash into Rob's chest.

"The fuck, Lis? Watch it—you practically ran over me." I step to my right and try to make sense of what's happening. Aidan's hand is planted firmly in the center of Francie's chest. Pushing him back from Rob and...Maryse? Everyone stops— talking, yelling, moving. Or it just seems that way to me. I don't know.

"Sorry. I-I didn't mean to—"

"Swear to God, felt like I got hit by a fucking linebacker."

Rob rubs at his chest. I didn't even hit him that hard. And Maryse wraps herself around him and giggles. She giggles. Fucking giggles.

It's only seconds—seconds that feel like they drag on forever—before I shift my eyes to Aidan. His expression is fierce, fists clenched and veins popping on his forearms.

Where Rob is all loud blustery bravado, Aidan moves with a quiet purpose. Each determined step hints at the promise of barely held restraint.

"It's time for you to go. Now." His voice is a low growl that raises goose bumps on my skin.

I glance at my sister and ex-boyfriend. They're stunned silent, like deer caught in the headlights of a truck.

Rob rips the door open and practically runs out, leaving Maryse behind.

"I called you, left you a voicemail and you didn't call back." Her eyes flick toward Aidan as she settles her hand on the push plate of the door. "I came looking for you. I don't appreciate the way my fiancé and I were treated by your friends."

Her bitch factor is off the charts as she sweeps a diamond-crusted hand game show-style. "Our wedding is next month. See if you can lose a few pounds, I'm not sure your ass'll fit in the dress I picked for you."

And she's gone.

The bright sun flares in my eyes momentarily blinding me when the door closes, throwing the room into a cool darkness. I don't know what just happened. The only thing I can do is laugh—high, thready and shrill. Aidan's hands wrap around my shoulders and he dips down, eyes darting back and forth between mine.

"So, that was my sister." Oh. My. God. "And her fiancé."

"Are you alright? Come, sit down a minute." He slides his hand around my back, pulling me in close.

The twenty feet between the entrance and the bar is all it takes for me to push the shock aside. Most of the shock. Aidan ushers me to a barstool and Francie sets a pint in front of me. With a nod toward the glass, he apologizes. "They weren't to ever be here again. I made that bloody clear to both of them way back."

"I know." Elbows on the bar, I rub my fingers at my temples. "Can I have a whiskey?" Francie sets the bottle on the bar with a couple of glasses, pouring for each of us. "That was not what I was expecting. Not in the least."

"Sláinte." The whiskey burns its way down burning off the rest of the ick from Maryse. Francie checks his watch as he comes around to me. He pulls me into a hug and plants a kiss on the top of my head, squeezing me tight. "I'll leave you, then. Lock the door 'til later if you need." That sends shivers through my already tense body.

I pour myself another shot and down it before pouring one for each of us. Aidan pulls me around to face him, my knees tucked up between his. Hands on the side of my thighs. "I don't know whether I want to pity him or kill him."

Aidan

I know what I want to do—exactly what I want to do. I want to kill the bastard and her sister too. Hearing the stories about her family was bad, but this? Seeing how they treat her. Tossing out insults like she doesn't matter.

This girl fucking matters.

It comes out on a huff, a sad little laugh, mostly through her nose. "What happened?"

I try to get some control over the anger simmering in my belly. It's making my skin itch. "Lisbeth—"

"Seriously, why were they here? Why can't they just leave me alone?" Her cheeks are flushed and her eyes are dark. Really dark.

"Francie told them never to come here. I'm allowed—I can make the choice to screen my calls. Avoid people who treat me like shit. I don't owe her anything. Not a fucking thing." She pulls her phone out and taps at it until her sister's voice starts in.

Lis, you need to call me. Rob and I have exciting news...

The high-pitched nasally whine is too much. I reach over and hit the bin icon and delete the message. "We know what she had to say. There's no reason to have to listen to that again."

"And a dress? She picked out a dress for me? Does she think, for a minute, I'm going to be a part of that three-ring shit show? I'm not sure I'm even going to it—why should I? God—if I go it's only to get in on the betting action on how long it'll take before one of them cheats on the other. Holy shit."

The words are just pouring from her. Spilling like there's no containing them. I want to lock the doors so no one stumbles in on this. I want to let her punch and hit and throw things until she gets it all out. I want to pull her to me and make it go away. Because what I see, what I watch helplessly, is Lis start to crumble.

Tears shine in her eyes as she curls into herself. Her shoulders fold in, her arms tight across her chest. Hair swings forward like a curtain, a protective shield around her face. She's hiding, this is her retreat. "I—excuse me a minute. I just need—"

I hold tight to her hips as she tries to wiggle away. "No. No more running. You have your separation from that arsehole and sister. They're gone. You want to cry? Hide your beautiful face, you do that here—with me." Sliding out of my seat, I pull her into my chest and wrap her up in my arms.

I hold her. Just hold her as she falls apart. Her body melting from a tense ball of stress to mold perfectly fitting against mine. When she finally weaves her arms around me, gripping the back of my shirt, I feel fucking accomplished. The talking we've done, all the touching and loving over the past few months, and this is the moment. She let me in.

And I'm not letting her go.

27

Aidan

"Thank you." The sound is small and a little sad. She's tucked up under my chin and I feel her words against my chest more than I hear them.

"Of course. I told you last night I'll do anything for you." I pull back and wipe at her tears with my thumb. "Anything at all, Lisbeth. I hate that you're sad, that you're hurting. But I will drop everything to hold you. To help you through whatever it is."

With a finger under her chin I tilt her face up to mine. I need to know that she understands this.

"You own my heart." I kiss her lips, swollen from crying, red from chafing against my shirt.

"If I promise that I'm not running or hiding, can I go to the restroom?" Little by little she unwraps herself from me. Running her hands from my back and up my chest, pushing away. "I just want to splash cold water on my face. God, I got tears all over you." She sniffles as she runs her hand over the tear stains on my shirt. "I'm sorry—"

"You have nothing to apologize for." I watch her go and pull out my phone and ring Finn. I scrub at a thoroughly clean spot on the bar, waiting for him to answer.

"What d'you want, Aidan? I thought you were taking my shift."

"I was—I did—but I need you to come in. Take it back."

"Mmm. I don't think so. Pretty happy wit' where I am right now." I hear the sheets rustle and what sounds like a sharp slap and a yelp.

"Christ, Finn. Just fucking get here. I need to go. I'll take whatever shift you want next week, but just fucking get here."

I toss my phone to the bar as Lis comes out of the loo. Her face shiny and free of makeup. She looks absolutely perfect.

"Oh my God, Aidan. I don't have a choice, do I? I have to go to my sister's wedding. And that dress—I really am going to have to squeeze my fat ass into it."

She looks to her untouched pint still sitting on the bar. Her shoulders droop again as she pushes it away.

"Lisbeth, there's not a thing you have to do. Nothing. But whatever you decide to do, that you want to do, I'll be there with ye. If ye need a reason to be out of town, we'll go. Anywhere you want. If you decide to go, I'll go too—if you want me there."

My hands slide down past her hips, gripping tight, I pull her close. "And you're perfect, love. Fucking perfect. Not another word about your arse. I love you the way you are, and wouldn't want you to change a thing."

She slides her hands around to the back of my neck, scraping her fingers through my scalp, pulling me down to meet her lips. "Thank you."

This time the words are spoken against my lips and become a sweet kiss. Until I feel her teeth nip at my bottom one, driving me insane.

I grip her tighter, spinning so her back is to the bar. I have her caged in, just arching her back over the bar. Every inch in contact from our thighs to our lips, holding her, taking the kiss deeper. The groan that escapes me, and the press of our bodies leaves no doubt that I need Lis.

I need to be alone with her.

Finn needs to fucking get here in a hurry.

"Hate how we left things last night. I wanted to wake up with you this morning." I press my hips into her as I trail kisses from behind her ear, down to her delicate collarbone. "Want to wake up with you every day, love. But I'll wait, if that's what you want. I'll wait for you as long as it fucking takes for you to be ready."

The scent of her lotion is intoxicating. The feel of her curves, electrifying. But the sound of her gasps and sighs and moans whispering across my ear is absolutely dangerous. I'm lost in her, absolutely consumed.

"Is this why you wanted me here so fast?"

Finn is leaning on the doorframe, arms crossed over his chest, watching us. The shitty smirk on his face says he's been here longer than I thought.

I grab Lis' hand and pull her out into the bright sun. We stand there for a beat, my thumb drawn to her wrist. While I'm looking around, deciding where to go, Lisbeth steps in front of me, sliding her hands up my chest, resting her fore-head between them.

"Are you done here? Is Finn—"

"Finn was supposed to be here anyway, I just couldn't be still this morning, so I opened the bar. I took a couple days off

—planned on spending them with you." My words come out low and gravelly.

She tugs me down the street toward her flat. "Come on. Gracyn is home, but we need to talk. She's—I talked with her this morning. God—that's why I came to the pub. I was going to grab us some donuts and then come find you. Your car was there, so—And then Rob and Maryse—"

She starts and hops through her thoughts too many times for it to make any sense. I pause at the steps leading to her door. Lis turns, up one step to face me. It's just enough height on her that I have to lift my chin to meet her eyes.

"Why did you come to find me?" She pulls on my hand trying to move me up the steps looking back and forth between my face and the door. I shake my head slowly. "Tell me, Lis. Why were you coming to me?"

"Yes. I wanted to tell you yes." She shifts closer to me, her cool palms on either side of my neck, her thumbs barely brushing my ears. It takes a minute, but then, with a whoosh of relief the tension that's been with me since last night, drains out of my shoulders.

I pull her body flush against mine and kiss her deeply. "You mean that? Truly?"

"Yes, I need to help Gracyn find a roommate, but I want to do this—I want to be with you."

With my hands on her hips, I squeeze, digging my fingers into the sides of her arse. "Go pack a bag, not a lot, just for a day or two. I'm taking you away—stealing you and keeping you with me always."

I fight with myself to let her go for even a minute. She said yes and God help me, I'm afraid it's a dream.

"I'll be back in an hour. You'll be ready, then?" My mind is whirring through the things I need to do—through the places

I can take her. Much as I love the vibe and pulse of New York City, I want something quieter, more intimate. I nip at her bottom lip, the one she bites when she's thinking hard about something, and I back away.

"Where are we going? What do I need to bring?"

Nothing. You don't need to bring a fucking thing. "Beach, whatever you need for the beach." I take two steps back to her and kiss her like I can't stand the idea of being apart. Because I can't.

Her laughter follows me as I run back to the pub to grab my car. I add finding a nicer vehicle to my list of things to do. Not for today. I only have an hour, less than that really.

On the way to my flat, I call a client from a couple weeks ago. He'd told me of a quiet little beach town on the Connecticut coast. He offers to have his assistant book us in for the next two nights. The confirmation for the Madison Beach Hotel pings through on my phone as I log in to my Airbnb account to take care of renting the townhouse Lisbeth likes.

I shove clothes in my bag—shorts, swim trunks, a couple t-shirts. My phone pings with an email as I debate bringing my trousers and a nice shirt. Just in case. Christ, we really don't need to bring a fucking thing. Room service is all we need.

I take the steps to Lis' flat two at a time, reading my email as I go. Three sharp knocks to the door, and I wait. And wait. Gracyn's voice filters through the door, "Lis—can you get that?"

As soon as the door opens, I stalk in. Hands weaving through her hair as I push her up against the wall. Her hands come up underneath my arms, gripping tightly. The kiss is hungry, desperate, and full of how much I missed her in the past hour.

"Aidan. Oh my God." She's breathing me in, just as much as I am her. When I'm sure I don't care that her roommate is here, Lis pushes at my chest. I pull back just enough for her to speak. "Let me grab my bag." I pull her in, kissing her again before I release her.

But I don't really let her go. Hands firmly on her hips, I follow her to her room. Gracyn steps out of Lis' room, looking like she's holding tight to a secret.

I drag my hands from Lis, not wanting to let her go. "I owe you a lifetime of gratitude. I promise to take good care of her and always put her first."

Gracyn looks me up and down, trying hard to look parental. Hands on her hips, toe doing a little tap-tap-tap on the floor. "I warned you months ago what will happen if you don't. Just keep that in mind, and treat my girl right."

With a kiss on her cheek and a wink, her smile peeks through.

"Love, before we go, can I use your printer? I want to sign and send the contract for the flat back." I flip open her laptop and see a familiar picture saved in the lower right-hand corner.

I print the contract and sign it. While it scans through and into my email, I click on the image. It's me. My school photo from primary.

"Were you stalking me?" I tap at the screen eyebrow cocked, smirking at Lis over my shoulder. "I'm flattered."

"I Googled you—God, ages ago. I thought you were adorable and saved it. I might have cropped out one of your school friends, though." Nose wrinkled and her eye-closing smile takes over her face. "I guess that is kind of stalkerish. Do you mind? Want to email, canceling that contract?"

"Hmmmm—I don't. I want to take you away. I want to spend every minute with you—loving you." I grab her hand and her bag, pulling her along behind me.

Lis

Tension hangs heavy in the car. The two-hour drive through Connecticut is an exercise in patience and self-control. One that I'm not prepared for. One that I'm failing miserably at.

"So, you're not going to tell me where we're going?"

"I'm not. You'll have to wait and see," he quips like he knows what I'm thinking—that I have no patience.

"I really suck at surprises. Maybe you should give me a hint?" I turn in my seat and lean toward him. I absolutely hate the car's console right now; I feel like it's separating us by miles.

The scruff on his jaw rasps as he runs his hand up and down. "I don't know. I planned this trip, packed for it, and secured our flat in less than an hour. I think you should let it be a surprise. Maybe let me take care of things. Maybe let me treat you to a few days away, where you don't have to worry about a thing." He struggles to hold a serious look on his face, and his cheeks start rising in a smirk. "Maybe, you should just lean back, enjoy yourself, and thank me for wanting to treat you to something special."

"Maybe." It rolls off my tongue as I sit back and watch this man. How am I this lucky?

Before I can reach into the back seat to grab my bag, Aidan's pulled it out on his side of the car. The strap resting across his chest pulls at his t-shirt highlighting all the peaks and valleys. The lines and the muscles I know by heart.

I didn't know that men like him existed in real life. Kind and protective, a gentleman—but not spineless or weak. He ushers me into the lobby and checks us in.

The concierge explains the hotel's amenities as she clicks away at her keyboard. The beach, the restaurant, complimentary cocktail hour.

I hear her talking, trying to pull Aidan into conversation, hanging on his responses. He's polite, but short, clipped almost, trying to move things along.

"Thank you." He tucks the plastic room keys between his teeth while shoving his wallet back in his pocket with one hand, pulling me toward the elevator with the other.

When the doors are closed, Aidan hits the button for the fourth floor. And all politeness is suddenly gone. He crowds me into the corner, hands on the walls on either side of me. Caging me in.

"Lisbeth, we're not goin' to make that cocktail hour. Ye okay wit' that?" His eyes are dark, his voice is darker, accent thicker.

He steps back as the doors open at our floor. I smile at a couple with a toddler and baby, loaded down with beach bags and a cooler as we exchange places.

"Probably a good thing they're headed out. Nap time would definitely be ruined," he mutters as he pulls me down the hall.

Stunned, a little off kilter, I look from the elevator to Aidan and back again. The woman hands her toddler a shovel from their beach bag and winks at me as the doors slide shut.

28

Lis

Our room faces the ocean and the view is breathtaking. I gaze at it briefly before hearing the thud of our bags hitting the floor.

I turn just as Aidan reaches me and backs me up against the glass door. His arms are braced on the glass by my head, his body pressing mine into the glass. "I want to do this right. Last night didn't go how I hoped, but I don't want to wait to have you." His eyes are dark, like the sky at midnight. They bounce between mine. "I will take you to dinner to celebrate. I will show you off to the world, but I need you, love."

It takes a moment, a heartbeat more, for my brain to catch up with his body, but when his lips crash against mine, nothing else matters. Not a thing. I wrap my hands around his back, pushing his shirt up. His muscles shift and flex as he slides a hand behind my neck. He palms the back of my head before tangling his fingers in my hair. Gripping it tightly, he tilts my head back holding me just where he wants me, deepening the kiss. And my need for him takes over.

His shirt is tight to his body and I struggle getting it out of my way. Aidan reaches back and pulls it off, breaking away only long enough to pull it past our lips.

"Jesus, Lisbeth, I can't get you close enough." He dances his finger across my skin, popping open my bra as he kisses from my jaw down my neck to the crook of my shoulder. And just like that, my shirt and bra are gone and his huge hands are palming my breasts. Pushing them up and together, he sucks a nipple into his mouth. Sucks hard and bites down sending a zing of pleasure and pain straight through my core.

I arch my back and slide down the glass, caught up in the exquisite things Aidan is doing to me. My nipple releases with a pop from his lips as he reaches down, wrapping his hands around the back of my thighs, lifting and turning me toward the wall.

"No fucking way anyone gets to see you, only me ever again. Lisbeth, you're mine now, yeah? Only mine." His growled words send shivers down my spine.

I wrap my fingers into the front of his waistband, pulling him to me while pushing him away at the same time. He groans into my mouth as my fingers brush against his cock. His skin hot to my touch. I pop the button and zipper, shoving at his shorts.

"Need these gone, please." My voice is husky with lust. This passion, desire, is not something I have ever felt before. I can't get him in me fast enough. It's almost desperation.

With his hips pinning me to the wall, he pushes at his shorts until they're gone. Kicked to the side with his shoes. He sets me on my feet, flicking the button on my shorts and slides his hands around my hips, pushing, gliding along my skin. As the last of my clothing slides down my legs, Aidan grips tightly to my hips, fingers stretching across my ass. My breath hitches as even his big hands can't span that far. This is so not the time for my doubt to show itself. I try to fight it, but I know I tense.

"Don't you dare get self-conscious on me, Lisbeth. I love every-fucking-thing about you."

He wraps my legs around him again, lifting me up against the wall. After tearing at each other's clothes it's a relief to feel his skin on mine, feel the head of his cock drag across my clit as he tilts his hips. Slow, crazy friction makes me pant in anticipation.

"Aidan, please..." I beg, "...Oh God, please... I need you, I need..." My words cut off as he fills me with one thrust. My mouth falls open, my gasp brushing across his neck.

My world is centered here, in this moment. There is nothing but heat and desire. Full to the brim with Aidan and need and love.

He pauses, for a fraction of a moment, giving me time to adjust. Getting himself under control. It doesn't last more than a heartbeat and he flexes his hips, pulling and pushing, each thrust punctuated with a groan and a gasp. Building and climbing, each of us desperate for the other.

All the pent-up frustration from last night, from the long drive, erupts with a snap of his hips and I fall apart. I gasp as I try to pull in a breath, shuddering around him, pulsing and trembling. Clinging to him with all that I have. Aidan draws out my orgasm, thrusting, chasing his own. With his face buried in my neck, panting and gasping, I feel his cock swell even more. His movements erratic, fingers digging into my flesh, he groans as he shudders and spills deep inside me.

My hands grip at the muscles of his shoulder and the

back of his head, holding this man as tightly to me as I can. Oh my God.

"Jesus, love." His words vibrate against my ear sending another wave of shivers through my whole body.

Pulling his face from my neck, Aidan leans back to meet my eyes.

"Do—do you need to put me down?" I start to squirm, but end up moaning as his dick twitches inside me.

Aidan chuckles and does it again—the twitching thing— and gets rewarded with another moan from me.

"I don't. You need to quit that shite, Lis. You're gorgeous, so just leave it, yeah? Hold tight." As I brace my arms around his neck, he pulls us back from the wall and heads to the bathroom, carrying me like it's no big deal.

He sets me down on the cold countertop and pulls his cock out of me. His hands are heavy on my thighs as he leans back to watch. "Fuck, Lisbeth. I—we didn't—" The realization crashes into him. We've always used a condom before. His wide eyes snap up to mine, panic evident all over his features.

"It's okay, Aidan. Stop." My hands on either side of his neck, thumbs caressing his cheeks trying to soothe his worry. "I have an IUD. We're okay—it's okay." I guess we've not talked about this. We just have always, religiously, used a condom. His eyes bounce back and forth between mine, searching—almost pleading. "I promise, it's okay."

The relief whooshes out of him in the breath he was holding. "I promised you I would take care of you, always. I shouldn't have done that. I've always used protection. Always. You put your trust in me and I—Christ." His words still carry the sharp edge of panic.

"Stop. Trust *me*, Aidan. I would have stopped you if it

wasn't okay. Please let it go, we have to trust each other, it's not just you proving yourself to me."

I pepper his lips with small kisses, willing him to relent and relax into me. But he's not done.

"I do—I trust you with everything I am, but you have to know. You *have* to know that I would never do anything to fuck with your dreams. Everything you've worked for—that's what matters." His words go straight to my heart. He's so intent on putting me first, making sure I'm okay. That I'm taken care of.

"I know." I pull him to me and quiet him with a kiss, sweeping my tongue along the seam of his lips. Wanting to show him we're good, begging him to open up to me and let this go.

Finally, *finally* he returns my kisses—letting me in with a groan. Our tongues tangle, the kiss growing in intensity.

He hikes my leg higher, my calf over the top of his ass. He keeps his hand on my leg, the other winding around my back. Fingers skate upward tracing designs I can't quite figure out with the way he's kissing me. I can't think about anything other than the way he's holding me, wrapping me up in him. I don't need anything else, just this. Just Aidan.

He angles his hips, hard again, his cock sliding through my slick center. Teasing me, getting closer and closer. Closer to where I want him with each pass, but not quite there.

I squeeze my hand between us, running my palm down my belly. He rocks back, dragging the head of his cock down, teasing, driving me mad. A gasp escapes me as my thumb circles my clit, rubbing in lazy circles. I'm waiting, waiting for that moment when he moves to drag his dick back to my clit. As he drives up again, I push down with my fingers guiding him where I want him. Where I need to feel him.

"Christ, Lisbeth. You feel like heaven. You're sure this is okay? I don't ever want anything between us again, but Jesus, Mary and Joseph..." He starts rocking gently, small concentrated movements, but with the way he's locked his arms around me I can't move. He's got complete control.

The teasing, the buildup, the rock of his hips—where his cock is hitting me.

"Yes...yes...oh God, Aidan...please..." I beg for him—to do what, I don't know, but I'm breathless and needy. And I feel myself coming apart all around him. Pulsing and panting, I come undone.

With my legs wobbly like jelly, I step under the hot steamy water. Aidan keeps hold of me, knowing I could melt into a puddle of goo at any moment. How did I get so lucky?

It's still so hard for me to believe this is all real. Aidan's soapy hands glide over my shoulders and knead at the muscles of my back before skimming down my sides. I yelp as he tickles me, grabbing tightly to him so I don't slip and fall.

"Hmmm—this is a waste of time. I'm just going to spend the rest of the night getting you dirty all over again." His hands are all over me, running up and down me, around my ass and down the backs of my thighs as he lowers to his knees. My fingers tangle in his hair as he presses hungry kisses to my belly, his fingers sliding in toward my center.

I feel it before it happens and there is nothing I can do about it. My muscles stiffen and Aidan looks up searching my face for the problem. I don't know whether to laugh or cry when my stomach chooses this totally sexy moment to growl —loud.

Aidan's eyes crinkle and the laugh that launches from him echoes through the shower. I could die of embarrassment—just die right here.

"I'll be quick, love. And then we'll get you fed." He mumbles something more but it doesn't matter as he licks and nips his way to my pussy. I'm so sensitive, it takes no time for my orgasm to rip through me. He slides his body up mine as he stands, holding me tight the entire time. "You ready for dinner now?"

WRAPPED in a towel and brain still fuzzy from orgasms, I open my bag to grab panties and a t-shirt. Sitting on the top of the things I packed, are a cute dress and my maroon shoes.

"What do you want me to order for you?" Aidan calls from the other side of the room.

There's a piece of paper tucked into one of the shoes. I close my bag, biting my lip to hide the smile I know will scrunch up my eyes.

"Lis, what do you want for dinner?" Bag in tow, I head for the bathroom to get ready.

"I thought you were taking me out tonight. Showing me off to the world?"

His head whips up just as the door slams shut behind me.

29

Aidan

The restaurant takes my reservation, though at this hour, I probably don't need one. I'd have been more than happy to stay in, wrapped up in Lis and order room service. But when she opened her bag, and closed it as fast as she could, she asked if we were still going out to dinner.

Yes, I'd told her I couldn't wait to take her out and show her off to the world. I meant that, but tonight I just want to be with her. And love her.

I do—I love her. But I'm afraid that telling her will spook her again.

I check my watch and push myself out of the chair. "Are ye ready, love? They've a table for us, we should go soon."

Not a fucking thing could prepare me for the sight of her walking out of the bathroom. There is nothing revealing about the black dress she's wearing—high neck, sleeves to her elbows, full skirt to her knees. But it hugs her tits, cinching in at her tiny waist, flaring over her hips and arse. Sweet Jesus.

My eyes blaze a trail down her body, lingering on every delicious curve, but the best part? She's wearing those fucking shoes. The dark red ones from last night. The ones I couldn't get out of my head.

Licking my lips, I drag my lascivious gaze back up over every one of those bloody curves until she extends her arm, a slip of paper in her hand.

"Not sure if this is for you or me, but it's from Gracyn." She's got a brow cocked and the smirk on her blood-red lips is distracting as all hell.

I'm rooted to where I stand, knowing that if I move, it'll be to scoop her up and take her back to bed. Fuck the dinner reservations.

The sway of her hips as she saunters toward me, skirt swishing back and forth, toes peeping out of those sexy-as-fuck shoes. By the grace of God, I get myself together enough to take the paper from her delicate fingers.

You're Welcome!

My chuckle is low and husky, I wrap a hand around her waist and pull her to me.

"I'll be sure to thank her, but if we don't go right now, we're not going anywhere." I lean all the way in and kiss her cheek, just below her ear. I've time to taste her red lips later.

HAND IN HAND, we walk the few blocks to the restaurant. The soft evening air, salty from the breeze off the water, swirls Lis' skirt around her legs. Sailboats bob and sway in the moon-light, the rigging whispers and sighs across the night.

Every head turns as we walk through the restaurant. She's that stunning.

As I requested, we're shown to a table that looks out over the water. The room is intimate despite the full tables. The lights are low, and with very little effort, it feels like we're alone.

The waitress delivers our drinks—whiskey for each of us. They don't serve it nearly as elaborately as Lisbeth does, but the amber liquid fuels the fire in me as it slides down my throat. Christ, the fact that she doesn't order a fussy, frilly drink, but whiskey on the rocks, is another plus for her.

"Thank you, again, Aidan. This—this is amazing." I watch as she brings the tumbler to her perfect red lips, and I'm fucking jealous. Jealous of the glassware. *Jesus.*

Last night, I was consumed by nerves, terrified of the outcome of our dinner. It seems impossible that it was just yesterday. Tonight though, I'm much more relaxed. Leaning back in my chair, I sip my whiskey across from the woman I'm moving in with me. My ring sparkles on her hand as she swirls her drink around in her glass. The diamonds catch the light with each small movement. The stone in the heart, her lips, those bloody shoes—Christ, I can't get them out of my mind—are all the same deep sultry red.

"No one has ever done anything like this for me before, thank you." Her eyes wide and her face open and full of —love?

God, I hope.

"Lisbeth, anything—absolutely anything for you. Anything at all, love." That shoe peeks out from under the table with each bounce of her foot as we wait for our dinners. It's distracting as hell.

"So tomorrow, what's the plan? Are we spending the day?"

I nod, watching as she swipes a drop of whiskey from the rim of her glass.

My nod turns to a slow shake as she sucks the amber liquid off the tip of her finger. I don't even think she's doing it intentionally—driving me crazy. That's part of what makes her so alluring. None of it is contrived—it's just the way she is. Fucking perfect.

"We can take a boat out. I think there are a ton of little islands off the coast—hundreds, if the tide is out. Or hike? Maybe go to a brew house. I think there's a good one in the next town over," she suggests.

"We're booked here through tomorrow night, so we can do whatever you want."

The server tucks our plates in front of us, checking to see if everything looks okay. Lisbeth moans as she takes her first bite and the rest of the meal becomes a battle to control myself. And to make that struggle worse, she picks the same dessert from our very first date. Her lips wrapping around the chocolate cake, sliding it into her mouth is all I can focus on. I'm completely captivated. Until I feel a ghost of a touch on the back of my calf. She's staring out at the water, her expression neutral.

I think maybe I imagined it, but when it happens again, she smirks and sets her fork down, dabbing lightly at the corner of her lips.

"Maybe we should just get the check?" *Fuck, yes.*

Tonight, I want to feel those shoes on my arse when I wrap her legs around me.

THIS GIRL IS BRILLIANT. She drinks whiskey neat and can keep up with me through the restaurant and the few blocks back to the hotel, all while wearing those fuck-me heels. She's perfect.

We practically run through the lobby. Our laughter filling the small alcove by the lifts as I skid to a halt. Lis' skirt spins out around her, showing more of her gorgeous legs than I want to share with the men sitting at the hotel bar. Of course, she catches me staring them down over her shoulder.

"You going a little caveman on me?" she teases, winding her arms up around my neck. And my heart swells—amongst other things.

"Would that bother you? The last thing I want is to scare you away now that I have you." I'm only half joking. Getting to this point was a hard-won victory.

I grip her hips, guiding her backward into the open lift, set to take advantage of our ride up when a hand slides between the closing doors. They bounce back open and two other couples step in. Since the tension and desire isn't nearly thick enough between us, Lis tortures me by slowly swiping a fresh coat of gloss on her deep red lips.

It takes far too long to get to our floor.

Lis

Aidan climbs back in bed and pulls me tight to his side covering us with the crisp white duvet. The cool air in the room feels almost cold as it chills the fine sheen of sweat clinging to my skin. I nuzzle his chest painting it with kisses, and he settles my hand above his heart.

The past couple of days have been a roller coaster of emotions. My insecurities have more than gotten the best of me and I know I need to get them under control before they ruin this thing between Aidan and me. I'm getting better, stronger, and that can all be attributed to Aidan and his patience.

Never—never before—would I have been confident enough to flirt the way I did at the restaurant tonight. Licking whiskey off my finger, running my foot up and down his leg. I sure as hell did not need an extra layer of gloss on my lips in the elevator. That was all for him. For Aidan.

He has checked all the boxes. Every one of them would have a big old red check, if I had a list of things that a guy needed to do, to show, to complete in order to own my heart. He's done them all. He has made me a priority at every turn. Always making sure that I'm okay, that I have what I need and then some.

Maybe he feels my brain working overtime, I don't know. But he presses my hand firmly to his chest, the other hand twisting and sifting through my hair. Lulling me to sleep.

30

Lis

The smell of rich dark coffee pulls me from the kind of sleep I never knew existed. I stretch, feeling the twist of muscles I didn't know I had.

"That's an image I want framed on our wall." Aidan's propped against the wall, shorts slung low on his hips. I should be embarrassed by that comment—I would have been before him. But the first thought that pops into my head is that he said *our.*

Our wall.

We're going to have our own walls, our own apartment. I pull the fluffy duvet over my head and wiggle further down in bed laughing like a fool.

The bed bounces as Aidan climbs over me pinning me right there with the covers I wrapped myself in.

"What are you doing, love?" The smile I hear in his voice consumes me when he pulls the duvet down, just uncovering my face. Squirming does nothing to budge him off me, not that I want him gone. The weight of him on me, being completely at his mercy, I like it—love it. "You're hiding from me? How long do you think you'll be able to get away with that?"

"Uh, probably just for a few more days? When do you get the keys?"

"*We* get the keys next week." My heart. He has been so patient with me. So understanding of my hesitancy. And he's still here, taking care of me, putting me first—loving me. "I ordered breakfast, hope that's okay."

He brushes a kiss across my lips, lulling me into that sweet sense of security. "You're very vulnerable here."

"I am. I'm at your mercy." Sweet kisses rain down the side of my neck. I tilt my head, granting him more access. My body reacting to his, desire fluttering through me. I feel absolutely wrapped up in him.

"It would be a crime to let breakfast get cold, though. Why don't you get comfortable and I'll serve you?"

He hops off me with a smirk, and he throws me his shirt. *Wait, what?*

"I was perfectly comfortable."

Aidan adjusts himself as he crosses to the tray. At least I'm not the only one who thought this was going in a different direction. I tug his shirt on while he lifts the silver dome, I all but forget my disappointment.

The room fills with the sweet savory smells of French toast and bacon. This is the last little snowflake that causes the avalanche.

Tears well up in my eyes watching him fix my coffee with the perfect amount of creamer. They start to fall as he adjusts the silverware on the tray. And I blink at them, smiling when he places the tray across my lap.

"You alright?"

"I couldn't be any better." I try to rein the emotion in and fail spectacularly. "You are so incredibly good to me, Aidan. I—I can't begin to imagine what it is that you see in me. You keep breaking down my walls. I never thought—wasn't looking for this—any of this. I think, I've tried to push you away more than once, but you stuck with me anyway.

"And you know all my favorite things—how did you know this was my most favorite breakfast? I've had it once, maybe, when we've been out. You picked my favorite apartment to rent, everything we do, everywhere we go—they're all the things I love. You've done every little thing to take care of me." I sniff hard and let the breath out, lifting my eyes to meet his. "I tried to fight it, but I love you. I tried to keep you out, but I can't—I don't want to. For the love of God, I'm ruining the sweetest moment ever." The tray rattles on my lap as I press my shaky fingers to my lips. "I'm sorry."

Aidan beams at me and swipes at the tears that have escaped my lashes. "Lisbeth." He pulls my hand from my mouth, rubbing circles on my wrist. "I love you. That's the answer to every question you have. Because I love you. You make my life better in every way possible. I sure as hell was not looking for love when I came to the States. I came to escape something that came out of nowhere—something I never dreamed I'd have to deal with yet. My brother was my best mate, and I didn't think I'd ever get that back. You've given me so much more. I want you to let me love you, to show you every day that you're the most important thing in the world to me. And you have nothing to be sorry for—nothing." Careful not to topple the tray full of food, he presses the sweetest, most loving kiss to my swollen lips. "Just let me love you, yeah?"

All I can do is sniff and nod. I have no more words.

Breakfast is perfect. Aidan is perfect. Everything is perfect.

I know—*know*—there is no such thing as perfect, but all of this is as close to perfect as anything can get.

We spend the day walking through the little town of Madison, visiting shops, walking through galleries showcasing local artists and browsing through a book store. An actual real live bookstore. One that just sells books—no Starbucks, just books. Our pace is unhurried. There is nothing we have to do, nowhere we have to be, no school or work, no roommates. Just us.

There's no time that we're not touching in some small way. Holding hands, stealing kisses, wrapped up in each other. *I love yous* whispered against each other's lips, making up for all the time I spent trying to protect my heart.

There was no need, he owns it. And after all the ways he's shown me he loves me, I trust him with it completely.

After a light dinner on the deck of the hotel, we walk along the beach. Sand between our toes, collecting shells and smooth stones. Away from the lights of the hotel, Aidan pulls me to a stop and sits in the sand.

"Come 'ere, sit with me." He pulls me down, nestling my ass between his thighs and wraps his arms around me. "I don't want to leave tomorrow. I want to stay until we get the keys to our flat. I don't want to spend another night without you in my arms." His words are soft, just loud enough for me to hear over the sound of the waves.

I pull his hands around me, literally wrapping myself up in him. "I don't want to go either."

My life has changed so much over the past six months.

Feeling Aidan all around me, there's not a thing I would change. Not one thing.

I lean and twist just so my lips meet the scruff at the underside of his jaw. I breathe him in, bergamot and vetiver, spicy and rich, warmth spreading through me. "Love you more than anything."

"Hmmm...I love you too, so much."

The stars glitter across the sky, the constant shush of the waves and the warm body around me, lull me to the edge of sleep.

"Come on, love. Let's get you to bed."

The walk to the hotel, the ride to our floor, as we get ready for bed. All of it quiet and peaceful—perfectly in love, peaceful. Up to the moment that I crawl between the sheets and settle in next to Aidan. He rolls to his side, the simple kiss not quite enough. His teeth nip along my lower lip, sending electric desire through my core. And just like that, clothes are peeled away ending up in a heap on the floor.

As frantic as we are to get to each other, skin to skin, nipples brushing his chest, we go slow. So slow. An inch at a time, he enters me, infuriatingly, deliciously, slowly.

When Aidan's hips meet my thighs, he stops, pauses. This is different, so different. Our confessions this morning impact every move, every action. Every little thing holds all the meaning we've not put voice to yet.

I rock my hips slowly, staring into his dark blue eyes. Seeing myself reflected there, I hope, pray, he sees himself in mine. Sees how he has invaded my soul.

He keeps his thrusts slow and deep. Every single move intentional.

I feel the build in the tightness of my muscles, in the soft grunts he makes as he exhales. The thump of his heart against the palm of my hand, like it's beating just for me. My eyes drift closed, lost in the ecstasy of this moment.

"Lisbeth, look at me. Please, love, look in my eyes."

I only just get them open, meeting his gaze when the slow, beautiful burn of my orgasm rolls through me. I gasp, whispering his name like a prayer. He draws it out as long as he can, jaw tense, arms bracketing me in, holding me like I'm a precious delicate thing. And when he comes, it's with my name on his breath and my heart fully his.

Aidan

These two days, with just the two of us, have been everything I hoped they would be. I fell asleep with her tucked in at my side. Her head on my shoulder, hand pressed to my heart, legs twined together, her breath fanning across my skin.

I wake up to the featherlight designs she's tracing on my chest and her lips pressed to my neck. It doesn't get any fucking better than this.

"Mornin'." I pull her tighter to me, planning to take full advantage of the time we have before we need to check out.

"Good morning. I didn't mean to wake you. Just needed to kiss you." Lis shifts so she's straddling me, her lips on a slow, lazy path across my chest. Tongue darting out to circle my nipple just before she bites down. No wonder she arches her back and fucking moans when I do that to her. Christ.

What started out as a sweet wakeup becomes a feverish, frenzied need for each other. She takes complete control and uses me, riding me, making me feel like a bloody king.

She was so shy, so tentative the first time we fucked. Afraid to ask for what she wanted, to demand what she needed. My girl has come so far. Gripping my cock as she slides up and down, taking what she needs. The sight of her, the feel of her—this. It doesn't get any better than *this*.

I HATE PACKING up our things to go back to Beekman Hills and draw the trip home out as much as I can. Instead of the highway, I take the back roads, winding through every small Connecticut town I can. We stop often, acting like tourists taking in the shops, and farmer's markets along the way. Neither one of us want to go back to the real world quite yet. I want to fast forward to waking up with Lisbeth every fucking day.

31

Aidan

I plug the address into my phone's GPS and yell across the bar, "I'll be back in a couple hours, yeah?"

Finn tosses me an *up-yours* over his shoulder. He's been pissy since I let him and Jimmy know that I was moving out. Not at all happy about his rent change with one less person to split the cost. I, on the other hand, couldn't be happier. I got an email on Airbnb that my new landlord had to leave town suddenly and wanted to hand over the keys three days early.

I take the steps up to the flat two at a time and rap at the door.

"Hey, yeah, so thanks for doing this, man. Pisses me off, I had no warning that this trip got moved up and I, ya know, just wanted to make sure that everything was all taken care of and shit. Cleaning crew just left, so here're the keys, you've got my email, right? Okay, and if you have any problems, um just, yeah, email me and whatever. Might be gone longer than

I thought? So if you want it longer, um, just let me know, email, whatever, okay. Yeah. I gotta go, so um it's yours."

I swear the guy didn't breathe through his entire speech. But he shoves the keys to the flat in my hand and takes off out the door in a complete panic. I walk through quickly to make sure everything's in order before heading to grab my stuff from the loft.

I SHOWED up on Francie's doorstep almost six months ago with just my rucksack and a case full of clothes. It takes me a couple hours and two full trips to move all the shit I've acquired in that time, over to my new flat. Mine and Lis' new flat.

I shouldn't be this fucking excited. Shaking and nervous like a teenager with his first crush. I'm a couple years away from thirty, lived with a girl after college. But this is different. Lis is different. She means the fucking world to me and I can't wait.

Quickly putting my stuff away, I make sure to leave plenty of room for Lisbeth's things. Room for her clothes in the closet, empty drawers in the dresser, plenty of space in the bathroom for her shampoo and lotions.

My gaze falls to the claw foot tub. She went a little crazy over that tub—more than a little. And all I can imagine is her hair pinned on the top of her head, a glass of wine in her hand and bubbles hiding her curves from view.

Everywhere I look, I see some glimpse of our future. Side by side making dinner, working, or watching movies snuggled on the couch. Sliding into bed with her at night and tangled up in the sheets together every morning.

As soon as my things are all sorted, I send Lis a text. I have to work until the bar closes tonight, but I have to see her. I want to place her keys in her hand so she knows that this is us now.

A: Where are you?

L: Work.

A: Come to McBride's when you're done?

L: Hmm...miss me?

A: Always...see you later.

I shove my phone back in my pocket and with a last check to see that everything looks good, I head back to McBride's.

As busy as the bar is, time just doesn't seem to move at all. How many times can I look at the clock in an hour for the hands to only show the passing of minutes? At half past eleven, the air changes. I know she's here before I see her and palm the keys in my pocket in anticipation. I can't help the thump of my heart as I turn to take her in.

"Hey, handsome. That for me?" She nods at the pint in my hand, hopping up on the barstool I've saved for her.

"It is." I lean over the bar to steal a kiss as I set her glass and the keys in front of her, whispering, "And these are too." Her smile stretches wide, scrunching up her eyes.

"What? I thought we weren't getting in until Friday." She wraps one hand around the keys and the other rests on my chest, covering my heart. "I haven't finished packing, yet." Her eyes fucking sparkle as her lips brush across mine.

"Yeah, I got an email from the guy. His project date got pushed up and he had to leave early. I met him, Christ, almost twelve hours ago? Sorted my stuff before coming back here, so..."

"You're already moved in?"

"I am. So, I can help you tomorrow."

"THIS IS THE LAST BOX. What about your furniture?" I set the box on the island counter and press up against Lisbeth's back. Nuzzling at her neck.

It's cool and blissfully quiet in the flat. No roommates, just us. Pushing her hair aside I trail kisses down the back of her neck. Her gasp turns to a full-on laugh when my phone vibrates in my pocket—right up against her arse.

"I scheduled that call just for your pleasure."

Looking over her shoulder, she notes the name of my caller. "You asked your—mother to call? So I'd get a little thrill from your phone? Smooth." She turns and pushes at my chest. "Go talk to your mom."

And to add to our newfound domesticated bliss, she swats my arse with a kitchen towel. Flashes of payback, run through my mind as I swipe at my phone.

"Hey, Mum. How are you?"

"Aidan, love, how are you?" Mum tends to talk quite loud when she calls, as if her yelling into the phone will make up for the miles separating us.

I hear Lis snicker behind me and meet her gaze with a wink. *Eye-din*. She mimics my mum's pronunciation of my name, her big smile spreading across her features. "Am I interrupting your dinner? D'ye have a friend over? I can call you tomorrow, love."

"Mum, it's fine. Yes, Lisbeth is here, but we're fine to chat." I kiss Lis' cheek and head out the back door, so she doesn't have to listen to my mother yelling through the phone to me. "What's going on? How's everyone there?"

"Good. Everyone's fine. And you? We saw Lorna last week,

poor soul. She's looking a bit better, though. Taking care of herself, now. Said she was planning a holiday before the baby comes."

"Good. I'm glad. She needs that. A spa day, then? A beach holiday?"

"I don't know. I don't think she said—I'll have to ring her mum and see if she knows. But thank you for helping her with it. It was lovely of you to send her some money for that." We catch up on all the family stuff and I prepare for what I hear at the end of every conversation.

"When are you coming home, Aidan?" We've talked about Lis, about my life here, but I'm daft for having not broached this yet.

"Mum, I—I'm not sure. I'm working on switching up my visa, planning on staying in the States." I wait for the explosion, for the tears and pleading. All my siblings live close enough for Sunday dinner, and I'm not just telling her I'm moving out of Dublin. I'm telling her I'm moving an ocean away.

And like only she can do, my mum takes me by complete surprise responding, "I hope I get to meet her soon. She must be very special."

"She is, Mum. She truly is."

Lis

Aidan's mom is adorable. I roll her pronunciation of his name around in my brain as I watch him talking to her outside. *Eye-din.*

His face lights up when he talks to her, smiling and laughing at the things they're talking about. And it hits me just how much he's giving up to live here—with me.

Because of me.

With a glass of wine in hand, I walk to the bathroom. While the tub fills, I dig through another box for my bath stuff and candles. The tub is huge—giving me plenty of time to arrange all my pretty bottles and candles on the windowsill.

I add my favorite scent under the stream of water and peel off my clothes as the churning water makes a mountain of bubbles. I turn off the lights and light a candle that I found on our trip. It smells like Aidan, filling the air around me with a mixture of our scents. The steamy water swirls around my ankles as I step in and sink down, letting the hot, gloriously hot, water surround and soothe me.

I stretch out as far as I can and turn the water off with my toe. The air is thick and quiet, the setting sun throwing cloud-filtered light through the bottles on the windowsill.

The colors dance across the bubbles and as I scoop them up and make piles on the surface of the water, my mind drifts to my family. My fucked-up, stupid little family. Their selfishness knows no bounds, and it would be so easy to stoop to their level and refuse to go to Maryse's wedding. It's the last thing I want to do, and they sure as hell don't deserve a thing from me. Not one person who knows the real them would think badly of me for not going.

I used to wish that Maryse and I had the type of relationship that I do with Gracyn. Where we can talk about things, ask the hard questions, get mad at each other but still know that the other person loves you and everything will be okay. We have never had that.

Gracyn's told me that Maryse is jealous of me, that she always has been. And my mom, too. That that's the reason they're so hateful. I'm not sure they know how to be happy.

That they know how to think kindly of people and not put them down. That by putting others down, they are not actually lifted up and made better.

I have been so busy trying to survive them and their hatred, my whole life, I've never really taken the time to think how sad it really is. I swirl my glass and take a sip.

Aidan has a bunch of siblings, but when Michael got sick, Aidan dropped everything and went to be with him. I have one sister. One. I have to go to her wedding, be gracious and mature. I have to face my ex-boyfriend's parents and congratulate them on their new daughter-in-law.

As the last of my wine slides down my throat, the door cracks open and Aidan steps in with the bottle of wine and his camera.

"Fucking gorgeous." He kisses my lips and fills my wine, setting the bottle on the floor next to the tub. Pulling a lock of hair out of the pile pinned on top of my head, he drapes it over my shoulder, his fingers leaving a trail of goose bumps in their wake. "Look toward your glass, love. Let your eyes drift off though—yes—that, right there. Don't move."

His camera clicks as he takes shot after shot. Moving around the room, murmuring thoughts and directions the entire time. When it finally hits me that the camera shutter is silent, I look up to see Aidan step out of his shorts. As he stalks toward me, I slide forward making room for him to step in behind me.

I settle my back against his front, thankful for this man, the love I have found.

"Gonna print one of those and put it on the wall, right next to the one from the gardens." His silky voice sends shivers through my body.

He slicks his hands down my arms, taking my glass from

me. He drains it in one gulp and sets the glass on the floor beside the bottle. He skims his lips from my shoulder, up my neck, finally nipping at my ear.

"Turn around," he rasps.

I grip the sides of the tub, steadying myself as I shift to face him. Aidan pulls me toward him until I'm straddling his thighs, the bubbles cleared between us. Droplets of water cling to his chest, trembling but not quite ready to slide down to the water. I reach out, tracing a design across each of the bulges and valleys of his muscles, playing an aimless game of connect the dots with the shiny little drips.

"This is where we live now. Just you and me." My whisper muffled in the humid air surrounding us, my fingers dancing down his torso.

Aidan's hands are heavy on my hips, his fingers pressing into the flesh.

"Just us." I watch his tongue dart out and wet his lower lip. Those are the only words he utters, but his heated gaze and the hitch of his breath as I wrap my hand around his hardening dick speak volumes.

I stroke him slowly, almost lazily, languishing in the realization that we are well and truly alone. No roommates, no one. Just us.

Aidan slides his hand between us, his thumb circling my clit mimicking the same lazy pace I've set.

The sun has set and the room is dark, lit only by the candlelight flickering in the mirror over the sink. The only sound, our panting breaths and the gentle splash of the water.

Shadows dance across Aidan's heavy lids as I shift, leaning forward, and lining myself up with the head of his cock. His thumb stills as I slide down oh-so-slowly.

It's completely and utterly silent in the bathroom until Aidan's groan fills the air between us. I hold still relishing the way he feels, the fullness. Our connection.

Rolling his head back to the edge of the tub, Aidan squeezes his eyes shut and blows a breath out through his pursed lips. He's trembling.

I brace my hands on his shoulders, rocking slowly and whisper his name. He pulls me to him, our lips brushing softly. Everything about this is unhurried and perfect.

We rock against each other, movements small but the sensations layer and build until the most intense orgasm hits me, Aidan right there with me.

32

Lis

I reach to turn off my alarm, just for a minute and then snuggle back into Aidan's warm body. We have been running nonstop since we moved in and hardly see each other.

My clinical hours at the hospital are not overnight this time, but start early, so our mornings are rarely full of leisurely wakeups. More like jumping out of bed, scrambling into scrubs, and running out the door. Hospital. Shower. Bistro. Sleep.

At least, that's what the first week was like. I hated only seeing Aidan when we tumbled into bed at night and ghosting a kiss across his lips as I ran out each morning, not wanting to wake him.

I set my alarm for earlier this week, so I can do this. Take five minutes to soak in his strength and calm before my crazy day starts. I place a kiss over his heart and start to ease out of bed, when Aidan's arm snakes out and pulls me back in.

"Not yet." His voice gravelly still. He closed McBride's last night, only sliding in next to me a couple hours ago. He kisses my forehead and rubs circles on my back.

"I have to go. Go back to sleep, I'll see you tonight." He holds tight and rolls us over, settling himself between my thighs.

He squints at the time on my phone. "You have two, make that one more minute 'til your alarm." Pressing his hips into me, he peppers kisses along my neck. "More than that, really since your coffee will be made for you while you get ready. Think we have time for a proper *good morning*?"

I groan, knowing we don't have time for a *proper* anything, not even a quick something.

"Tonight, are you working?" He feels so good, his body pressed into mine, hands tickling up my sides. I want to stay in bed all morning wrapped up in him. But...*mwamp— mwamp—mwamp—* Aidan's alarm goes off and when he leans over to turn it off, I crawl out of bed and hear a mumbled curse as I grab my clothes and head for the shower.

After a lightning fast shower, I twist my still-wet hair into a bun, and slide into a seat at the counter. Aidan fixes my coffee and a peanut butter and jelly sandwich. "We need to talk about your sister's wedding. It's in a few weeks, yeah? Have you given any thought to what you want to do?"

I have, and it strikes me that I haven't shared those with him. I bite my lip, feeling bad for not talking this out with Aidan before now.

"I need to go. It's the right thing to do, no matter how much I'd rather spend the day anywhere other than there."

"What's the time, again? I'll make sure I'm covered at the pub." Aidan pops a bite of my sandwich in his mouth and makes a face. "How do you eat that shite?"

"You don't have to do that. I'll just make my appearance and leave." I hike my bag higher on my shoulder and grab my PB & J from him taking a big bite.

Aidan plants his hands on his hips, eyebrows pinched together.

"You think I would let you go through that alone? No, tell me again when it is and I'll make sure I'm free. Not letting you deal with that without me."

My heart flutters at his concern for me. "It's two weeks from Saturday." Popping up on my toes, I give him a kiss and murmur, "I love you," before I head out into the world.

I HAVE BEEN BLISSFULLY AVOIDING my mother's calls for the past couple of weeks. Our relationship is nothing short of toxic and I just don't want to play anymore.

Of course, just as Gracyn and I settle ourselves at McBride's, my phone rings. It's my mother, again. Aidan places our pints in front of us and stares at my mom's name on the screen.

"Just answer it. You're gonna have to talk to her at some point. The sooner you do, the sooner we can go look for a good dress. One we like." Gracyn nods her head at Aidan like they are teaming up on me. "Right?"

His lips pinch together and his eyes sparkle as he agrees with Gracyn.

I close my eyes and swipe at the screen. "Hello?" Passive aggressive, just for this moment, I will my voice to sound like I have no idea who is calling me. It's all I'll allow myself.

"Lisbeth. Have you been avoiding my calls?"

I roll my eyes and shift to climb out of my barstool.

Gracyn grabs my leg as Aidan grabs my hand, both of them holding me in place.

"We need to discuss your part in the wedding. Have you lost enough weight to fit in the dress we picked?" Two sets of eyebrows hit their respective hairlines with record speed and I just shake my head.

"Wow. Um, hmm." Gracyn is looking for a pen to scribble-yell her thoughts on my mother, and Aidan, bless him, sets a glass in front of me along with a bottle of bourbon. I smile at both of these amazing people I have supporting me.

"While I'm sure the dress you and Maryse picked is lovely, I'm going to find my own. Is there a color you'd like me to stick with or a specific detail? Length? Sleeve?"

My mother's displeasure is unmistakable, mostly because she launches into me on how ungrateful and selfish I am. Pot, may I introduce kettle?

I let her rant while I pour myself a little bourbon and before I can even pick up the glass, Gracyn dumps in enough to put me on my ass. Aidan drops in an ice cube and nods for me to take a drink.

I'm so caught up in enjoying these two hovering over me, I miss it when my mom's tirade comes to a close. "...Lisbeth are you even listening to me?"

"No. I stopped a bit ago. So, Bliss Bridal is where you got the dress? I'll consult with them for the color."

"I have your dress here at my house, you'll just have to make it work. You can pay me for it when you pick it up—" At *her house*? As if I didn't grow up there. But it has never been home to me. Never.

"Yeah, no. Sorry, I'll—" Is she for real? "I'll see you Saturday." I'm so over this mess.

"The rehearsal is on—" Can't do it.

I disconnect the call, throw back the bourbon and turn to my sister of choice. "*Shit.* Wanna go shopping?"

TURNS OUT, being a little bit buzzed is a great way to shop with Gracyn. Loaded down with dresses in the most boring shade of pink you could even imagine, I pull Gracyn into the dressing room with me. Much as I love my privacy, I need her in here with me.

"What the fuck is that?" She picks a dress from the hook and looks at it like it has personally offended her. "Nope. Not that one." She rifles through my *maybes* and pulls four more dresses out, chucking them in the corner. "Those are *nos* too."

Perfectly satisfied with herself, Gracyn rolls her hand at the remaining dresses in a "get a move on" gesture.

Miraculously, I find two dresses that look good enough. And while I don't love the color, I'm stuck with it. Thank God for small favors—it at least complements my hair and skin tone.

I plop down on the chair opposite the fainting couch where Gracyn is laid out and put my feet up on the end.

"What do you think? Which one?" She offers me a Twizzler from the package she pulled from her purse. I grab two, because they're Twizzlers.

"Any one of those look fine on you. Just pick one."

I check the price tags and they are all way more than I want to spend. I shrug, not really excited about any of these options.

Gracyn chucks me the bag of candy and stands. "Hang on a minute."

Six of the strawberry-flavored twists later, she comes back

and trades the candy for a dress. Heaving a sigh, I push myself up and look at what she brought me.

It's pretty. Like really pretty. Off the shoulder, rouched bodice, and a fitted skirt that ends just below my knee. It's similar in style to the dress I wore when Aidan asked me to move in—the first time.

It fits perfectly and looks drop-dead gorgeous.

"Where's the price tag?" I can't find it no matter which way I twist.

"At the register. It fell off when I grabbed it out of the rack. I think it was like eighty bucks?" She's doing her shifty thing again. "So, that's the one. Let's get out of here and get something to eat."

"G, don't lie to me."

Hands on her hips, attitude in full swing, Gracyn turns and pins me with a look.

"Fine. Francie and the bar boys gave me a wad of cash to make sure you got something beautiful that would knock your mom and Maryse on their asses." She puts her hand up cutting off my protest. "We all know you're all about doing everything yourself, but just take it this time. Really. Strut into that wedding looking like a rock star with your beautiful man and let them know—rub it in their fucking faces—that you got your Prince Charming."

33

To celebrate finding something fantastic to wear to the wedding, and mostly because we are out of Twizzlers at this point, Gracyn and I head to the bistro. We grab a couple of seats at the bar, and order a shit-ton of food. Sangria, fried calamari, goat cheese and tomato bruschetta, eggplant au gratin—and tiramisu. The dress is forgiving, so thankfully this splurge won't even matter.

"So, thank you, G—for today. I hate shopping unless you make me."

"Lis, you hate shopping regardless. God, you hate doing anything that's just for you. Seriously, be selfish once in a while. It's okay, you know."

"Yeah, I feel like I've gotten better at it—maybe? How are you doing?"

I scoop some eggplant onto some garlic toast, garlic and spices bursting in the air. "You miss me or are you liking living alone?"

"Mmm, I'm alright. I miss you always, you know that. It'd be nice to find another roommate though. I hate that you're still paying rent and don't even live there."

Gracyn grabs a fork and divides the plate of calamari in half, leaving a huge gap between the piles.

"Yeah. I hate that I'm not paying for anything with Aidan right now. He keeps telling me not to worry about it, but it's killing me, being dependent." I reach past her for the lemon and squeeze it on my half of the calamari.

I lean back in my seat and look out the front windows, watching people go by. There are couples walking hand in hand, families getting ice cream from next door. There is love out there and my friend needs to find some.

"So, what about Gavin? Heard from him?"

The eye roll she gives me is epic—Olympic quality.

"And how would I hear from him, hmm? No contact. That's—you know what? Forget it. He was fun, a fling. Just leave it alone already, please? Please?"

"Someday I'm going to get you drunk enough to spill. Are you dating at all right now?"

She grumps a *no* into her wine glass and grabs a lemon-less ring of squid, popping it into her mouth.

I shake my head and go back to staring out the windows, and watch as a girl crossing the street stops right in the middle. A car screeches to a halt, the driver yelling at her. She doesn't seem to notice, focused intently on something in front of the gelato place next door.

"Holy shit, what is she doing?"

Gracyn's head pops up just as the chick waves off the driver and dashes the rest of the way across.

"Weird. Hey, I'll be right back, I need to check when I'm working again." And she bolts for the back room with her phone clutched tightly to her chest. She's so making my head spin. I swirl the deep red wine around my glass, lost in thought.

"Hey, can I get a margarita, heavy on the tequila? Rocks and salt, please."

The girl from the street drops her clutch on the bar and slides into the seat next to me. Her phone vibrates inside the clutch, stops and starts in again. She pulls it out, swiping the screen angrily.

"There's nothing you can say that will make this right, so stop. I don't—" The last thing I want to do is listen to her phone call, but she's right there. And pissed. "—no, you do you. It's fine, I'll figure something out and get my shit out." She disconnects and tosses her phone on the bar.

She drains half her drink in one gulp and drops her glass back down on the bar. Gracyn wiggles back into her seat on the other side of me and looks back and forth from me to the girl with her eyebrows up in her hairline.

"Sorry, y'all didn't need to hear my mess." She slams down the rest of her drink and rattles the ice at the bartender. "Just keep 'em coming, sugar."

As she downs the second margarita, tension seeps out of her and sanity finds its way back in. And we all realize that Gracyn and I are just sitting there, watching this poor girl's shit show unfold.

She looks from me to Gracyn to me once again, empty glass and back up to me again.

"Wow. Um, sorry. Really." She reaches out her hand. "I'm Kate, and honestly, I'm not a psycho, I just... Holy shit, my day has gone to hell in a hurry."

Her Southern twang from earlier is working its way out of her voice, like she's willing it to go away. She slides her glass toward the edge of the bar and taps the rim as the bartender looks over.

"You gonna be alright? That's a lot of tequila," Gracyn asks.

"I don't know that there's enough tequila in the world to take care of this day. Month, really. *Shit*." She shakes her head and smiles. Then the giggles start, and by the time she's worked up to a full-on laugh, the last thing I expect are the tears.

Not laughing tears, but the real ones.

"Kate, are you okay?" I hand her a wad of cocktail napkins and slide her water glass closer. "What happened?"

"Oh, my Lawrt." She dabs at her mascara, not smudging it in the least. It's a skill that I absolutely do not possess.

She looks out the window and sighs. "I'm a walking soap opera. I was early, meeting my boyfriend here for dinner. I'm never early, y'all. Never. And I guess he was banking on that, because"—she swallows hard and stares at the ceiling until she gets herself together again—"because I found him making out with his boyfriend at the gelato place next door."

My hand flies to my mouth, trying desperately to hold in the shock. Just as the words whiz through my brain, I hear Gracyn bark out, "Well shit, Lis, you don't have the worst breakup story anymore."

The silence is deafening for all of ten seconds before Kate's laugh fills the bistro bar and her perfectly preserved mascara runs down her face.

Gracyn dumps the rest of her sangria down her throat and I can't hold it back anymore. The laughter bubbles out between my fingers, still firmly clamped over my mouth. We're for sure making a scene.

"I'm so sorry," I squeak out, "so sorry. It's not funny, but—"

"Oh, it's funny," Kate spits out. "It just fucking sucks. I need to find a new place, too, now." Sighing, she wipes at her eyes and mumbles, "*Fuck.*"

"Sorry, again." Nudging Gracyn with my elbow, I ask—silently—and she agrees—less silently.

"I'm looking for a new roommate. I'm Gracyn and this is Lis. She just left me for the love of her life."

"Are you serious? Because that would be amazing." Kate leans over me to Gracyn. "I teach kindergarten, well, I start next month, but I can prepay rent until then. I don't want you thinking I'm gonna mooch or flake or anything. When—how soon can I move in? God, I don't ever want to see that asshole again. Can you believe I moved up here to be with him? Shoulda known a fine dressing, pretty Southern boy wanting to move closer to the fashion district was too good to be true."

She's killing me, all quick wit and Southern drawl. Kate pulls out her phone and shows us a picture. Pretty is most definitely the word for him. His hair is not just styled, but coiffed. His smile is all veneers and the boy is sporting seersucker shorts and original Penguin polo that so needs to be a size larger. I think I saw in Urban Dictionary that it's referred to as a *smedium.*

"Isn't Aidan covering part of fashion week?"

Nodding through my last gulp of sangria, Kate shifts her gaze to me. "Is that your man?"

I show her the picture I took of him at the beach. Shirtless, scruffy, and rugged. Holding his hair out of his eyes and a hint of his crooked tooth where he's biting his lip.

I love this picture the way he loves the one of me from the reflecting pool. "Yeah, he's a photographer...very straight, I swear."

"Mmm—you hope."

Gracyn is shocked silent before busting out laughing, covering up my giggled *If you only knew.*

34

Aidan

She's not answered one phone call. Not returned a single text. No one's heard from her or seems to know where she is. She's disappeared.

I'm not sure how I became the one in charge of finding her, but I am. Lorna's been my best friend for years. I didn't think twice about being there for her and Michael after his diagnosis. Didn't flinch at helping her through the end. But I'm three thousand miles away. In another country. I can't just drop everything and go 'round her flat looking for her.

I'm not sure what else I can do.

For Lisbeth, though, there's no question. She's been working her hours at the hospital during the day. Shadowing the nursing staff, and loving every minute of it. But she's still putting in as many hours at the bistro as she can each week.

As hardworking as she is, she's just as stubborn. I've told her the rent is paid. The bills taken care of. I've got us covered with this flat. I want to help alleviate some of her stress, take the load off and give her the opportunity to finish her school and training without having to worry about paying day-to-day bills.

I laugh to myself as I fix her coffee in the huge travel mug she likes. She takes hers to the hospital with her in the wee hours of the morning, so I bought a second one. One for me to treat and spoil her with.

Gracyn pulls up to the curb, just as I lock the door behind me.

"Thank you, for doing this." I settle into my seat, and pinch the travel mug between my knees pulling the safety belt across me.

"No problem. I love that you're taking care of my girl." The drive to the hospital is slow with traffic at this hour. "We should get done at the same time. You don't need to sit at the bar all night."

Sliding my sunglasses down, I take a sip of coffee and shake my head.

"Erm, no. She's my girl." I wink at Gracyn forgetting that she can't see past my aviators. "And since she insists on working so much, I'll at least spend the evening in her presence."

"Good answer. Why—forget it. Stupid question."

"Why, what?" The red light gives her a moment to look at me.

"I was going to ask why she's killing herself working— what? Seventy hours a week between the bistro and the hospital when she could just accept some help? But we both know that she's not wired that way." She brushes away her question.

The car behind us honks and Gracyn turns her attention

back to the road. She pulls into the car park and drops me by Lis' car.

"Thank you, Aidan. Thank you for seeing how amazing Lis is. Thank you for loving her the way she deserves." Her voice is quiet and her knuckles pale as she grips the steering wheel tightly.

I wait for her to face me, but Gracyn doesn't break her stare out the windshield.

"I wouldn't have it any other way. Thank you for taking care of her until I found her. She's lucky to have you for her friend."

I lean against the trunk of Lis' car to wait for her, and as I watch Gracyn drive away, I swear I see her swiping at a tear.

The look of confusion on Lisbeth's face turns to sparkling eyes and smiling face when she sees me leaning against her car.

"What are you doing here?" She hikes her bag higher on her shoulder as she steps into my arms.

"I'm here to take care of you." Much as it pains me, I keep our kiss chaste, polite for her professional workplace. "You're changed already for the bistro?" I take Lis' bag and keys, and hand her the coffee.

"Yeah. I had to wash off the hospital germs before I go serve food and drinks. God, can you imagine?"

I settle her in the passenger seat and the relief washes over her as she takes her first tentative sip of coffee.

"You're incredible, Aidan. I needed this so bad."

I smile at the little humming sound she makes while she enjoys the moment to relax, to let the caffeine work its way into her system. To allow herself to be taken care of. She's getting better at it, but I want to do so much more for her.

"How was it today?"

"Good. It was really good. I learn so much every time I'm there." She sinks into the seat, head back, eyes closed. She needs this. Her alarm goes off before five o'clock every morning and she's been running for the past eight hours.

As she relaxes into a quick nap, I reach over to stop the travel mug from sliding out of her hands. I tuck it between my thighs and reach back to take her hand in mine.

I need to check my schedule, between McBride's and my expanding photography commitments, to make sure I can do this for her as much as possible. Make sure she has what she needs.

She blinks away the fog as I park and open her door. I offer Lis my hand, and she climbs out stretching the rest of the nap away.

"Do you need me to help you set up for the night?" I run my hand down her ponytail, giving it a little tug at the end.

"No, I'll be fine." She grabs at her coffee and leans in to brush a kiss across my lips. "Thank you, so much. I'll have G drop me off when we're done. But will you bring my bag in for me when you get home?" Home. It is home with her things strewn about.

"I will, but I'll be back to fetch you home." I stop her protest with a quick kiss to the lips that deepens into the promise of more. When I know she's good and breathless, unable to protest, I pull back. "Let me take care of you, Lis." My lips brushing hers with each word.

It's hard won, but her whispered "okay" is the only thing I want to hear. With a final kiss, I send her on her way and head home.

I throw her scrubs into the washer, well aware that she likes to wash them separately to keep the hospital cooties away from our other things.

While I wait, I run around the flat straightening things and tidying up. I set a fresh towel on the edge of the tub, place her favorite candle on the windowsill. I straighten the bed and grab her robe to hang by the tub so she can wrap herself in it before she falls exhausted into bed.

As soon as the dryer makes its awful buzz, I pull out her warm scrubs and hang them so they are ready for her in the morning.

Done with the domestic shit, I grab my rucksack and head back to have dinner with Lis, needing to carve out whatever time I can to spend with her.

35

I catch Aidan watching me in the mirror as I swipe on a final coat of mascara. He's laughing at my mascara face, the one everyone makes—brows up, but lids half closed, mouth open, tongue out.

"Would you stop? Making me laugh is not gonna move this process along." I screw the tube of black goop closed and chuck it in my makeup drawer.

I am doing my very best at dragging my feet. This wedding is the last thing I want to do on this gorgeous Saturday. I just don't want to go.

And like he can read the thoughts running through my brain, Aidan pulls my dress from the closet. "We can leave as soon as you've had enough. Before that, really. I'll entertain you, make you laugh."

He sucks a breath in, the sound hissing between his teeth, as I drop my robe and reach for my dress hanging from his finger. Aidan's eyes take in my strapless bra in pale pink with matching lacy boy shorts, lingering lazily until he finally meets my eyes. His are dark and heavy-lidded, almost black with desire.

"I don't see any reason for us to linger at the party after." He steps closer as I slide my dress over my hips. With his hands on my hips, Aidan turns my back to him and slowly slides the zipper closed. He places a kiss at the back of my neck, my hair pushed to the side. My skin tingles where his lips rest and I have to concentrate really hard on why we need to leave—soon.

Pulling myself together, I step away from him and into my shoes.

"We need to go. No more distractions."

I try to pull off sassy and all I hear is breathy and desperate.

With my hand firmly tucked in the crook of his arm, Aidan and I walk up the steps to the church. Not the church we attended on Christmas and Easter growing up. No, it's the big showy church in town, the one that will look better in the pictures.

"Doing alright?" Aidan asks with an extra squeeze of my hand.

I blow out a shaky breath and slowly nod.

"Sure?" I'm not sure. The closer we get to the back of the church where the ushers wait to seat us, the more nervous I get. I don't want to claim being here for either side. It's childish, but honestly, who can blame me.

"Didn't think you'd actually be here." His voice is far too loud and draws way too much attention. The muscles beneath my hand tense, as Aidan recognizes Tyler, Rob's best friend. "You here to make sure she doesn't spill any drinks later?" he laughs and slaps Aidan's shoulder like they're friends. "I'll, uh take her from here." He winks, jutting his arm out to escort me down the aisle and the loud and obnoxious becomes absolutely uncomfortable.

Outwardly, Aidan is the image of calm and serene, but I can feel his tension as he rolls his shoulders and shifts his body between us.

"You won't, actually." Tyler takes a step back and stares at us, not quite sure what to do. "I'll escort Lisbeth, if you'll just show us where we're to sit."

"Fff—wherever, man. Enjoy the show, Lis." Tyler puffs out his chest and tries to brush past Aidan to the couple behind us. What I'm sure he intended to be an intimidation, has Tyler looking like a fool as he bounces off of Aidan's shoulder, stumbling.

This stupid exchange, the posturing, has garnered far too much attention. Whispers are rippling through the church and like the wake of a pebble dropped in a still pond, bodies stretch and turn. People are staring at me, comments hush through the church.

"What do you want, love? Shall we strut to the front of the church or take a seat back here, and not worry about it?" Aidan's warm soft voice calms my racing heart.

I smile up at him, knowing there is no one I'd rather do this with.

"Let's sit back here. It'll be easier to make a quick getaway if we need."

Aidan

The look Lisbeth's mum tosses at her as she's escorted down the aisle is nothing less than judgmental. I don't understand the dynamics. They seem to thrive on judgment and condescension, going out of their way to make this strong, lovely woman doubt herself at every turn. I want to protect her—rescue her from them.

We definitely made a mistake in sitting at the back of the church. While it made perfect sense to not parade down the aisle, we do have to endure the stares and whispers of everyone as they file out after the ceremony. As guests file out, I feel Lisbeth getting tense, her discomfort floating around us like a cloud. I run my hand down her back, landing on her hip and pull her close to me.

"Do all of these people know it's you he was dating a few months ago?" I get a stiff nod, and she reaches back for my free hand.

My phone buzzes a text notification. It's the third one since the ceremony ended, but it'll have to wait. When it's finally our turn, we leave the sanctuary and make our way outside, breathing a sigh of relief when we are safely tucked into the car.

"That was awful. I'm not going to make it through the reception." Lis drops her head back to the seat and stares at the ceiling of the car. "Why did I bother getting a dress to match the wedding party? It makes no sense. This is ridiculous, I shouldn't have come."

I hate the doubt and self-deprecation. Shifting in my seat, I turn her face to mine, making sure I've got her attention. "You're here because it's the right thing to do, you know that. If I'm honest, your family is like nothing I've ever seen before. They are absolutely toxic." She rolls her eyes and huffs out a small snort. "I don't know how you're related to them, seriously. I can't for the life of me figure out why that arsehole picked her over you," I rush to smooth what was not meant as a hurtful comment, "but I thank God, every day, that he did. I may thank Rob personally at the party, buy him a drink. I definitely have the better of the sisters."

"Thank you." The smile, the peace spreading across her face makes me feel good. Like I've gotten through to her. "You're very sweet, but you know you don't have to say those things, right?" I start to protest in earnest when she winks. "And if you play your cards right, I'll even go home with you tonight. Let's just get this done. Make our appearance, have a couple drinks and leave."

The reception is even more of an event. It's not just a couple drinks type of party. There's a formal dinner with table assignments and dining partners.

I grab a couple whiskeys from the open bar handing Lis a glass as her mother sidles over to us.

"I didn't realize you were bringing someone with you. We'll have to make space at one of the tables for your friend." The dismissive flip of her wrist should have bothered me. But the fact that she has no interest, no respect for her daughter is what has my ire up.

"Aidan, this is my mother, Anna Rittenhouse. Mom, this is—"

I extend my hand, all my manners on full display. "Aidan Kearney, ma'am. It's a pleasure to meet you."

She reluctantly places her hand in mine. Her handshake is as cold as her assessment of me.

"You're not from here." The woman is brilliant.

"No, I'm not. But I've found the best reason to stay." I pull my hand back and place it possessively around Lis' waist.

Anna looks from my hand to Lis, from Lis to me and back again.

"Well. I'll figure out the seating." And away she goes snapping at the poor wait staff lugging a tray laden with champagne glasses. *"We've had an unexpected guest show up. You'll have to add a place to table—"*

"So, that's my mom." Lis takes a tiny sip of her whiskey and shakes her head. "And you've already met Maryse and Rob, so now is your chance to run. Take off before it's too late." Her small laugh and nervous smile trying to cover her discomfort.

"Love, it's already too late. I'm not going anywhere." The kiss is just barely on the right side of appropriate, flushing her cheeks a beautiful rosy pink.

My hand at her back, I guide Lis to our table when the announcement is made to please enter the dining room. As I pull her chair out for her, my phone buzzes a text—and immediately starts the phone call buzz. I pull it from my pocket and see it's Francie.

I decline the call and see a stack of text messages from him, the last demands CALL ME NOW.

"Lisbeth, I have to take this. I'll be right back, love." I set my glass in front of her and swipe to call Francie as I make my way out to the lobby.

"Christ, ye need to get your arse here, now. Did ye know? Did ye think to tell me she was comin'? How does Lis feel about this?"

It's rapid fire, question after question.

"Francie, what are you talkin' 'bout? Slow down."

"Aidan, Lorna is here. In the pub. Said she's here to bring

234

ye home. Ye want to tell me what this is about?" I can practically hear his blood vessels popping through the phone.

"I don't know. I've been trying to reach her for weeks and have heard nothing. When did she get there? And what the fuck—she wants to bring me home?" My mind is racing. What is she doing here? Why now? Should she even be traveling?

"She's been here an hour or so. I tried to feed her, but the girl's exhausted. Looks like she's been up for days. Aidan —"

Pinching the bridge of my nose, I huff out, "Tell her I'll be there in a minute. Let me—let me tell Lis I have to go." I end the call and see Lis' sister smirking at me over her glass of champagne.

Fuck.

36

Aidan

The look on Lis' face nearly killed me. The disappointment. The resignation. And ultimately the acceptance that I was leaving her to the wolves. I could see them circling with their teeth bared, ready to descend on her.

I hope with all my racing heart that Maryse didn't hear as much of my phone call as I think she did. I can only imagine how she would spin things if she had half a mind to.

I cringe thinking of the way she smirked at me like she had the world's juiciest secret.

This day could fuck right off.

I'M RELIEVED that she's okay. She looks fantastic, actually. She's sitting at the small table at the back of the pub, feet on the chair across from her, smiling down at her phone.

"Hey, how are ye?" Lorna's head pops up at the sound of my voice and a huge smile breaks across her face.

"Aidan—God, it's good to see you." She struggles a little as she stands, rolling her eyes at my offered hand. "I've got it, come here and give us a hug. I've missed you."

I wrap her up in my arms, relief washing through me.

"What are you doing here? Should you be traveling like this?" I pull back and look at her round belly.

"Yeah, I'm fine for a few more weeks." She smiles softly as she rubs her hand across her bump. "I missed you, Aidan, a lot. I needed to see you before—before this has me all tied up. How are you doing?" She sits back down, reaching for the other chair to prop her feet up again.

"I'm good, really good. Can I—let me get us a couple drinks, are you hungry?" She shakes her head and I pop into the kitchen to grab myself a sandwich and crisps.

The hors d'oeuvres from the cocktail hour are long gone and I'm starving. I throw a couple extra pickles on my plate, not because it's a pregnant cliché, but I've known Lorna forever and pickles are her thing.

I set the plate down and grab a water for her and a pint for myself.

"Did ye put extra pickles on here for me? You're a prince, man. God love ye." She's tearing into my plate without abandon.

"Jesus, d'ya want your own?" Lorna smiles at me and around the bite of turkey sandwich—my turkey sandwich. I push the plate in front of her and head back to the kitchen to make another for myself.

Francie pokes his head out of the tiny office off the kitchen. Pinning me with a glare, eyebrow cocked, he silently questions me. "Francie, she's just here for a visit before the baby comes. That's all."

"Not the way it sounded earlier when she showed up." He

folds his arms, resting them on his paunch trying to make himself look the part of the stern father.

"Lisbeth?"

I cringe, knowing I deserve his judgment for this. "She's at the wedding reception, her sister's. I'm sure she'll be here soon."

"I don't like it, Aidan."

I feel like an arse for leaving her there, but what other choice did I have?

My thoughts run in a muddled mess as I turn back to rejoin Lorna.

Holding my plate out of her reach, I drop a few more pickles to hers.

"You're lovely, ye know that? Mmm, so good." She mumbles, brushing the crumbs off her hands. "Sorry, didn't realize I was so hungry until I saw yours. So, you're good? Better? Ready to come home?" Lorna bobs her head from side to side while taking me in. "You're dressed awfully posh, were ye out, then?"

"I am good, much better, and I was out. At a wedding, actually."

"You're working again then? That's fantastic. You're far too good at what you do to waste time tending bar and mucking about."

"I am, but—" My words forgotten when Lorna grabs my hand and places it on her belly, pressing it flat.

"Was that? That's the baby moving?"

"It is. He's really strong." She says gently.

He. It's a boy.

"I'd like to name him Michael Aidan. After the two men who mean the most to me."

"Lorna, that's—I-I'd be honored."

It's not fair that my brother is missing all this. He wanted to be a father more than anything. It kills me knowing the last thing he did before finding out his death sentence, was create this life. He should be here. He should have his hand on his wife's belly, feeling his boy kicking and rolling and moving. These moments should be Michael's.

Lorna slides both hands over the top of mine, holding me in place. She talks quietly, telling me everything will be okay. Soothing me, like I'm the widow facing this alone. I cover my face with my free hand, letting the tears come.

Not the wracking sobs from right after his death, but silent sad tears mourning Michael's loss of this gift. Tears for this child having to grow up not knowing his father and the man he was. Not truly knowing how desperately he was wanted.

The slamming of the pub door against the quiet of the room, pulls me out of my moment. I wipe my tears and take some deep breaths, pushing down the pain in my heart.

"I'm sorry. I thought I was over it, but—God, he's really gone. And this sweet child will never know him." I brush at the tears that continue to fall.

"I know. Believe me, I understand. I've done nothing but cry and ask *why* for months." Lorna slides my pint across the table. I take a healthy draught and steel myself.

Of course, she has. She's been alone through all of this. Dealing with the pain and the guilt and the loss of her husband. Knowing she's going to have to be both mum and dad to this child.

"There is a way." I lift my head and meet her eyes, hesitancy clouding them.

"There's a way for what?"

"For his father to be in his life. For him to know Michael in a sense." Lorna's voice wavers with uncertainty.

I shake my head, not understanding what she's trying to say.

"Come home, Aidan. Come home with me and...we're a good team. We can do this. Together." Her plea, the only thing sounding in the pub.

"What?" Not sure that I heard her right, I search her face, fear written all over it.

"You were close to Michael. You were there with me through everything." She can't mean it. "Aidan, you're the only one who truly understands. He would want you to be a part of his son's life. You're so much like him it would be like his father was here. Please."

Nonononono. "Lorna, I can't take Michael's place. I—"

"Sorry. No, you're right. I shouldn't have asked. Shouldn't have even implied."

She's a flurry of nervous hands and false laughter, not meeting my eye. "I should have gone on a beach holiday instead. This was a mistake. I'll—I'll just call a cab and go. I'm sorry."

"Lorna, stop. You can't just turn around and go. You've got to be exhausted." She's staring at her bag, sniffling quietly. "Come on. Let's get you settled and we'll talk in the morning, after you've slept."

She nods and wipes at her cheeks.

"Where are you booked in?"

Still not meeting my eye, she replies barely audibly, "I didn't book anything. I-I thought I could stay with you."

I run my hand down the scruff on my jaw and nod once, pulling my phone from my pocket. I need to call Lis and let her know we have a guest tonight. Shit, I need to call my mum and let her know that Lorna's alright. That she's here, I'm not sure that she's alright. Swiping at my screen I see a text from Lis.

L: At Gracyn's. Staying here tonight.

A: Sounds good. Need to talk in the morning.

I grab Lorna's bag and guide her out the door, feeling eyes on me the whole way. Holding the door, I catch Francie leaning in the doorway of the kitchen, the corners of his mouth turned down. I know he's worried, but it's Finn who makes me pause. Hands braced on the bar, his eyes are narrowed and full of disgust. And they're aimed right at me.

He throws the towel to the bar and brushes past Francie, muttering *feckin' bastard*. I'm all but certain I hear the sound of his fist hitting the wall as the door shuts behind me.

Lorna falls asleep on the short drive to my flat, exhausted, I'm sure from the travel and emotions resurfacing. Wanting to wake her gently, I smooth her blond hair back from her forehead. "Lorna, we're here. Come on, let's get you to bed."

I take her bag straight back to the bedroom pointing out the bathroom and kitchen on the way. With Lis spending the night at Gracyn's, it makes sense for Lorna to have the bed. I grab a pair of shorts and a t-shirt from the dresser before turning to face her.

"I'll take the couch. My girlfriend is spending the night at her friend's flat, so just make yourself comfortable. I'll, erm— I'll let her know you're here and we'll all chat in the morning."

"Girlfriend? You're living with her? Is it—is it serious?"

She wraps her arms around herself, again keeping her gaze from meeting mine.

"It is. Go to sleep, we'll talk tomorrow." I drop a kiss on

her forehead and wish her a good night. My heart breaks for Lorna as I head down the hall.

I loosen my tie and grab some blankets and a pillow from the hall closet, throwing them to the couch.

Relieved to see nothing new from Lis, I call my mum, peeling off my suit while I fill her in on Lorna.

Lis

I can't stay at this reception any longer. I have smiled and nodded politely through all the comments about everyone assuming it would be me and Rob getting married. I have answered all the tacky questions about when Rob and Maryse "started" dating. I stuff down my desire to tell every single one of them what a lying cheating bastard he is and how much they deserve the misery of each other.

But I don't.

I sip my drink, far slower than I want to. It's the same one I started the night with. Aidan was supposed to be by my side for this. He was supposed to be my buffer from all of these shitty meddling people. When he told me he had to leave, that Francie called with an emergency, I tried to be understanding. I tried to have a brave face.

I tried.

I set the watered-down whiskey on the table with a sigh and reach for my bag to order an Uber and meet Aidan at McBride's.

Somehow, I've been able to avoid Rob's parents. Do they know he cheated on me? Do they care? I don't know. I've managed to avoid Maryse and Rob, too.

Until now.

Like she's on a mission, Maryse bustles through her audience cutting off my escape. "You weren't going to leave without saying goodbye, were you?" Hand on her hip, champagne glass in the other, she literally blocks me from leaving.

I paste a smile on my face. "Of course not, Maryse. Congratulations to you both and thank you for inviting me to celebrate with you. Your wedding was just lovely." My words are as fake as our relationship and it shows.

I try to step around her, but she's not done with me.

"Where'd your date go? Couldn't keep hold of him either?" she sneers.

"What? For the love of God, Maryse, leave it alone. You won, okay? You have Rob, and really, Aidan wanted to thank you both for that in person, but he had to leave unexpectedly. There was an emergency and he had to rush off."

I have never understood why she hates me so much, but this is the end.

"Mhmmm—his *emergency*. I heard him on the phone earlier, have fun dealing with that...again."

Why? What is wrong with these people?

The Uber driver tries to make conversation, but I have nothing more for him than an occasional *uh-huh*, and a *thank you* when I hop out at the pub. Thinking my night can't get any worse, I step through the door and my heart—my heart stops.

I close my eyes, trying desperately to convince myself that I'm not seeing this. When I open them again, my heart cracks, the pain slashing through my chest almost convinces me I've died from this.

I drag my gaze to the bar and see Finn seething at Aidan. The sound of a pregnant woman soothing Aidan as he rests his hand on her belly, his shoulders shaking. Telling him they'll be okay.

That's what truly breaks me.

Hopeless and destroyed, once again, in less than a year, I turn and walk away from the man I love. But it's worse this time. So much worse.

Tears stream down my face as the door slams behind me.

What am I going to do? Where am I going to go? I can't go home. Home. God, I can't do this.

On autopilot, I head up the street to my old apartment praying that Gracyn is home. My mind is blank but spinning a hundred miles an hour. My car, he has my car. Kate. Gracyn has a new roommate. I shake my head, running up the stairs. I don't know what I'm going to do if they're not here. I knock on the door and wait. It's Saturday night, they're probably out.

I knock again, *pleasepleaseplease* falling off my tongue.

"Gracyn—please." I call into the crack of the door.

"Lis, honey, what happened? Come here." The sound of her voice, here at the door of this apartment—Gracyn ushers me in and when my back hits the wall, I slide down to a heap on the floor. Down into the misery of another broken heart. Down into the familiar place of despair and confusion.

I let the sobs wash over me and cling to Gracyn. Just barely registering when she hisses, "I'm gonna fucking kill him."

I CRY.

I sob.

I fall apart tucked into Gracyn's side. And once again, a wad of tissues is thrust into my hand as my best friend soothes my hair out of my face and rubs my back.

"Hey, come on, Lis. Tell me what happened. Where's Aidan?"

All I can manage through the hiccupping sobs is to shake my head. I can't say the words. I can't. I want so much for this not to be real.

"Oh shit." Kate huffs out as she walks out of my bedroom —her bedroom. *What am I going to do?* "Do we know yet if this is a chocolate cry or are we going straight for the tequila?"

"I sure as hell need some tequila, maybe a dull steak knife to castrate the bastard," Gracyn grits out. "I warned him—I told him I'd cut it off if he broke her heart. Jesus."

It should bother me that Gracyn and Kate are talking about me like I'm not here. But their murmured threats and plans to take care of me, protect me, calm my sobs to a steady stream of tears.

"C-can I stay here tonight? I can't go home, G." Kate's face is filled with sympathy as she pushes up off the floor and heads down the hall. "Sorry. I don't—I can find somewhere else."

"Why would you do that?"

Glasses clink in the kitchen before Kate comes back around the corner. Dropping a t-shirt and leggings on the back of the couch as she passes, with her hands filled with tequila, my bottle of bourbon, and a couple shot glasses.

"Go get changed, Lis, we're gonna need the whole story."

After changing into Kate's clothes and scrubbing my face, I shuffle back into the living room and drop down in the corner of the couch. Gracyn hands me a box of tissues and a tumbler of bourbon while Kate finishes sending a text—from my phone.

"What—did he send a message?" I hate the hope bleeding through my question, my voice still thick with tears.

"You let him know that you're spending the night here." Kate glances down as my phone pings. "And he says he wants to talk in the morning. You ready to spill?"

She powers my phone down and sets it in the kitchen.

"This whole day can eat a dick." I gulp down half my bourbon and revel in the warmth as it slides down my throat. "I was leaving the reception to catch up with Aidan, and Maryse had some shit comment about him running off and that she heard all about his emergency and—"

"Wait, he left you at the reception? What the hell?" Gracyn plops herself on the other end of the couch.

"Yeah, he had a bunch of texts and missed calls. Francie was blowing up his phone. Said there was an emergency and he needed Aidan at McBride's immediately. So, he left and, the things people will say—unreal."

As bad as the wedding was at the time, relaying the horrors of it are far better than thinking about what comes next. I know the wait is killing Gracyn, but she gathers all her patience and fills my tumbler while I tell them about Tyler at the church, the comments at the reception. I even laugh at some of the shit people thought it was okay to ask me.

"But why did he leave you, Lis? What was the big issue at McBride's?" Gracyn pushes me, knowing I'll avoid this as long as I can.

It's not cold in the room at all, but I pull the blanket off the back of the couch, wrapping it around me. When I have that settled, I reach for a throw pillow still feeling far too exposed. Hugging it to my chest, I blow out a big breath readying myself for opening the scabs and scars on my heart.

"I walked into McBride's and he was bent over a pregnant woman with his hand on her belly, crying."

I almost can't get the words out. Tears stream down my face again, the little details I couldn't process at the time are all I can focus on now. The way they held hands, the soft way she looked at him. The sweet lilt of her voice as she talked about this baby—their baby.

"She's Irish, I heard her talking, shushing him while he cried over her. Telling him..." I have to pause. I grab tissues from the table and wipe my tears.

I'm so sick of crying.

"Telling him what, sweetie?" Kate folds her long legs into the chair across from me.

"...that they can get through this together. That everything will be okay, now. They were both folded into each other, crying and holding on to the baby between them. This is worse—so much worse."

The pain where my heart used to beat is excruciating. It's off the pain scale. The pile of tissues on my lap is growing with each passing minute.

"Maybe...maybe it's not what it looked like?" Kate offers hopefully. "How pregnant do you think? Could it, I don't know..."

"It doesn't matter. Tonight, we drink and eat ice cream. Tomorrow, we'll deal with this shit." Gracyn nods, her plans made, everything in its tidy little box.

I just can't with this whole thing. I reach for the bottle, filling my tumbler again.

I FELL ASLEEP CURLED into the couch with Gracyn tucked into the opposite end. My face is swollen from crying, my head hurts from bourbon and I drag myself into the bathroom to see just how bad the damage is.

One quick glance in the mirror and I get the shower going. With my forehead on the cold granite counter top, I dig deep, building the wall back up around my heart. With repetition, comes strength. There are so many sayings for moments like these. Lemons and lemonade. Bootstraps. Not getting more than you can handle. I run through them like a mantra as I shower and grab some clothes from Gracyn's room.

I braid my hair, and tiptoe to the kitchen, grabbing my phone. There are no new messages when I power it back on. Just the one Kate sent last night and Aidan's response.

I order an Uber and jot Kate and Gracyn a note. Gracyn would go with me in a heartbeat, but I need to do this alone. I grab a coffee from the bakery across the street and send Aidan a text that I'm on my way.

37

Lis

I haven't heard from Aidan, but the door is unlocked like he's waiting for me. I shouldn't feel nervous walking into our apartment, but my palms are sweating and the hairs are standing up on the back of my neck.

"Aidan?"

He doesn't answer, but I hear water filling the tub. Could I have totally misread what I saw? Maybe it's not what I thought. I drop my purse on the counter next to where he left my keys and head down the hall.

The sheets are rumpled on my bed, my candles are lit in the bathroom. And the woman he was with last night walks out of my bedroom with my robe wrapped around her perfectly round pregnant belly.

Nonononono.

"Back already, love? Did you forget your wallet?" Her singsong voice slices through me and I can't help the gasp that escapes me. Startled, her hand flies to her chest and, "Jaysus wept, ye scared me."

I have no words. My mouth opens and closes, but nothing. I stand there like an idiot staring at her, my heart trying to decide whether to race—or just stop.

"You're Lis, then." She looks me up and down, appraising me. Her tone is not as sweet as when she thought I was Aidan. Her eyes narrow. "He's not here. He ran out to grab a few things, for the next couple days, just until we go to the city this week."

"Who—wh-what do you mean?" There they are, those words I've been waiting for. And they are absolute gibberish.

"Aidan and I are going to the city. He's a job there this week and then we're on to Dublin. Did he not tell you?" Her hand rubs lazy circles on her belly drawing my attention to the baby growing in there.

She knows his schedule. She's in my house.

Cocking her brow, she jeers, "He didn't tell you about this then, either? To be fair, it happened just before he left. Aidan didn't even know about the baby for a few months. He needed to get away and I love him enough to have given him that. But you have to understand, we always planned to raise our kids together. Always. And that didn't change with Michael's death."

Her hands are splayed across her, smoothing my robe. Showing off the innocent child that will kill me.

There is no way in hell that I can come between them. I can't do it. Aidan was obviously hers first. They have a past.

And that past is growing into Aidan's future.

Nodding my head, listening to her words, it becomes clear to me. I love him too much for there to be any other choice.

"I-I need to grab some of my things. I—"

"Of course. I'll just pop in to take my bath, stay out of your way." She smiles victoriously.

I won't keep him away from this baby.

The quiet click of the bathroom door launches me into action. I grab my suitcase and fill it with clothes, throwing shoes on top of my scrubs, clearing out as much as I can jam in there. Shoving my makeup into my computer bag.

With a quick look around the room, my eyes land on the picture on Aidan's nightstand. It's from the beach. He's squinting at me, the bright sunlight glinting off the water. We're laughing, his arms thrown around me. Arms I thought would keep me safe, give me comfort.

Arms that will soon be holding and loving a new baby.

Willing my tears away, I twist off the beautiful ring he gave me and set it in front of the picture frame. My bags behind me, I rush through the apartment stopping only to grab my purse and keys.

I stumble on the stairs, laden down with my heavy bags, barely catching myself before I fall. I need to go. I need to be gone before Aidan comes back.

I shove everything into my car and drive straight back to Gracyn's curling up on her couch and losing what's left of my heart.

Aidan

My love-hate relationship with the pub is strong this morning. Finn insisted on ripping my arse, face to face, and I missed Lis' text while he was stressing just how badly I'd fucked up with her.

"Fuckin' watched 'er 'eart break when she walked in the door."

His fist takes me by surprise, snapping my head back.

"Told ye I'd kick yer arse, if ye fuckin' dicked 'er 'round."

As his fist struck my jaw for the second time, it pounded home the fact that what she walked in on may have looked very different from what it was. I thought I would be introducing my best friend and the love of my life, but now I need to do a little crisis management instead.

Busting through the door of the flat, I call out for Lisbeth.

"She's come and gone already. I was in the bath, but it sounded like she packed a bag and left," Lorna answers around her cup of tea.

I push past her, striding into the bedroom. The bed is perfectly made, everything looks in order, but her case and computer are gone. Her drawers and closet empty. I pull out my phone and click on her contact. Six rings. Six hundred beats of my heart, and no answer. I try again. And again. I try until my calls are automatically rejected.

I send text after text. I'm on the tenth message when I see they're not being delivered.

"What happened? What did she say?"

This is so much worse than I ever imagined. I turn, facing Lorna, pleading for her to help me make sense of this. My skin is too tight, and my jaw aches from Finn's right hook.

Lorna gasps as she feathers her fingers over my swelling cheekbone. "Oh my God, Aidan what happened? Were you attacked?"

I push her hand away, shaking my head.

"Lorna, what happened?"

Tears cloud her eyes. "I'm sorry, Aidan. She said she made a mistake. That you were just a distraction." She puts her hand on my arm trying to ease the bomb she just dropped on me. "She said if you love her at all, you'll respect her need for time and a little distance. She suggested you go home, visit your parents while she sorts herself." Tentatively, she wraps her arms around my waist, hugging me.

Resting a hand on her shoulder, I close my eyes trying to figure out what to do.

How often have I told Lis that I don't want to be a distraction? That I won't come between her and school. Maybe I pushed her too hard. Wanted her too fast.

She pulled back after our first dinner out, it took her weeks to come back 'round and talk to me. The time we spent in the garden and then the darkroom. That's when things really changed. I should have held back, not taken advantage of the heat of that. Fucking hell, I couldn't even help her study for her class, without having to push things further.

And then pushing her to move in—make this commitment.

I look at the wall above our bed. The picture I took of her in the garden, sunlight filtering all around her. The one of her soaking in the tub, bubbles spilling over the edges. Moments of love captured and frozen in time.

"Can you give me a minute? I need to talk to—" My voice thick with emotion, I realize the only person I want to talk to, is the one who needs space. The one who needs time away from me. I untangle myself from Lorna and wait as she closes the door softly behind her.

I sag down on the edge of the bed, elbows on my knees. I shouldn't have left her last night. She needed me and I left. Finn was fucking right. I failed her when she fucking needed me the most.

I call Gracyn, desperate to know where Lisbeth is, but the call goes nowhere. She must have blocked my number.

The only thing I can do is give her what she's asked for. All I've wanted was to help her, to make things easier for her. To give her the love and support she needed to reach her goal —and I fucked it all up.

I drop my head into my hands making peace with what I know I have to do. The light streaming in through the window glints off the photo Lis took of us at the beach.

I pick up the frame and knock something to the floor. When my fingers meet cold metal, the lump in my throat becomes too hard to swallow around. I clutch her ring over my heart. My arse hits the floor when I slide down off the mattress, my back propped against the side of the bed. I don't know how long I sit there, the symbol of all I hoped for clutched to the spot Lis always rested her hand. I held it right fucking there yesterday.

Scrubbing the tears from my face, I stand and slide the ring on the little finger of my left hand. Without thinking I reach for Lis' school bag knowing she keeps a pad of paper in there. My hand drops to my side and with a shuddering breath it hits me again that she's gone.

I shuffle out to the kitchen and pull my credit card from my wallet, letting it fall to the counter. I slide it to Lorna. "I have to run out, need to let Francie know I'm leaving. Can"— Jesus, I can't believe I'm doing this—"can you book me a flight home? End of this week, if you can get us on the same flight. I'll be done with the shoot late Thursday, so—I don't know, as soon as possible."

My eyes never leave the counter as the images of eating breakfast—making dinner—with Lis flash through my memory.

. . .

FRANCIE OPENS his door after three raps of my knuckles and zeroes right in on the bruise blossoming on my cheek.

"Looks like Finn talked to you already. Come in and tell me your troubles, then."

Francie's little house backs up to the pub and looks like an eighty-year-old grandmother lives here. He straightens a lacy circle on the back of a chair before offering me a seat on the dainty floral couch.

It's my first time here and I can't help looking for the twenty-three cats he's probably collecting.

I perch on the edge of the uncomfortable couch, hating what I came here to say. There's no reason to put it off any longer. I twirl my key ring around the key to McBride's.

"I'm leaving."

He leans back into the uptight chair he's sitting in, his forehead wrinkled in surprise. "That's not what I expected. Have ye told Lis?"

"It was her idea, Francie. Said I was a distraction. To go home and see my family while she sorts herself."

I feel him staring at me, but I can't face him. I can't look him in the eye.

"I leave in the morning for a photo shoot in New York City and then we'll fly out Friday. Don't know when I'll be back."

I pull the key to the pub off the ring and place it on the glass-topped coffee table.

"We?"

"I'm booked on the same flight as Lorna." My voice catches and I have to swallow back the tears that burn behind my lids. "It just makes sense to travel home with her."

"Not a thing about this makes sense and ye know it." He fixes me with the same look he gave me last night.

"Leaving Lisbeth is the last thing I want to do," I grind out, pain shooting through my bruised face as I work my jaw back and forth.

"Then why are you doin' it? Stay. Tell 'er how important she is. That you'll do what she needs, stay out of 'er way, if that's what she wants. But do it from here."

He's spent so much time in the past six months threatening me—pushing me away from her. The change of heart throws me off.

"Why? She doesn't want me here. Why are you so invested in this now? You've been warning me off at almost every turn."

"Because I love that girl like she's my own. And I've not seen her this happy, this settled in all the time I've known her. Let me talk to her, find out her reasoning before you go."

He's right. Nothing makes sense anymore.

I pull the envelope from my back pocket, her ring safely tucked inside. "I'm going. I'll visit my family, then...I don't know, then I'll come back if she wants me. Will you give her this, though? Please?"

He makes me wait a lifetime, before he reaches out to take the envelope.

A tight-lipped nod.

A heartfelt hug.

A silent farewell.

And I go back to the flat I shared with Lis for far too little time. Avoiding Lorna, I go straight to the bedroom and pack my bag, only what I need for work and a visit to my parents. The rest of my stuff I box up and move to the storage room off the kitchen.

38

Lis

Five days. He's been gone five days and I'm pretty sure I'm dying.

He's not even really gone, though. Or maybe he is. I don't know.

I knew he would be in the city all week, I was prepared for that part. I was prepared to spend all weekend just being with him, neither one of us scheduled to work.

I never imagined that I would lose him.

Stupid.

So instead of hanging out all weekend with Aidan, I wake up on Gracyn's couch again. Not that I really slept. I can't.

"Hey, what are you doing awake so early?" Gracyn shuffles out and drops down in the corner of the couch.

"Not really sleeping all that great." I push up so I'm sitting in the opposite corner, blankets all wrapped around me. "What did I miss? I just don't understand, G."

She doesn't have the answer any more than I do.

There is no answer.

"You should come out with us tonight, Lis. Just for one drink—" She starts pushing as soon as I start shaking my head.

"I don't think so. I...I have things I have to take care of today. I need," Lord, this hurts, "I need to find a place to live."

I twist the blanket around my fingers, avoiding looking at her.

"Nuh uh. This is your apartment too. You can stay here as long as you need."

"I can't. It's not fair to you and it sure isn't fair to Kate. She moved in here to get away from relationship shit, she doesn't need mine."

I'm feeling so sorry for myself, I can't even pretend to hide it.

"Fine. Look for a place, but you can't commit to anything today. Promise me. And come out for a drink with us. You can't sit here all weekend, you have to get out."

I open my laptop and start looking for a place to live while Gracyn makes coffee. There's nothing. Nothing I can afford alone.

"Mornin'." Kate stumbles out in a hungover haze and heads straight for the kitchen.

I know it's fruitless, but I do a search for roommates wanted and come up empty there as well. Kate and Gracyn bring steaming cups of coffee and the rest of last night's pizza, dropping the box on a stack of magazines on the table.

Kate dives into the pizza, not saying another word until she's downed two slices. "So, you're going out with us tonight?"

Jesus, it's not even ten o'clock in the morning and the

hungover kindergarten teacher is making drinking plans for the night.

I tilt my head side to side, not ready to commit. "Maybe? I guess?"

Kate nods like it's a done deal—set in stone—while I'm still trying to think of ways to get out of going.

"I'm gonna run some errands this morning, I-I'll be back later."

I climb off the couch, starting back toward Gracyn's room. She cleared some space in her closet for me but this needs to end. I can't stay on the couch for much longer.

"Want me to come with you?" Gracyn is right behind me. Ready to catch me, like she knows I'm gonna fall.

"No, I just..." I don't know what I need. Well, I do, but he's gone. "I just need some alone time. I need to figure this out, G."

I grab some clothes and shower as fast as I can. I miss my bathroom. I miss my tub. I miss Aidan.

I get in my car and drive aimlessly. People are out, living their lives and I'm—I'm what? Sleeping on my best friend's couch, because someone else is living in my old room.

Just like someone else is loving my old boyfriend.

I stop at the farmer's market on my way through town and grab a couple peaches and a scone. Cold pizza didn't do it for me earlier.

Without thinking, I drive north toward the river and head to the mansion. I sit on the massive stone deck, leaning against a marble column. Usually this place gives me such peace, a sense of calm. Today, my heart hurts and being here, looking out over the water does nothing for me.

I wander down to the gardens. *The gardens.* If I can't get him out of my mind, I might as well surround myself with him. Make myself sick on the memories of us. Maybe then, I can purge them. I sit on steps where Aidan stood taking the picture of me that hangs on our bedroom wall.

My mind won't stop racing through our time together. Looking for the signs I obviously missed. The signs that there was someone else and once again, I am temporary and easily replaced.

"LISBETH, YOU HAVE A MINUTE?" Francie calls to me from the bakery across the street. I'd stayed in the garden far longer than I had planned and of course, got nowhere on finding a place to live. "Come, let me buy you a cuppa and a treat, yeah?"

With a quick check for traffic, I cross the street and run straight into Francie's arms. He holds me tight and pats my back, shushing me until my grip around him relaxes a bit. He guides me inside and to the counter.

"Hey, Roxie, can I have a large iced coffee with almond milk?" I place my order and move to the side.

"A cuppa black for me and two of those chocolate tortes for us. Thanks, love."

I hit the trifecta—groan, eye roll and smile at sweet Francie. "The chocolate. How'd you know I need that?"

"Figure we need it for our chat. How're ya?"

He steps back giving me the lead to find a table. We settle in by the window and Roxie places our yummies in front of us and skips away. I want to feel that carefree again.

"I'm alright." I shrug a shoulder and pick at the smattering of raspberries centered on the torte.

"Yeah? You're not a very good liar. Never have been."

Francie eyes me over his steaming mug and chuckles. "Haven't seen much of ye this week."

I fight the tears and push a big sigh out through my nose, lips rolled in between my teeth. I shrug again.

"I didn't really feel like peopling this week."

"Stop playin' wit' your food and eat it already. Where've you been? Stayin' wit' Gracyn? Doesn't she have a new roommate now?"

I nod, taking a bite of the dense chocolate cake. Trying hard not to think of all the times Aidan and I shared this dessert—the heat in his eyes as I slid the decadent confection off my fork.

"Mhmmm. I looked online for a new place, but I can't afford anything on my own, and the whole strange roommate thing freaks me out. I-I miss—"

"I know. Still don't understand what happened," he says.

I have nothing to say. I don't really know what happened either, so I stare out the window and avoid looking at my friend. When enough time has passed, that he knows I'm not going to make eye contact, Francie pulls an envelope from his shirt pocket and places it on the table in front of me.

"He came by Sunday. Asked me to make sure ye got this. I held off hoping he'd come to his senses, but..."

I tear my eyes away from the pot of flowers I've been staring at and look at the envelope. My name is scrawled across the front of it. Aidan's ridiculously beautiful writing over the top of an odd bulge.

"I don't want it. I don't need his excuses."

I push it away, the bulge taking shape.

Nonono.

Tears form and hang on my lashes. "I can't, Francie."

"Lissy, I don't know much about anythin' other than nothin', but I can recognize when things have gone tits up. You're both thinkin' the worst and maybe...maybe you're both wrong." He slides a napkin across the table to me. "Do you want me to leave ye while ye read it?"

I dab at my tears and shake my head. "Stay." I hold the envelope, feeling the weight of it, knowing that it's going to rip the scab off the barely stemmed flow of my fragile heart.

I unfold his note, placing the ring on table next to my plate. The words blur as my hands tremble and shake.

Lisbeth,

This ring is yours, always. How you wear it is up to you. I want it all, but I'm afraid I've driven you away and that was never my intent.

I'm away to Dublin to see my family and give you the space you need. The last thing I ever wanted was to become a distraction. You and your needs were always first and foremost in my mind.

Our flat is paid up through the end of your school term. Stay there. I want to know that you've a safe place to stay. I'll stay at the loft when I get back.

"Too many people know the price of everything and the value of nothing." I value every moment we've spent together, and every memory we've made.

I love you always,
Aidan

OSCAR WILDE—HE quoted Oscar Wilde. My heart tap dances beneath my ribs.

"I don't know where you both got lost, but I've not seen that man as devastated since he showed up in my pub after his brother died, Lis. Sure, it didn't help that Finn got his fists to him first, but Aidan was ruined."

I twirl the ring around on the table, lift it and test it out on my pointer finger, spinning it around. "What do you mean? Finn hit him?"

Something feels off—wrong—somehow.

"Called him to the pub Sunday morning and laid him low. Told him how things might've looked to ye, not knowing Lorna." Francie stacks his empty plates and pushes them to the edge of the table.

"What?"

39

Aidan

"These were the only seats available when you booked us?"

I fold myself into the postage stamp-sized space. In the center of the plane. In the middle bank of seats. In the center of the row. And all I have running through my head is the song "Stuck in the Middle with You," Bublé's version, not the old one. We're so tucked in here, changing seats with Lorna won't win me any extra leg room.

"There were the two seats in first class." She smirks at me.

This last-minute fare set me back a ridiculous amount of money, no way was a first-class upgrade even an option. I push myself back into my seat as far as I can, hating everything about this trip.

I check my phone for the millionth time this week, the millionth time today. Not that I really expect Lisbeth to call or text, not if I've been labeled a distraction. I have seven hours of absolutely no distractions to think about what happened. To think about Lis.

The past week had been so busy with shoots, editing the final product and getting things squared away for the week or so that I'll be gone. I don't intend for it to be any longer than that. I've started building my life—the life I want is here in the States.

I scrub my hands over my face, and check my phone one last time before turning it off for the flight. I try again to relax and get comfortable, but it's just not going to happen. The flight attendants run through their bit and I really only pay attention when they get to the part about the booze available.

"You excited to go home?" Lorna tries to chat with me, but I'm tired. I'm cranky.

"Yeah. Sure." I close my eyes, hoping she'll stop. I just don't want to talk.

"Your mum will be so happy to have you back." She's not getting it.

I tune her out for a bit as the plane taxis and takes off, counting the minutes for the pub in the sky to open and let me drown my sorrows.

It's pretty obvious I've been ignoring Lorna when my eyes pop open at the formal offer of a beverage. I order whiskey for me and the three pregnant women in my row, not that I plan on sharing with them.

How does that even happen? How is it that I'm squished into this tiny space with three women growing tiny humans? Maybe that's why it feels so damn crowded in here.

"Thanks," I mumble as the four little bottles of liquor are distributed through the row, along with the drinks the ladies actually wanted. I'm not fooling anyone and we all know it.

The stewardess, Marta, must feel for me, or something. The little bottles appear on my tray table as soon as Marta moves on to the next row.

As the third one empties down my throat, Lorna starts again, trying to draw me out of my fit.

"It's been almost six months, Aidan. It's time you're home. Your family needs you. The life you have in Dublin is still there for you."

"My life is in New York," I huff out, disgusted with this whole thing. "What—what exactly did she say to you, Lorna? It's killing me. I feel like I finally found what you and Michael had. I love her, fought so hard to get her to trust me, to give me a chance."

I roll my head on the seat back to face her. I line the empty bottles up in a nice neat row across the top edge of my tray. "What did I do wrong? How did I screw this up?"

We've been friends for so long. So. Long. Surely Lorna can help me understand where I went wrong. Her cool hand picks up mine, stilling it from the nervous fiddling with the bottles. She holds it possessively on her belly, my nephew moving and stretching. The pressure calming both of us, lulling both the baby and me into a state of security.

Lorna's melodic voice is quiet, soothing. She practically coos at me.

"She said she made a mistake. That she was wrong about your relationship. Said you're not right for each other, and she was going to go home, spend time with her family as well, and focus on herself. That she needed time for her."

Lies. Nothing but lies and they roll off her tongue effortlessly.

I pull my hand back and glare at her while keeping my voice even and low. "You're full of shite."

Lorna and the woman on the other side of me both gasp.

"Wh-what? I—no—that's what she said." Lorna's face is turning red and her left eye is twitching. It's her tell.

This girl and I lied our way out of all kinds of mischief growing up, I've seen that eye twitch more than I care to think of right now.

"Her family's not in her life. Certainly, they're not her 'safe' place. Not where she'd go to sort herself." I turn toward her as much as I can in this tiny seat. "What really happened? Tell me the fucking truth, Lorna. The truth."

HER DECEPTION IS TOO MUCH. The way she played Lis, the lies she wove, there's no excuse for those. Having to sit next to her for the remainder of that flight while she cried and I seethed was uncomfortable for everyone around us.

All of that is enough to send me off the deep end. As soon as the plane lands, I pull the airline website up on my phone and try as I might, I can't make a reservation on a flight back. I close down my phone and tuck it away as I approach the customs area. The anger vibrating inside me is barely contained as I stride through to the next available agent.

"Papers."

I shove them across the counter.

"Can you help me? I tried to make a return reservation as soon as I deplaned and the system won't let me. Do you know what that's about?"

I need to get back to the States as soon as possible. I need to explain to Lis what happened—that Lorna lied.

To both of us.

"Sir, there seems to be an issue with your last visa. How long were you out of the country?" *Fuck.*

"Since March? But I started the process of renewing it—changing the designation before I left the States. I need to get back."

He flips my passport closed, hands it back to me and waves me through.

"You'll want to go to the state department and start working on that to get things sorted. Should be able to travel back in a couple months. Next."

"What? No, I can't wait. I have to go back soon—now."

He yells, "Next" again, and I'm absolutely fucked.

Lorna sniffles as she takes her papers from the agent next to mine and moves slowly toward baggage claim to collect her case.

"Did you hear that? Did you, Lorna?" I'm doing everything not to draw attention, but I'm livid. "I'm stuck here, for months. Months until I can get back to Lis and try to fix this shit."

I'm tired. My face is red and I am shaking all over and no matter how much control I want to have, my voice is rising. I'm not surprised to see a TSA agent striding toward us.

"Is there a problem here? Ma'am, do you need us to escort this man away? Is he threatening you?" He's got a hand on his baton and one on his walkie, ready to call for backup.

"No, I'm fine. Thank you." Thank Christ.

"About fucking time you start telling the truth." I grumble it low. The last thing I need is to be detained in the airport.

"I'm sorry, Aidan. I'm so sorry."

I'm done with her. Done. But I'm not a complete asshole. I grab both of our cases from the conveyor and head for the exit.

It's pissing rain and my phone pings as I move off to the side of the door.

It's my dad.

Traffic is snarled and he's going to be a bit.

It's the middle of the night in Beekman Hills, but I don't care. I send the first of what will be a million texts to Lisbeth, hoping she'll listen—that she'll forgive this mess.

40

Lis

My phone has been pinging with incoming texts since two o'clock in the morning. I only hung with Gracyn and Kate until about midnight. We'd had dinner and gone to a club dancing, but when they decided to go to McBride's, I just couldn't.

Not yet.

Instead I grabbed my bag from their apartment and drove home.

Home.

All of Aidan's stuff was in the storage room behind the pantry. His closet empty, his drawers cleared, toiletries gone. I had a new understanding of how he must have felt when he saw the empty spaces I had left last week.

Only a week has passed. How was that possible? It feels like a lifetime.

I twist my ring in my pocket. I still can't put it back on, but also can't bear to not have it near. I'm not sure I'll ever be able to.

Searching for signs that *that woman* left some mark while she was here, I dragged my bag back to our—my room.

I hate her.

There was no way I was willing to take any chances that she'd had the decency to change the sheets before she left, so after taking care of that, I crawled into bed. I flipped and rolled until I finally got comfortable only to hear the pinging of my text notification. I had turned it off, but now—now it's time.

THERE ARE MORE than twenty messages. Mostly from Aidan, telling me he loves me, needs to talk to me. They are full of excuses, claiming I don't understand. *No shit.*

The last one though, is long. Desperate, almost. His tone is different, prompting me to really read it, not just scroll through it like I did with the others.

A: Please call me as soon as you get this. I'm stuck. I can't get back to you. This is the biggest cockup ever and I need to talk to you, I need to see you and I fucking can't. Please, Lis. Please call me.

I lay there thinking. Do I want to talk to him? Do I want to give him a chance to feed me lines and bullshit excuses?

I feel so overwhelmed between the letter yesterday and all of these messages. I don't know what I want.

That's not true. I know what I want, I just don't know that I can have it, that it's still in my reach.

The messages and calls continue, making my phone buzz and ping until I just turn it off again.

I let days pass—weeks. I'm getting ready to start my last

semester of college. I can't piss away all my hard work because of a bump in my road. Because I made a mistake. I gave too much of myself, too soon and it ended poorly.

He's all I think about. It's taken until tonight to even step foot back in McBride's, and it was awful. I was nervous walking in there, but it was so much worse than I'd imagined.

The unfamiliar face behind the bar caused my steps to falter. The accent, the lilt of his voice wasn't right when the new bartender asked for my order.

It surprised me, shocked me, that this is what affected me so severely. This was Aidan's place. This was where we started, and in a way, it's where we came undone.

I felt his loss like a heavy blanket, weighing me down. Suffocating me. I couldn't stay, everything about being there felt wrong. I turned and left without a word, shaking the tears away.

Safe in my bed, I read each of his messages. I've read them so many times, I have them memorized yet they give me nothing, no direction. No idea of how to put this behind me and move on. Gripping the case so hard it creaks, I swipe the screen waking the display and see another text from Aidan.

Please.

My thumb hovers over the button, and something in me cracks. I need closure.

The message was sent hours ago. Probably as he was lying in bed. I talk myself in and out of calling him a thousand times before I do it.

"Lisbeth." He answers right away, like his sole purpose since he left was waiting for my call.

It's three o'clock in the morning in Dublin.

"Hey." Now that I've done it, broken down and finally

called him, all my thoughts fly from my head, leaving me with nothing.

Silence drags, weighing the air between us. There is so much he needs to explain to me, so much I need to say and suddenly, it doesn't feel right, doing this over the phone. We're too far apart, too disconnected.

"I need to see you." I hardly breathe as I force each syllable past my lips.

"I can't come back, I—there's an issue with my visa. I—"

The words tumble from my mouth. "I'll book a flight. I have a few days right before classes start. I need to know what happened, what I did, where I went wrong. This is my last semester and I can't afford to flake on this now. You owe me this."

I don't know where that strength came from, but the lead blanket that has been sitting on my chest for the past couple of weeks seems to have shifted.

"I'll pay—please—anything." His voice washes over me wrapping me in his sadness.

I'm glad. Glad he's upset, glad that I'm not alone in this.

"No. I've got it. You've paid the rent on our apartment, I can do this. I-I'll send you my arrival information in the morning, but I have to finish up some things here before I leave."

"Of course, yeah." Relief with a touch of desperation, bleeds through the miles.

"I love you, Lisbeth."

"Okay. Um...I'll text you in the morning. Bye." I disconnect quickly, harshly, but that's all I can handle right now.

I pull my computer off the nightstand and book a flight to Dublin.

. . .

WHY AM I DOING THIS? The customs area is jam packed with tired cranky people wanting to get their luggage and breathe fresh air for the first time in hours.

I pull my phone out to let Aidan know I've landed. The guy behind me in line taps my shoulder and point to the sign that mobile phone use is strictly prohibited in this area. With a tight smile and a nod of thanks, I put it back in my bag catching the glare of a customs agent.

The line creeps forward so slowly. The thoughts I've barely suppressed since I boarded the plane bombard me. Tired and nervous, I shuffle my feet, one step forward, wait, wait, wait.

Am I going to have to see her? Being civil to that woman is not something I think I can do.

It takes almost an hour to make it through this mess and to baggage claim. The conveyor is empty, bags lined up along the wall—all of them except mine.

My bag sits on the floor next to the man I'm here to see. Hands shoved deep in the pockets of his jeans, he shifts on his feet and smiles tightly.

"Hi." I wipe my sweaty hands on my pants.

"Hey. Did ye have a good flight?"

His gaze bounces from my face to the ceiling, the wall behind me, finally landing on mine.

Pressing my lips together, I nod and lean in to grab my bag.

Aidan stoops, grabbing it before I can get to it, settling it on his shoulder.

All I want is to step into him, his arms wrapped around me—enveloped in him. Instead, I follow silently out to a small blue SUV.

We stand staring at each other over the top of the car, neither of us saying a word.

Things have changed. Every single time we've gone out together, Aidan has always—always—opened my door for me. Until now. I blink back the tears threatening to fall; I shouldn't have come.

"Think you're up to drivin' after your flight?" His voice is soft and a little hesitant. Maybe I'm not the only one feeling off balance right now.

"What? No, I..."

Of course. I'm on the wrong side of the car. My lip between my teeth, I walk around to where Aidan has the door open for me and climb in. I watch him stride around the car, appreciating the way he moves, missing everything about him.

"I brought you a coffee." He nods at the cup holder as the aroma makes its way through my foggy brain. "You probably want to nap, but it really is best to just try and get on the local time." Hotels and long-term parking fly by as I sip. It's perfect —of course it is.

"Thank you. This is great." I don't know what to say, the awkwardness is creeping in. I should have planned this better, I'm here for three days and I didn't think to get a hotel room. Never considered how this would go beyond getting on a plane and seeing Aidan. Talking to him.

I lean my head against the window as we wind through the city, eventually pulling onto a tree-lined street more than an hour after leaving the terminal. "I'm sorry, I didn't know you lived so far from the airport. I could've taken a cab or something."

With my bag in his hand, Aidan guides me through a

bright red front door and whispers, "I just wanted to have a quiet moment with you before the pandemonium."

I almost miss his words as he tucks my bag inside the door and a toddler comes tearing around the corner, hands in the air squealing. Aidan scoops him up and tosses him in the air, blowing raspberries into his tummy.

"JAYSUS WEPT, was yer flight delayed getting in? What took ye so long? Come in, love, come in. Och, Aidan, don't wind 'im up like that. We've got 'im all day."

Aidan's mom swoops in and wraps me in a warm strong hug. "I'm so glad to meet you, love. Come in and have a seat. Can I get ye something to eat? Did Aidan show ye through the city in the morning traffic, then?"

She's a flurry of efficiency, taking my jacket, setting my purse on the table by the door.

I try to keep up with her, I do. But I miss half of what she says, unable to focus.

"Um, I-I'm fine, thank you. Mrs. Kearney."

Swaying slightly, I reach for the closest solid surface to steady myself, and find my hand on Aidan's arm.

She smiles as she takes me in. Is it significant that I reach for Aidan when I'm unsteady?

"Love, it's Ann. Come on, then." She's lovely, of course she is.

"D'ye need a moment? To freshen up after your flight?" My breath catches in my chest at Aidan knowing I need to catch my breath.

I turn to him and nod, grateful for him.

"I'll show you up. Henry, go with Granny for a treat, yeah?"

He sets the sweet boy down and grabs my bag, leading me upstairs to a bright sunny bedroom at the back of the house. The pale creamy walls are covered with pictures of Aidan and his siblings. And as much as I want to fall into the soft ivory bedding, I step closer to one of the more recent photos, studying the faces.

"Are you a twin?" I glance over my shoulder knowing that Aidan is still with me.

He's leaning against the doorjamb, arms folded across his chest, looking past me to the framed photograph.

"That's Michael. He was fifteen months older than me."

It hits me then; how little Aidan has talked about his brother with me.

"I'm so sorry." I take a step toward him and stop. I want to go to him, put my hand over his heart. Comfort him.

His gaze settles on mine and he sucks in a deep breath, almost like he's bracing himself. "I want to do this now—talk —get things sorted, but." He glances at his watch and scrubs a hand down his face. "But all hell is about to break loose and we need time."

I scrunch my brows together, not really getting what he's saying, when the front door flies open and the sound of love and laughter float through the house.

"They're all dyin' to meet you, insisted on it, so we'll not have a quiet moment for quite a while." Meeting his family is not what I came here for. This is not how I imagined this would go. Not at all.

"Take some time. The bathroom's just across the hall. I'm so sorry for the chaos, I'm sure it's the last thing you want to do after traveling and...everything." Aidan backs out of the room shaking his head, his smile forced. "Just come down when you're ready, yeah?"

I flop down on the bed, disappointed, annoyed as shit. I feel dizzy, light-headed. Closing my eyes, I breathe deep, trying to calm my racing heart and push down this bitter pill.

Did he plan this? Is this to throw me off balance? Why am I here? Why the fuck am I spending the day with his family? I'm here to say goodbye—to let him go.

I allow myself ten minutes to wallow and curse and mentally stomp my feet before dragging myself to the bathroom. I wash my hands and brush my teeth, trying desperately to center myself for what is, no doubt, going to be the longest day ever.

I swipe on some lip gloss, hoping it's enough armor for what I'm about to face.

41

Aidan

Chaos is the only way to describe it. My niece and nephews are running around the house. My mum and sisters are waiting to pounce the minute Lisbeth comes down the stairs. And I just want to have her alone. I hate every minute that we have to put off talking. Clearing this mess up.

Good or bad, our day has been taken over by my family. Just as Lis comes down the stairs, Henry rounds the corner at full two-year-old speed. I catch him as he slips, falling on his arse. This is the best age, when they fall and can't quite decide whether they should cry or not. Eyes wide, he looks to me for a hint at what he should do.

Lis claps her hands and smiles huge. "Good job, Henry— look at you!"

It's exaggerated and so over the top, but does the trick and the little monster giggles and reaches for her.

I'm jealous, and horribly in love, as he wraps his chubby little arms around her neck. I want this. Christ, how I want to have this with her. Babies, and little monsters and all the love in the world.

"Thank you," I murmur.

"Of course. He's darling, two-ish?"

"He is. My oldest brother, Sean's, son. They'll be by later." I take a deep breath and blow it out between pursed lips. "Actually, they'll all be by for dinner. I'm sorry. I tried to get them to hold off a day, but—"

"Everyone? What does that mean?" I've not seen her face this hard, tense, not ever. She narrows her eyes at me, her voice cold. "*She* won't be here, will she?" Lis is practically vibrating, she's so tense.

"No. Of course not, they wouldn't do that to you—I wouldn't do that."

The air is thick with tension. I'm ready to grab her hand and pull her out the door. Take her out of here so we can sort this.

My mum's voice rises above the clamoring in the kitchen. "Aidan, bring Lisbeth in here and let us have her a bit. You'll have plenty of time tomorrow." Any hope I had of talking to Lis today dissipates immediately.

I shake my head, afraid to meet Lis' gaze. Her frustration is written all over her face.

Lis slips into the kitchen pasting a polite smile on and sits at the table. Mum and Bridget start asking about her trip and school and how we met while my youngest sister, Kathleen, splashes a little whiskey in each of their coffee mugs.

"Uncle Aidan, will ye take us to the baker for a treat? Mum and Granny said ye would while they talk to yer pretty friend." Eagan's big blue eyes are joined by his big sister's and Henry scrambles down out of Lis' lap.

"Me, too. Wanna go too."

I throw Bridget a look and am met with a bright evil smile and a five-pound note.

"Here's a list for me as well, love. Pick this up while you're out." Mum hands me a scrap of paper and waves me off.

I end up trotting the kids down the lane and back. The baker, the grocer—Mum's planning is impeccable. She's kept me out with the kids until they're all starving and it's Henry's much needed naptime.

"Erin, take this for me." I hand the baker's satchel to my niece and scoop a whining Henry into my arms where his thumb goes straight to his mouth and his blond curls tickle my neck as he nestles in. It takes about four steps for his breathing to even out and he relaxes into me, his bum resting in the crook of my arm and his little legs tucked up between us.

"You gonna marry her? Can we call her Aunt Lis?" Erin lisps over Lisbeth's name, not quite used to the gap in her smile. Ever since she lost her first tooth, Eagan's been working on his.

It's not that I haven't given this question a ton of thought over the past few weeks—longer, if I'm being honest.

"Erm...well..." We've been talking about school, and the zoo, and her friends and dance class. She's hardly spent any time with Lis. "I'd like to, but I'm not sure she feels the same."

"Why?" And here we go, Eagan's favorite game.

Sighing, I try to figure out how to put the quickest end to his questions. "I might've hurt her feelings, made her mad at me." As soon as the words leave my mouth, I realize my answer is far too open ended for a five-year-old boy.

"Why?"

I stop outside the house and wait for Erin and Eagan to look at me.

"Because I'm but a simple man, and while my love is big and strong and my intentions are good," their attention is fleeting and both kids are looking up toward the door, "I made a mistake and now I need to beg forgiveness."

Erin scowls at me. "You should buy her flowers and chocolates. That's what Da does when he messes up." And with that bit of advice, she skips up the steps and into the house.

Eagan, however, is very serious in his response. "You should share something very special with her. That's what I did in school when I hurt Josi's feelings." This must be his little friend that Bridget was telling me about. "I shared my most favorite crayons with her, the ones I don't let anyone use because they're my favoritest. Girls have to feel special sometimes, Uncle Aidan." He nods like he imparted the world's greatest secrets on me. And maybe he has.

The rest of the day is filled with my family occupying Lis in every way. We eat and talk and the kids fawn over her, wanting every bit of attention they can get.

Lisbeth is polite and engaging. I'm sure no one can see how hard she's working to keep it together. I see it. I don't miss a thing. Each time she looks at me, I feel her stress, her frustration straight through to my soul.

And at dinner it starts all over again. The introductions as my brother Declan and Bridget's husband, Cian, follow my dad in from work, chatting Lis up. Sean and Aileene waltz in a half hour later beaming with happy news of another baby on the way.

Dinner winds down and Mum shoos us out to the lounge while she and Kathleen clean up, and Lis grows quiet. She's settled in at the corner of the couch with Henry on her lap and his sturdy book in her hand.

I take in the way she cradles my nephew to her, not just reading him the little book, but asking him about the animals on the pages. Both have heavy eyes, and I watch as they slip into sleep, his head on her chest and her check nestled against his curls. And my heart squeezes. I hope it's not too late.

"Aidan, why don't you get Lisbeth settled, you've a big day tomorrow." Mum rests her hand on my shoulder, drawing my attention. "She's lovely, I'm glad we had today with her." She pins me with her mum look. "Be honest, but don't let her go. She's one worth fighting for."

"She is." I squeeze my mum's hand and stand. "What was this about today? We could have had this sorted by now, if you'd have just let us be."

I need to know why she bombarded Lis like this.

"I want her to know your family, the good in us. If Lorna's the only one she's met, after the mess she's made, Lis would have no problem telling you to piss off." She wraps her arm around my waist and nods toward the faces staring at me from around the room. "The way you've talked about her since you got home, it's obvious you love her and that she has your heart. I love Lorna, but she had no right to do what she did and I won't let her be the reason you lose the woman you love."

Sighing, I scoop Henry up and deposit him still asleep into Sean's arms. "Thank you, Mum. I hope it works."

I shake Lisbeth gently, waking her. "Lis, let's get you to bed."

Her eyes go wide and dance nervously around the room. Much as I would love to take her to bed, we're in my parents' home and we have a lot to sort before we're ready for that. I smile and shake my head slightly, ruefully.

She says her *goodnights* and heads up the stairs.

"I'll be back down as soon as I've got her settled."

Sean stands, adjusting his son's sleepy body. "I think we're away, then. See you tomorrow." Aileene gathers up Henry's things and they file out. But not before she has her say. "I like her, Aidan. Make things right."

It's late morning when I finally give in, I can't stay away any longer. I lie on the bed, watching her. Every cell in my body drawn to her. Wanting to take her pursed lips, kiss her senseless.

I slide a lock of hair off her cheek and through my fingers causing her to stir awake.

"Morning," she mumbles.

"Not for much longer." I tuck the hair behind her ear, caressing her cheek. "Are you up for a drive, or d'ya want to stay in? Everyone's gone for the day."

I don't want to do anything to pop this bubble of time where there's no stress, no fuckups and nothing but sleep-rumpled Lis.

"Yeah. Let's go out. Just give me thirty minutes to clean up?" She doesn't make any move to get up.

"Lis, I'm sorry. I didn't know she was coming to visit. I —" She rolls away from me, throwing her arm over her face.

"Stop. Just forget it, this was a stupid idea." Her words are muffled, but she sounds defeated. Like she's giving up.

Christ, I don't want to lose her.

"She's my sister-in-law. Was my best friend growing up. But none of that excuses me leaving you when you needed me. I should never have walked out of that wedding without you. I broke my promise, and you have every right to be mad, but..."

Her arm flies off her face, and she sits up clutching the duvet to her chest.

"You don't get it, do you? I'm not mad, Aidan. I'm hurt. You discarded me, threw me away like everyone else has. You made me trust you—fall in love with you. I gave you my whole heart and you went running without a word."

I sit up facing her. "Lisbeth, I—"

"No. I came here for me. So I could have my say." She blinks away the tears glistening in her eyes. "You didn't say a word to me about what that emergency was. Did you think that I wouldn't understand? That I'd hold you back from a friend? All of this could have been avoided, if you'd just talked to me.

"Instead, you left me clueless. Guessing at what I was seeing in McBride's with you bent over her, crying. Why? Why would I have thought it was anything other than what it looked like? You hadn't even told me Lorna was pregnant. Have you asked yourself why? Why you didn't share that really important tidbit with me?

"Because it's just about all I've thought about. All that's been going through my head. That and why I'm not enough. Never enough." Tears gather, threatening to spill.

"Lisbeth. My God, I love you. I was thinking of all the things I need to do to create our life together. Lorna and Michael's baby never crossed my mind aside from a few phone calls with my mum. I was so focused on us—you and me. Getting work to support us. Sorting my visa. Finding a way to make me irresistible to you—so that you'd have no other option but to choose me."

I want to touch her, need the connection with her. Wiping

the tears from her cheeks, I push on. "I wasn't hiding anything from you. Not intentionally. It just wasn't relevant. I'm so sorry. I fucked this up with us. I made you feel less than the most important thing in the world to me." I run my hands down her arms, taking her hands in mine, rubbing circles on her wrist. "You are my world. I failed miserably, but please, please give me a chance."

She tugs at her hands, trying to pull them away from me. I hold on for dear life, not wanting to let her go.

"Sh-she said you were going to raise the baby together. She—"

"Yeah. I found out what she said to you halfway across the ocean, stuck in a seat next to her for another three hours. I was livid, tried to get right back on the next flight out. She had no right to try and play us like that. The shite she told me you said—"

I shake my head, shoving the anger back down. It won't do us any good now.

"Lis, I don't know why she thought she needed to do that, be manipulative. That's not how she was growing up, that's not anything I would have ever expected from her. I think...I think the grief, the loss of Michael—maybe the raging hormones?—made her act irrationally. I don't want to make excuses for her, but it's just not who she is.

"This whole thing is a mess and you're absolutely right. If I'd told you, if I'd stayed with you..." I lift her chin so she's looking at me, so she can see my sincerity. "You're my world. Lisbeth. My bloody world, and I will do anything to prove that to you. Please tell me it's not too late. Please tell me we've a chance—that I've a chance to share your life with you."

Her gaze bounces back and forth between my eyes for far

longer than I'm comfortable with. My heart forces the blood through my veins.

That's it.

I close my eyes and nod slowly, sure that this is the worst day of my life. Far worse than burying my brother, my best friend. He was taken from me by an awful disease, one that has no cure. I've lost Lis through no fault but my own.

"It's not." My head whips up, searching her face. "It's not too late. I-I want to try, I want to be with you, Aidan. I love you." She leans in, brushing her lips across mine.

42

Lis

The minute my lips touch Aidan's I feel the spark, the shock of electricity as it courses through my body. I'm finally able to breathe for the first time in almost a month. My world spins in the right direction and my heart fills with hope and possibility. It hits me, just how lost I've been without him. My heart only stuttering, not truly beating, until now.

Before Aidan, love was conditional, sometimes even cruel. I let Lorna's words get to me, affect me, because that's what I've known for most of my life. Much as I thought I'd given my whole heart to Aidan, I realize that I've still been holding back, shielding myself. Only giving him pieces of me. This is it, though, it's time to bare my soul and give him all of my heart— cracks, scars, flaws—all of it.

He releases my hands, grasping either side of my face and pulls me to him deepening the kiss. Not wanting any space between us, I crawl forward onto his lap, my knees firmly planted on either side of his thighs. I need to be close, need to feel our connection again. Show him how much he means to me.

Aidan groans deep in his throat as I settle myself, grinding against him. My skin tingles as he runs his hands over me, touching me everywhere. Pulling me closer until there's nothing between us but thin layers of cotton. His touch, warm and comforting, singes my skin through my thin sleep shorts and t-shirt. His warm palms press my ass closer, closer, closer as I push his shirt up his torso, revealing the bumps and valleys of his muscles.

My need for him making me forget all rational thought. I pull back just long enough to get his shirt over his head and out of my way, crashing my lips back to his as soon as it's clear. His muscles shift and flex across his back as his hands glide up my thighs and dig into the flesh of my hips—pushing me, pulling me.

I work my hand between us and fumble desperately with the button of his jeans. Frantic to feel him, to be with Aidan, I struggle with the closure and groan in frustration.

"Lis—" he breathes across my lips. "Jesus, I can't believe I'm saying this. Lisbeth, stop." Aidan grabs my hands and stills them, clasping them tightly.

I pull my head back panting and search his eyes, not understanding. "What? Why...?" Surely, I didn't misread him.

He leans back, putting even more space between us.

"The last thing I want is to take you in a rush, fuck you like a secret in my parents' house." He looks to the clock on the nightstand and then over his shoulder to the open bedroom door. "I'm not sure when they'll be back, but I sure as hell don't want that to be on my mind while I show you how much I've missed you. I want you to myself, Lis. Completely to myself."

I look past him, out the door, biting my lip.

"Yes. But—" My brain is fuzzy with lust and I blink several times trying to make sense of what to do next. My body physically aches for him. My heart thunders in my chest, pushing the blood through me in the familiar rhythm I've come to associate with Aidan. His grip on my hands loosens. I feel his thumb graze the skin on the underside of my wrist like he's measuring the beats.

Aidan brings my knuckles up to his lips and stops, staring at my fingers. "Where's your ring? Did Francie not give you the letter?"

"It—it's in my bag. I brought it to give back to you. I couldn't...I just couldn't wear it," I whisper, not wanting to give the words life, to admit that I was coming here to say goodbye.

With one arm wrapped around, holding me tightly to him, Aidan leans to the side grabbing my purse from the nightstand. "Where? I need it." His words rumble through my chest, making me catch my breath.

I pull out my wallet, unzip the inner pocket. Fully prepared to return this ring, I never expected to wear it again. The thought that I will, brings tears to my eyes. I place the ring in his waiting palm, giving him my right hand. He kisses my knuckles again and places it over his heart, before reaching for my left hand. "Lisbeth, this is more, so much more than just dating. I won't lose you again."

He flips the ring so the point is out, toward my fingertips and slides it on sealing it with a kiss over the ring and one to my lips. "This is just a place holder until I'm home with you. But I won't—let—you—go."

Each word is punctuated with a brush of his lips across mine.

I feel like time has stopped. And once again, the thought flies through my head, that this is not why I came here—but it's so, *so* much better.

"You good with that? Or we can go to the jeweler right now and get you a proper engagement ring."

"No. No, this is perfect. I don't need anything else, just you." The beat of my heart syncs with the thump of his beneath my palm. I bow my head and press a kiss to his chest, tasting the salt of the single tear that escapes my lashes. The veil of my hair covering my emotions.

Aidan lifts my face to his with a lone finger under my chin. I want to hide, but I know I need to let him in. Let him see me.

With a shuddering breath, I look up into his eyes. This single moment is so much more intimate than any we've shared. The recognition of what this is, what is passing between us, spreads across Aidan's face, changing his look of confusion to one of tenderness and love.

His gaze slides down, landing on my lips. His kiss filled with the love and emotion his features hold. Breaking the kiss, he rests his forehead on mine, sighing. "Let's get dressed and go. I'll show you a bit of Dublin before we can check in." His words give me all the pause I need to collect myself.

TWENTY MINUTES LATER, I meet him by the front door catching the tail end of his phone call. "...right, so that's the soonest? You've nothing earlier? Right, yeah, that'll be fine. Thank you." Aidan slings his bag over his shoulder and grabs mine from me.

"You ready?"

"Where are we going?" My stomach growls as we walk out, locking the door behind us. I slap my hands to my stomach and feel my cheeks flame red as he turns, a smile stretching across his beautiful face.

"Erm—we're going to get you something to eat and then I'm going to share one of my favorite things with you." I cock an eyebrow at him trying to suppress a giggle-snort.

Aidan chucks our bags in the back of the car and straightens up. Hands low on his hips, shaking his head as he laughs. His eyes sparkling with mischief and desire.

"Yeah, I intend to share *that* with you later. But Eagan gave me his views on love yesterday and how to win over the girl. I want to test his theory."

"Really? Advice from your five-year-old nephew? You're that desperate?" Chuckling, I climb into the correct side of the car this time.

"If I were truly smart, I'd have taken Henry's lead and wrapped myself around you last night." He pulls my hand to his lap and drives us into Dublin. We park near the Woolen Mills at Ha'penny Bridge and go in to the café there.

WE SETTLE in to our lunches and watching the people pass outside the huge plate glass windows.

"Is this what you're sharing with me? Your favorite thing in Dublin?" I sip at the best pint of Guinness I've ever tasted. "For the love of God, this is amazing. It tastes so—so different."

"Yeah, it's fresh here. Better, right?" He smirks at me; our easy conversation is back. God, I missed this. I missed him. I think a part of me knew all along that I was coming back to clear things—that I couldn't live without him. "And, no. This is just lunch to keep you from scaring off my next surprise." He pops a bunch of fries in his mouth being particularly obtuse.

"You're not going to tell me. Is it that awful?" I'm teasing, baiting him when suddenly my blood runs cold. He wouldn't, would he? I press my shaking hands flat to the tabletop, and stare at him.

She's his best friend. And she sure as shit should be scared of me, but I'm not doing this today. No way in hell. I take a bracing breath and bite back the anger and disappointment that threatens to bubble up and overflow.

"Lisbeth, what? What's wrong?" Aidan's fork clatters to his plate as he reaches for me.

A hot flush climbs up my neck, setting my cheeks on fire. "I can't see that woman, Aidan. I won't do it. Not yet."

His roaring laughter snaps my attention.

"What the fuck is so funny about this?" I'm seething.

"Lis, no. Give me some credit, I'm not that daft."

I'm not so sure.

"I want to take you to Howth, a fishing village up north—to feed the seals. Sammy's a local celebrity, loves getting a fish head thrown to him, waving at all the pretty girls. He's quite a flirt." He gazes at me over his pint glass, and I'm not sure if he's being flippant.

His eyes go dark then, intensely serious—dangerous.

"Then I'm going to take you to spend the night in a castle and remind you—repeatedly—how much I love you."

Oh.

43

Aidan

Over and over and over again.

I show her how much I've missed her. How much I love her.

I drink in every single moment I can with Lis, savoring the time we have. I don't want to spend even a minute sleeping.

Her laughter as she fed the seals was musical. Hearing my name on her lips as she comes undone, is something I will never get enough of.

The pale light of early morning filters through the castle window, highlighting Lis' kiss-swollen lips, and her messy hair.

I don't want to let her leave.

I check my watch and think of how little time there is until we have to leave for the airport.

I have her. But I have to let her go.

I still have to say goodbye.

"Hey, you let me fall asleep." Lisbeth's voice is raspy from sleep. I feel her graze my neck as she runs her finger down to rest over my heart. "I didn't want to miss out on any time—I didn't want to waste this, any of it." Her warm palm rests on my skin and her fingers toy absently with my nipple.

"What's...what's the plan? How are we going to do this, until you get back?" And there it is. Her need to know and my complete and utter lack of answers. It could be weeks, yet. It could be months.

Sifting my fingers through her hair, watching the light play with the silken strands, I press a kiss to her forehead. "We'll do whatever we need to to see each other. I'm going to bust my arse to get everything taken care of here as quickly as possible, but..." I move her on to my chest, needing to have her closer, hating the words that hang between us, "...but it could still be some time. Are you going to be okay?"

I search her face, cradled between my palms needing reassurance that this will work. That we'll be okay.

"I will be. I'm going to dive into my classes, get lost in studying for the nursing boards. I'll be busy, but I will miss you every single moment." Lis leans forward brushing her lips across mine in a slow sensuous kiss. One full of all the emotions that neither of us seem to be able to put into words.

I roll us gently so I'm braced above her, breaking the kiss only enough to whisper against her lips, "I love you, Lisbeth. Don't want to imagine being without you."

I want her, but more than that, I want her to know it's with my heart—not just my cock.

She shifts beneath me, pulling me closer.

"I came here to say goodbye. To be done with us, to move on." Lisbeth slides her hand down my torso, fitting it between our bodies. She wraps her long slender fingers around my cock and strokes me gently. "I never imagined that we would be here. Together but still saying goodbye."

I kiss a trail down her neck, across her collarbone, tasting her, breathing her in. Memorizing every detail until we are together again. There's nothing between us, not a fucking thing. No history, no past, no misunderstandings.

"Not goodbye. This isn't goodbye, Lisbeth. This is forever."

She gasps as I slide into her, twining her legs around me. With my heart beating against her hand, I hold the other one above her head, my thumb rubbing circles on her wrist. Each of us feeling the pulse of this love that neither of us expected to find.

I rock slowly, not wanting an inch of space between us. Wanting to draw this out as long as possible. Wanting to stay here forever in this perfect bubble and never let her go. I suppress every primal urge to mark her as mine for all the world to see.

Instead, I love her, worship her body, and thank God she's given me another chance.

Lis' gasps mix with mine as we move against each other—with each other. Climbing. Building. I want to touch her everywhere all at the same time, desperate to show her how much I love her, how she owns every piece of my heart.

Slowly, we reach the top of the wave, our orgasms thrumming reverently through us. The world falling away leaving only the two of us, nothing else.

WE'VE DELAYED IT—WE'VE actively avoided it.

And now we're late to the airport.

"Ohmygod ohmygod... I'm not gonna miss my flight, am

I?" Lis is frantic, bouncing and shifting in her seat. "Aidan, I cannot miss this flight. My classes start tomorrow."

Her eyes are wide and pleading, all the serenity from the hours of losing ourselves in one another, gone.

I whip the car into a spot blessedly open in the front row of the car park. Lisbeth jumps out and meets me at the boot of the car.

I grab her bag and her hand and we run like mad for the terminal.

"You won't miss it. Boarding isn't 'til half ten. You'll"—I glance at my watch and grind my teeth—"you should be okay."

Hands clasped, we weave and dodge through the crowds of slow-moving people—people who actually showed up on time. People who are on holiday. People who don't have to put half of their heart on a plane across the ocean not knowing if it will be two weeks or two months until they can be together again.

We're both panting, breathing heavy as we skid to a stop at the airline desk.

"I-I need to check in for a flight to New York?" Lis is digging through her purse for her passport spilling bits and things onto the desk and floor. "Um—sorry, I know it's here. Aidan? Where did I put my—oh God, here it is. Sorry."

"Well. You are cutting it close, then. Checking any baggage with us today?" The attendant is obviously put out by our tardiness.

"No. I just have a carry-on."

"Gate 414. Security is to your left. You'll want to hurry."

This is the part I've been dreading. The line through security is short, almost nonexistent.

I want to beg her to stay. And I absolutely can't. Instead, I walk with her as far as I can, clinging to her hand, spinning my ring around her finger.

When I've gone as far as I can, I turn her so that she's facing me, mere inches between us.

I'm stalling.

Time is running out, and all the things I couldn't find the words for earlier, are fighting their way to the surface. I open my mouth and close it again. There's too much to say and not nearly enough time.

"You'll call, yeah, when you land?" I pull the lapels of her jacket together, not wanting to let her go. "When you get back to the flat?"

I'm fighting to be strong for her, fighting to keep my tears at bay.

"I will. I promise." She settles her hands on my forearms, a tear rolling down her cheek. "You'll come back to me soon?" Her eyes overflowing with emotion.

I swallow hard and nod, echoing her words. "I will. I promise." I kiss her thoroughly, tasting the salt of her tears, only letting go when I absolutely have to. With whispered *I love yous*, our fingers slowly sliding apart, I watch Lisbeth—my entire world—walk through security and away from me. I watch her as long as I can, until she disappears in the sea of people. Only then, when she's no longer visible, do I let go and let the tears stream freely.

Lis

Once I'm through security, I do my best to get lost in the throngs of bodies moving toward the departure gates.

I need to catch my breath.

I need to talk myself into getting on this plane.

I need to see his face one last time.

Twisting to look over my shoulder, I see him. I see the moment he thinks I'm gone, consumed by the crowds.

My tears matching his, flow down my cheeks.

Leaving Aidan like this is the hardest thing I can imagine. The only thing making it bearable, is knowing that our love is strong enough to endure whatever gets thrown our way.

EPILOGUE

Gracyn

Lis stumbled through the door late this morning, arms full of pies and wine for Thanksgiving. She practically dropped everything trying to get her boots off. I had to hide in the kitchen, slugging back the rest of my mimosa afraid of what would come flying out of my mouth.

She bitched at me for not helping her. Laughed at me for trying to pull off Thanksgiving dinner. To be fair, I don't know what I was thinking. I figured fried chicken was close enough to turkey and we'd make it work, but Kate vetoed that and went on a cooking spree. Food was never the point of today anyway.

Lis wanders back into the kitchen as Kate takes the turkey out of the oven. "Smells amazing in here. Kate, what can I do to help?" Neither of us did much cooking when we lived together, but Kate is ah-freaking-mazing.

"Nothing, really. Gracyn just needs to set the table and we

should be ready pretty soon. Wait, can you open the champagne I have in the fridge?"

Lis goes to the fridge digging around for the bottle I hid behind every available condiment jar.

I check the big clock over the bookshelf and grab plates and silverware, hurrying out to the table we set up behind the couch.

The cork makes a deep satisfying pop and Lis brings the bottle out setting it on one end of the table. "Are we—is there someone else coming?" she asks as she scans the table set for four. "Oh shit, is Kate still on that dating site? Do we finally get to meet one of them?"

Kate slides out of the kitchen, leaning a shoulder on the wall, not wanting to miss anything.

"We do have someone joining us, but it's—"

And right on time, almost like we planned every little detail, the door swings open.

It takes all of four strides for Aidan to cross the room, weave his fingers into her hair and kiss Lis silly.

Aidan asked me to help him surprise Lis when he got his visa mess fixed. He wanted this to be a special moment. One that will become so much more.

And by the shock on her face it looks like we did it. This is worth all the planning and lying and scheming I've done over the past three weeks.

Their love is palpable, seeing them finally together after so long. Lis touching his face, his arms, his chest like she can't believe he's really here.

Aidan beaming at her, his fingers threaded through her hair, pulling her in for a kiss that promises so much more.

I drag Kate into the kitchen, feeling bad, like we're intruding, giving them a little privacy.

No one deserves this kind of love more than Lis. She's been through enough and seeing her happy makes my heart swell and my eyes leak.

Someday, I want what they have—the kind of love they share.

I brush at my tears, stowing my emotions quickly, trying to keep my thoughts from running straight to Gavin. This moment is all about Lis.

I love it.

Love her being in love.

Love the ring I know he has in his pocket.

Love that she's going to say *yes*.

Thank you for spending time in Beekman Hills with Aidan and Lis.
I would love to know what you think of these two! If you can,
please drop a quick review on your favorite retailer for me!
To stay up on releases and happenings, make sure you're signed
up for my newsletter at www.kcenderswrites.com

...now, jump into **Twist** for more of Finn and Addie, or
Tombstones to meet Kate and Jack.
If it's Gracyn's story you're looking for, grab **In Tune**
(formerly Tunes).

ALSO BY KC ENDERS

For information on additional titles and to release alerts, please visit www.kcenderswrites.com and make sure to sign up for my newsletter.

Beekman Hills Series

Troubles

Twist

Tombstones

Stand Alone Titles

Sweet on You

Broken: A Salvation Society Novel

The UnBroken Series

In Tune *(formerly Tunes)*

Off Bass

Coming Soon

Beat Down

Out Loud

ACKNOWLEDGMENTS

Thank you from the bottom of my heart to each and every one of you that have touched my life along the way. You all mean the world to me.

Kate. This would have never happened without you.

Lynsey. Your inspiration and input are what started this mess. Credit or Blame...it's up to you.

Marisol, Kate S., Shawn, Chad B., and Chelsea. Your support, encouragement, and feedback have made this book what it is. Thank you.

The ladies in McBride's on Main, A Novel Bunch KC, and all the real-life bartenders at Cinder Block Brewery, thank you for the words of encouragement, your enthusiasm and the pints poured and endured while I wrote at the bar. Someday I'll try to figure out the bottles of bourbon and the barrels of beer that went into the writing of this!

When everything started to crumble and the world demanded I quit this crazy adventure, thank you for seeing me through to the finish.

ABOUT THE AUTHOR

Karin is a New York Girl living in a Midwest world. A connoisseur of great words, fine bourbon, and strong coffee, she's married to the love of her life and is mother to two grown men that she is proud to say can cook and clean up after themselves, and always open doors for the ladies thanks to the Rules of Being a Gentleman (you're welcome, world). Her one major vice is rescuing and adopting big dogs. Tons of personality, not so good on manners. She loves talking books, hearing from readers, and hosting the occasional virtual Happy Hour in her reading group.

www.kcenderswrites.com

facebook.com/kcewrites
instagram.com/authorkcenders
bookbub.com/profile/kc-enders
goodreads.com/author

Made in the USA
Monee, IL
22 July 2023

39561662R00174